W9-DCI-922

FLORENCE

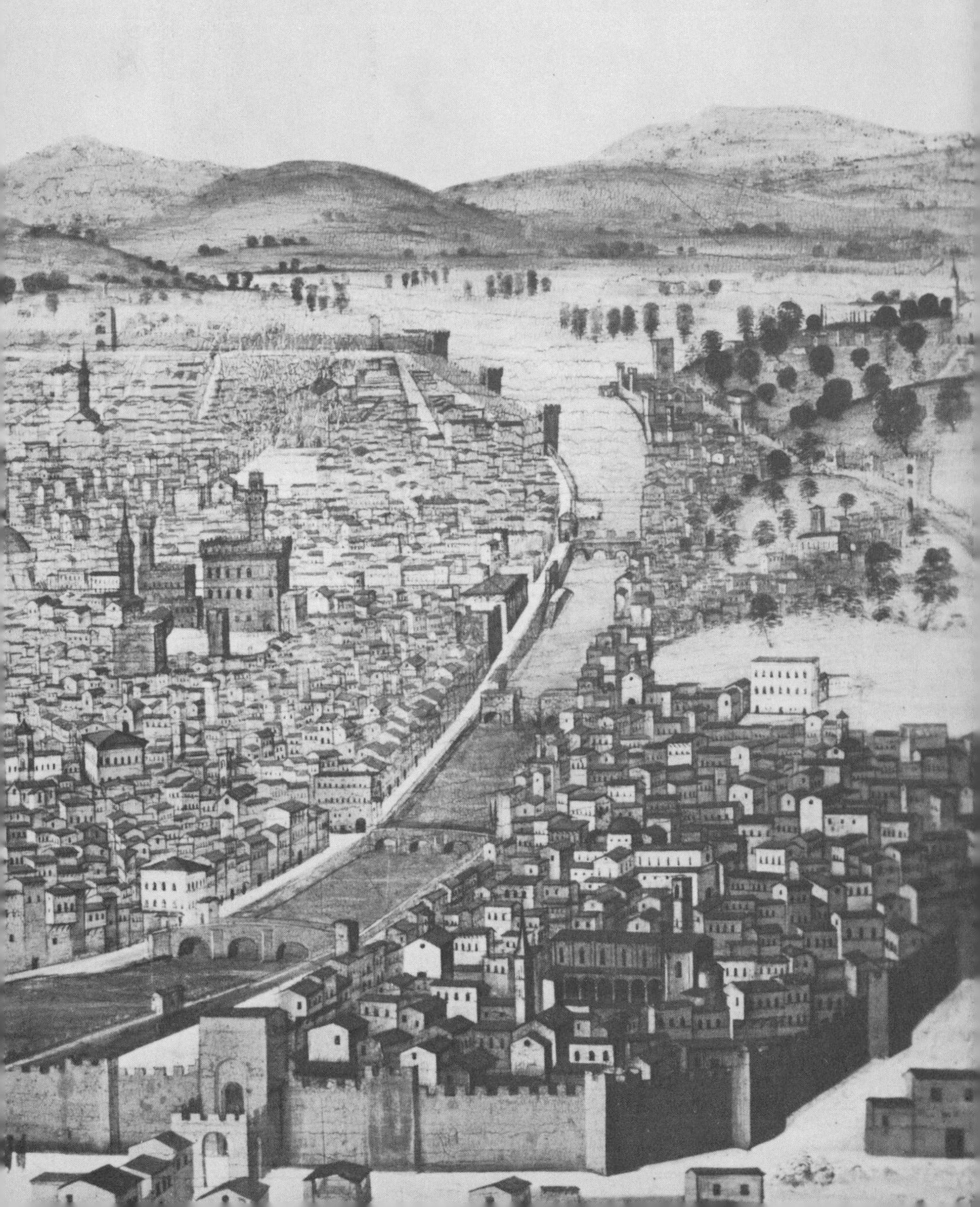

The Great Adventure of Michelangelo

Also by Irving Stone

BIOGRAPHICAL NOVELS

LUST FOR LIFE
(*Vincent Van Gogh*)

IMMORTAL WIFE
(*Jessie Benton Fremont*)

ADVERSARY IN THE HOUSE
(*Eugene V. Debs*)

THE PASSIONATE JOURNEY
(*John Noble*)

THE PRESIDENT'S LADY
(*Rachel Jackson*)

LOVE IS ETERNAL
(*Mary Todd Lincoln*)

THE AGONY AND THE ECSTASY
(*Michelangelo*)

BIOGRAPHIES

SAILOR ON HORSEBACK
(*Jack London*)

THEY ALSO RAN
(*Defeated Presidential Candidates*)

CLARENCE DARROW FOR THE DEFENSE

EARL WARREN

HISTORY

MEN TO MATCH MY MOUNTAINS

NOVELS

PAGEANT OF YOUTH

FALSE WITNESS

BELLES-LETTRES

WE SPEAK FOR OURSELVES
(*A Self-Portrait of America*)

WITH JEAN STONE

DEAR THEO *and* I, MICHELANGELO, SCULPTOR
(*Autobiographies through letters*)

COLLECTED

THE IRVING STONE READER

1. Michelangelo Buonarroti.

THE GREAT ADVENTURE OF MICHELANGELO

IRVING STONE

An Abridged Illustrated Edition of
THE AGONY AND THE ECSTASY
Especially for Young Readers

Illustrated by Joseph Cellini

Fic
Sto

Learning Resource Center
Wawasee High School
Syracuse, Indiana

DOUBLEDAY & COMPANY, INC.
GARDEN CITY, NEW YORK

Library of Congress Catalog Card Number 65–10617
Copyright © 1961, 1965 by Doubleday & Company, Inc.
All Rights Reserved
Printed in the United States of America
9 8 7 6 5 4 3

For VINCENT

Newly born into this world.

Thinking of the wonderful stories
He will have to read
Written by authors of all lands
And in all languages.

February 11, 1965

THE BOOKS

List of illustrations

Black and white photos

Picture Credits

Nos. 1, 2, 3, 5, 6, 7, 9, 12, 13, 16, 17, 18, 20, 21, 22, 23, 24, 25, 27, 32, 33, 34, and 35, Alinari.

Nos. 4, 8, and 19, Alinari-Brogi.

Nos. 10, 11, 14, 15, 26, 28, 29, 31, and 30, Alinari-Anderson.

All photos from the Alinari are reproduced with permission by the Art Reference Bureau.

The best of artists hath no thought to show
which the rough stone in its superfluous shell
doth not include; to break the marble spell
is all the hand that serves the brain can do.

How can that be, lady, which all men learn
by long experience? Shapes that seem alive,
wrought in hard mountain marble, will survive
their maker, whom the years to dust return!

Beauteous art, brought with us from heaven,
will conquer nature; so divine a power
belongs to him who strives with every nerve.

If I was made for art, from childhood given
a prey for burning beauty to devour,
I blame the mistress I was born to serve.

—MICHELANGELO BUONARROTI

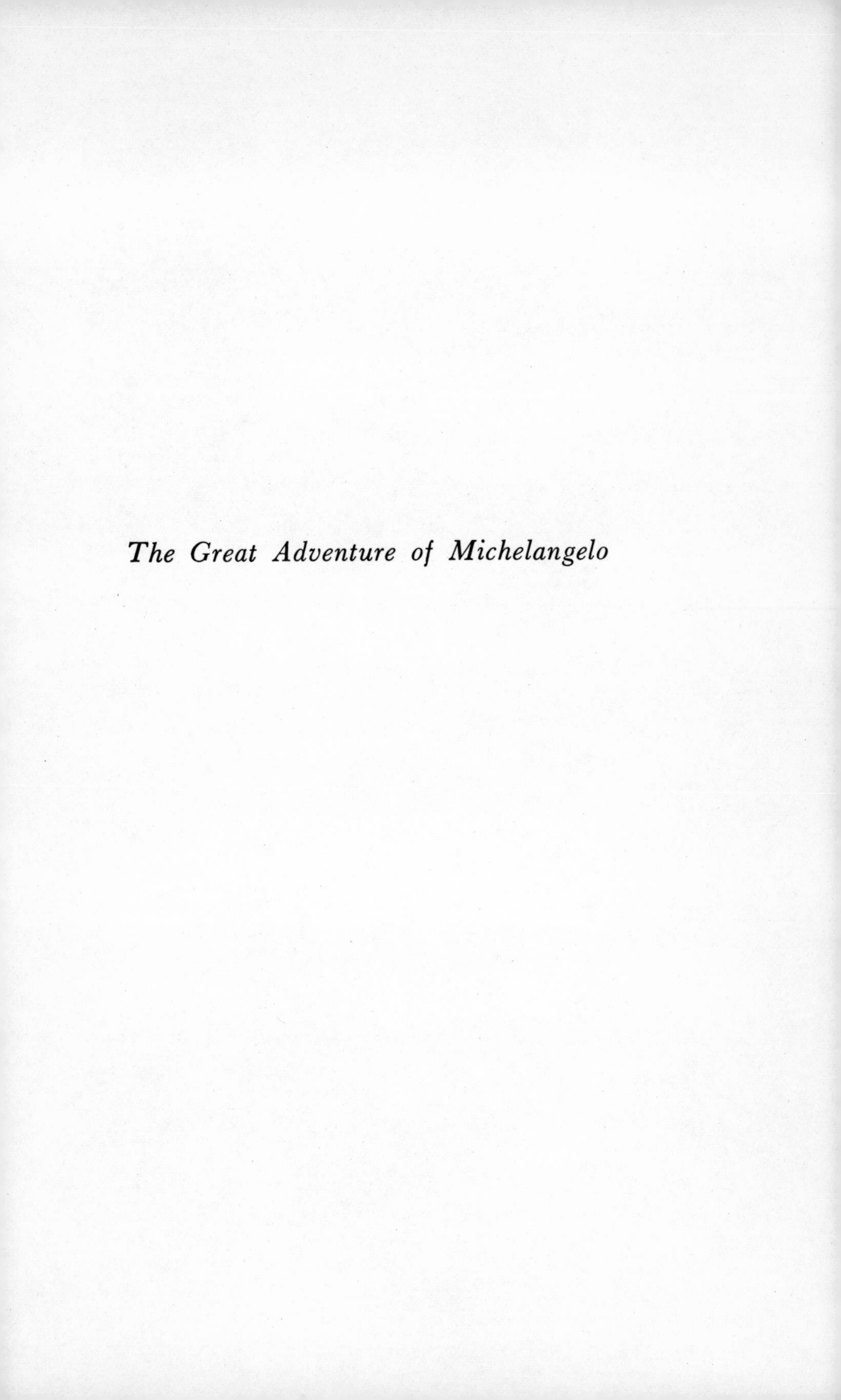

The Great Adventure of Michelangelo

BOOK ONE

THE STUDIO

He sat before the mirror of the second-floor bedroom sketching his lean cheeks with their high bone ridges, the flat broad forehead, and ears too far back on the head, the dark hair curling forward in thatches, the amber-colored eyes wide-set but heavy-lidded.

"I'm not well designed," thought the thirteen-year-old with serious concentration. "My head is out of rule, with the forehead overweighing my mouth and chin. Someone should have used a plumb line."

He shifted his wiry body lightly so as not to waken his four brothers sleeping behind him. With rapid strokes of the crayon he began redrafting his features, widening the oval of the eyes, rounding the forehead, broadening the narrow cheeks, making the lips fuller, the chin larger. "There," he thought, "now I look better. Too bad a face can't be redrawn before it's delivered, like plans for the façade of the Duomo."

Notes of a bird's song came fluting through the ten-foot window, which he had opened to the cool morning air. He hid his drawing paper under the bolster at the head of his bed and went noiselessly down the circular stone stairs to the street.

His friend Francesco Granacci was a nineteen-year-old youth with hay-colored hair and alert blue eyes. For a year Granacci had been providing him drawing materials and sanctuary in his parents' home across the Via dei Bentaccordi, as well as prints borrowed surreptitiously from Ghirlandaio's studio. Though the son of a wealthy family, Granacci was apprenticed to Ghirlandaio.

"You're really coming with me this time?" Granacci demanded excitedly.

"It's my birthday present to myself."

"Good. Remember what I told you about Domenico Ghirlandaio. Be humble. He likes his apprentices to appreciate him. Let's hurry."

To reach Ghirlandaio's studio they had to cross the Square of the Old Market, where fresh beeves hung on pulleys in front of the butchers' stalls. From here it was but a short walk to the open door of Ghirlandaio's studio.

Michelangelo stopped for a moment to gaze at Donatello's marble St. Mark standing in a tall niche of the Orsanmichele.

"Sculpture is the greatest art!" he exclaimed, his voice ringing with emotion.

"I don't agree with you," Granacci said quietly. "But stop gaping; there's business to be done."

The boy took a deep breath. Together they entered the Ghirlandaio workshop.

The studio was a large, high-ceilinged room with a pungent smell of paint and charcoal. In the center was a rough plank table set up on horses around which half a dozen sleepy young apprentices crouched on stools. In a near corner a man was grinding colors in a mortar, while along the side walls were stacked color cartoons of completed frescoes, the Last Supper of the church of the Ognissanti and the Calling of the First Apostles for the Sistine Chapel in Rome.

On a raised platform sat a man of about forty, his wide-topped desk the only ordered spot in the studio, with its neat rows of pens, brushes, sketchbooks, and implements hanging on hooks, and behind, on the wall shelves, volumes of illuminated manuscripts.

Granacci stopped below his master's desk.

"Signor Ghirlandaio, this is Michelangelo, about whom I told you."

Michelangelo felt himself being spitted by a pair of eyes reputed to be able to see more than any artist in Italy. The boy too used his eyes as though they were silver-point pens, drawing for his mind's portfolio the artist sitting above him in an azure coat and red cloak thrown over the shoulders against the March chill and wearing a red cap, the sensitive face with its full purple lips, prominent bone formations beneath the eyes, deep cheek hollows, the black hair parted in the center and worn down to his shoulders, the long supple fingers of his right hand clasped against his throat.

"Who is your father?" demanded Ghirlandaio.

"Lodovico di Lionardo Buonarroti-Simoni."

"I have heard the name. How old are you?"

"Thirteen."

"We start apprentices at ten. Where have you been for the past three years?"

"Wasting my time at school, studying Latin and Greek."

A twitching at the corner of Ghirlandaio's dark wine lips showed that he liked the answer.

"Can you draw?"

"I have the capacity to learn."

Granacci said:

"He has a good hand. He made drawings on the walls of his father's house in Settignano."

"Ah, a muralist," quipped Ghirlandaio. "Competition for my declining years."

Michelangelo was so intense that he took Ghirlandaio seriously.

"I've never tried color. It's not my trade."

"Whatever else you may lack, it isn't modesty. Very well. Suppose you sketch for me. What will it be?"

Michelangelo's eyes traveled over the workshop, swallowing impressions the way country youths break bunches of grapes in their mouths at autumn wine festivals.

"Why not the studio?"

Ghirlandaio gave a short laugh. "Granacci, give Michelangelo Buonarroti paper and charcoal."

Michelangelo sat down on a bench to sketch. His eye and hand were good working partners. For the first time since entering the studio his breathing was normal. He felt someone leaning over his shoulder.

"I'm not finished," he said.

"It is enough." Ghirlandaio took the paper, studied it for a moment. "You have a strong fist." Michelangelo held his hand in front of him. "It is a stonecutter's hand," he replied proudly.

"We have little need for stonecutters in a fresco studio. I'll start you as an apprentice, but you must pay me six florins for the first year—"

"I can pay you nothing."

Ghirlandaio looked at him sharply.

"The Buonarroti are not poor. Since your father wants you apprenticed—"

"My father has beat me every time I mentioned painting."

"But I cannot take you unless he signs the Doctors and

Apothecaries Guild agreement. Why will he not beat you again when you tell him?"

"Because your willingness to accept me will be a defense. That, and the fact that you will pay him six florins the first year, eight the second, and ten the third."

Ghirlandaio's eyelids flared.

"That's unheard of! Paying money for the privilege of teaching you!"

"Then I cannot come to work for you."

The apprentices made no pretense of working. Michelangelo stood his ground, his manner respectful both to the older man and to himself, gazing straight at Ghirlandaio as though to say, "I will be worth it to you."

Ghirlandaio felt a grudging admiration. He lived up to his reputation of being a man "lovable and loved" by saying:

"It's obvious we shall never get the Tornabuoni choir finished without your invaluable help. Bring your father to see me."

Out on the street Granacci threw an arm affectionately about the smaller boy's shoulder.

"You broke every rule. But you got in!"

"Never shall I live out of sight of the Duomo!" Michelangelo cried.

They reached the carpenter shop which occupied the ground floor of the house the Buonarroti clan rented in the Via dell'Anguillara.

"*A rivederci,* as the fox said to the furrier," Granacci twitted.

"Oh, I'll take a skinning," he responded grimly, "but unlike the fox I shall come out alive."

He turned the sharp corner of Via dei Bentaccordi, waved to the two horses whose heads were sticking out of the open-top door of the stable across the street, and climbed the rear staircase to the family kitchen where his stepmother was making her beloved *torta.*

"Good morning, mother."

"Ah, Michelangelo. I have something special for you today: a salad that sings in the mouth."

Lucrezia Buonarroti rose at four o'clock in order to reach the market square at the same time the farmers arrived through the cobbled streets with their pony carts filled with fresh fruits and vegetables, eggs and cheese, meats and poultry. She selected the tenderest, slender green beans and peas, unblemished figs, peaches. Michelangelo and his four brothers called her The Best, because every ingredient that went into her cooking had to be The Best.

He knew she was a docile creature in every phase of her marriage except the kitchen; here she was a lioness in the best fighting tradition of the Marzocco, Florence's guardian lion.

Michelangelo walked through the empty family room with its heavy oak bench facing the fireplace, the six-foot bellows propped against the stone, its wall chairs with leather backs and leather seats. The next room was his father's study. Here Lodovico sat cramped over his gray-parchment account books. As long as Michelangelo could remember, his father's sole activity had been a concentration on how to retain the ragged remnants of the Buonarroti fortune, which had been founded in 1250 and had now shrunk to a ten-acre farm in Settignano and a house with a legally disputed title close by this one which they rented.

Lodovico heard his son come in and looked up. He sported a luxurious mustache which flowed into his beard, cut square four inches below his chin. The hair was streaked with gray; across the forehead were four deep lines. His small brown eyes were melancholy. Michelangelo knew his father as a cautious man who locked the door with three keys.

"Good morning, Father."

Lodovico sighed. "I was born too late. One hundred years ago the Buonarroti vines were tied with sausages."

Lodovico knew to the last florin how much each Buonarroti generation had owned of land, houses, business, gold. The family history was his occupation, and each of his sons in turn had to memorize the legend.

"We were noble burghers," Lodovico told them. "Our family is as old as the Medici." Michelangelo was forbidden to sit in his father's presence without permission, had to bow when given an order.

Michelangelo had been taught by his father that labor was beneath a noble burgher; but it was the son's observation that Lodovico worked harder in figuring out ways not to spend money than he would have had to work in earning it. Within the Buonarroti fortress there had remained a few scattered resources, enough to let him eke out his life as a gentleman providing he spent nothing. Yet in spite of all the skill and dedication Lodovico brought to his task their capital had dribbled away.

Standing in the recessed wall of the eight-foot window, letting the thin March sun warm his bony shoulders, the boy's image went back to their home in Settignano, overlooking the valley of the Arno, when his mother had been alive. Then there had been love and laughter; but his mother had died when he was six, and his father had retreated in despair into the encampment of his study. His aunt Cassandra had taken over the care of the household, and Michelangelo had been lonely and unwanted except by his grandmother, Monna Alessandra, who lived with them, and the stonecutter's family across the hill, the stonecutter's wife having suckled him when his own mother had been too ill to nourish her son.

For four years, until his father had remarried and Lucrezia had insisted that they move into Florence, he had fled at every opportunity to the Topolinos. He would make his way down the wheat fields among the silver-green olives, cross the brook which marked the division of the land, and climb the opposite hill through the vineyards to their yard. Here he would silently set to work cutting the serene stone from the neighboring quarry into beveled building blocks for a new Florentine palace, working out his unhappiness in the precision blows in which he had been trained, along with the stonecutter's own sons.

Michelangelo pulled himself back from the stonecutter's yard in Settignano to this stone house on the Via dell'-Anguillara.

"Father, I have just come from Domenico Ghirlandaio's studio. Ghirlandaio has agreed to sign me as an apprentice."

During the silence that pulsed between them Michelangelo heard one of the horses neigh across the street and Lucrezia stir the embers of her fire in the kitchen. Lodovico used both hands to raise himself to a commanding position over the boy. This inexplicable desire of his son's to become an artisan could be the final push that would topple the shaky Buonarroti into the social abyss.

"Michelangelo, I apologize for being obliged to apprentice you to the Wool Guild and force you to become a merchant rather than a gentleman. But I sent you to an expensive school, paid out money I could ill afford so that you would be educated and rise in the Guild until you had your own mills and shops. That was how most of the great Florentine fortunes were started, even the Medici's."

Lodovico's voice rose. "Do you think that I will now allow you to waste your life as a painter? To bring disgrace to the family name! For three hundred years no Buonarroti has fallen so low as to work with his hands."

"That is true. We have been usurers," angrily responded the boy.

"We belong to the Money Changers Guild, one of the most respectable in Florence. Moneylending is an honorable profession."

"I have as much pride in our name as anyone. Why can't I learn to do fine work that all Florence will be proud of, as they are of Ghiberti's doors and Donatello's sculptures and Ghirlandaio's frescoes? Florence is a good city for an artist."

Lodovico put his hand on the boy's shoulder, calling him *Michelagnolo,* his pet name. This was his favorite of the five sons, for whom he had the highest hopes.

"Michelagnolo, Ghiberti and Donatello began as artisans and ended as artisans. So will Ghirlandaio. Their work never raised their social position an arm's length, and Donatello was so destitute at the end of his life that Cosimo de' Medici had to give him a charity pension."

The boy flared at this attack.

"That's because Donatello put all his money into a wire basket hung from the ceiling so his assistants and friends could help themselves when they needed. Ghirlandaio makes a fortune."

"Art is like washing an ass's head with lye, you lose both the effort and the lye. Every man thinks that rubble will turn into gold in his hand! What kind of dreaming is that?"

"The only kind I know," cried Michelangelo. "Bleed me of art, and there won't be enough liquid left in me to spit."

"I'll teach you to be vulgar!" Lodovico cried.

He started raining blows on the boy, his right elbow crooked stiffly so that he could use his arm as a club. Uncle Francesco came running into the room. Not wanting to fail his nephew in this critical moment of his youth, he also began hitting the boy, boxing his ear with the heel of his palm.

Michelangelo lowered his head as dumb beasts do in a storm. There was no point in running away, for then the argument would have to be resumed later. Deep in his throat he sounded the words of his grandmother:

"Patience! No man is born into the world whose work is not born with him."

Then, suddenly, all words and blows stopped and he knew that his grandmother had entered the room. She was a retiring woman in black, not beautiful but with a finely modeled head, who exercised her matriarchy only in moments of family crisis. Lodovico did not like to give his mother offense. He slumped into his chair.

"Never let me hear again about this being apprenticed to artists," he said.

Monna Alessandra went to her son's side at the account desk.

"What difference does it make whether he joins the Wool Guild and twists wool or the Apothecaries Guild and mixes paints? You won't leave enough money to set up five geese, let alone sons. All five boys must look to their living; let Lionardo go into the monastery as he wishes, and Michelangelo into a studio."

"I am going to be apprenticed to Ghirlandaio, Father. You must sign the papers. I'll do well by us all."

"We have not a scudo to pay for any apprenticeship to Ghirlandaio."

This was the moment for which Michelangelo had been waiting. He said gently:

"There is no need for money, Father. Ghirlandaio has agreed to pay you for my apprenticeship."

"He will pay!" Lodovico lunged forward. "Why should he pay me for the privilege of teaching you?"

"Because he thinks I have a strong fist."

After a considerable silence Lodovico lowered himself slowly into his leather chair.

"Truly I have conquered myself in more battles than a saint!"

Domenico Ghirlandaio's was the most bustling and successful studio in all Italy. Ghirlandaio, who never sought a commission, could refuse none; on Michelangelo's first day in the studio he told him:

"If a peasant woman brings you a basket that she wants ornamented, do it as beautifully as you can, for in its modest way it is as important as a fresco on a palace wall."

Michelangelo found the place energetic but good-natured. Twenty-eight-year-old Sebastiano Mainardi, with long black hair cut to imitate Ghirlandaio's, a pale, narrow face with a jutting, bony nose and protruding teeth, was in charge of the apprentices. He took Michelangelo in tow.

"The purpose of painting," explained Mainardi to his newest apprentice, "is to decorate, to bring stories to life pictorially, to make people happy, yes, even with the sad pictures of the saints being martyred. Always remember that, Michelangelo, and you will become a successful painter."

If Mainardi was the major-domo of the apprentices, Michelangelo soon learned that sixteen-year-old Jacopo, with the monkey-like face, was the ringleader. He had a gift for appearing to be busy without doing a lick of work. He welcomed the thirteen-year-old boy to the studio by warning him gravely:

"Doing nothing else but hard work is not worthy of a

good Christian. Here in Florence we average nine holidays every month. Add Sundays to that and it means we only have to work every other day."

Two weeks flew by until the magic day of his contract signing and first pay dawned. Michelangelo suddenly realized how little he had done to earn the two gold florins which would constitute his first advance. So far he had been used as an errand boy to pick up paints at the chemist's, to screen sand to give it a fine texture and wash it in a barrel with a running hose. Awakening while it was still dark outside, he climbed over his younger brother Buonarroto, sprang out of the bed, fumbled in the bed bench for his long stockings and knee-length shirt.

Ghirlandaio was surprised to find the boy on his doorstep so early, and his "good morning" was short. He had been working for days on a study of St. John baptizing the neophyte and was upset because he could not clarify his concept of Jesus.

Michelangelo was apprehensive: would he forget what day it was? Granacci saw his friend's expression. He went to David, Ghirlandaio's brother, and murmured something in his ear. David reached into the leather purse he kept hooked onto his wide belt, crossed the room to Michelangelo and handed him two florins and a contract book. Michelangelo quickly signed his name alongside the first payment, then wrote the date:

April 16, 1488.

Joy raced through his veins as he anticipated the moment when he would hand the florins to his father. Then he was aware of an enthusiastic hubbub among the apprentices and the voice of Jacopo saying:

"It's agreed, we draw from memory that gnome figure on the alley wall behind the studio. The one who draws the most accurate reproduction wins and pays for dinner.

Cieco, Baldinelli, Granacci, Bugiardini, Tedesco, are you ready?"

Michelangelo felt a dull pain in the chest; he was being left out. His had been a lonely childhood; he had had no intimate friend except Granacci. So often he had been excluded from games. Why? Because he had been small and sickly? Because there was not enough laughter in him? He so desperately wanted to be included in the companionship of this young group, but it did not come easy.

Now, at the apprentices' table, Jacopo was completing the details of the game.

"Time limit, ten minutes. The winner to be crowned champion and host."

"Why can't I compete, Jacopo?" Michelangelo cried.

Jacopo scowled. "You're just a beginner; you couldn't possibly win, and there would be no chance of your paying. It wouldn't be fair to the rest of us."

Stung, Michelangelo pleaded, "Let me join in, Jacopo. You'll see, I won't do too badly."

"All right," Jacopo agreed reluctantly. "But you can't have a longer time. Everyone ready?"

Excitedly Michelangelo picked up charcoal and paper and began hammering down the outlines of the gnarled figure, half youth, half satyr, which he had seen several times on the rear stone wall.

"Time limit!" cried Jacopo. "Line up your drawings, center of the table."

Michelangelo ran to the table, put his sketch in line. Jacopo stared at him with his mouth wide open.

"I can't believe it. Look, everyone, Michelangelo has won!"

There were cries of congratulation. Cieco and Tedesco smiled at him. He glowed with pride. He was the newest

apprentice, yet he had won the right to buy everyone dinner. . . .

Buy everyone dinner! His stomach sank as though he had swallowed his two gold florins. He counted heads; there were seven of them. They would consume two liters of red wine, soup-of-the-country, roast veal, fruit—making a sizable hole in one of the gold pieces that he had waited for so eagerly to turn over to his father.

On the way to the inn with the others rushing ahead, laughing heartily among themselves, a loose thread began flapping in his mind. He ran the spool of his thoughts backward, fell in step beside Granacci.

"I was gulled, wasn't I?"

"Yes."

"Why didn't you warn me?"

"It's part of the initiation."

"What will I tell my father?"

"If you had known, would you have made yourself draw badly?"

Michelangelo broke into a sheepish grin.

"They couldn't lose!"

There was no formal method of teaching at Ghirlandaio's studio. Its basic philosophy was expressed in a plaque which Ghirlandaio had nailed to the wall alongside his desk:

The most perfect guide is nature. Continue without fail to draw something every day.

Michelangelo had to learn from whatever task each man had at hand. He moved from table to table, doing odd jobs. No one had time to stop work to teach him.

The next noon he ate sparingly of Lucrezia's veal roast and returned to the studio, empty now because the others were taking their afternoon nap. He had decided that he must study the drawing of his master. Under Ghirlandaio's desk he found a bundle labeled Slaughter of the Innocents, took it to the apprentices' table and spread out the dozens of sheets for the fresco. These rough studies had simplicity and authority. He began copying the drawings and had made a half-dozen sketches in quick succession when he felt someone standing behind him. He turned to find a disapproving frown on Ghirlandaio's face.

"Why are you prying into that bundle? Who gave you permission?"

Michelangelo put down his charcoal, frightened.

"I didn't think there was any secret about it. I want to learn." He regained his composure. "The quicker I learn, the quicker I can help. I want to earn those gold florins."

The appeal to his logic served less to banish Ghirlandaio's anger than the intensity in the boy's eyes.

"Very well. I'll take some time with you now."

"Then teach me how to use a pen."

Ghirlandaio took his newest apprentice to his desk, cleared it and set up two corresponding sheets of paper. He handed Michelangelo a blunt-nibbed pen, picked up another for himself, started crosshatching.

Michelangelo followed the older man with quick movements of the hand. A look of rapture came over his face. This was the happiest he had been. With pen in hand he was an artist, thinking out loud, probing his mind, searching his heart for what he felt and his hand for what it could discern about the object before him. He wanted to spend hours at this work desk, redrawing models from a hundred different angles.

Ghirlandaio was aware of the eagerness in the boy's face, the excitement in his hand.

"Michelangelo, you must not draw for its own sake. This figure is not usable in a fresco."

Seeing how well his apprentice followed him, Ghirlandaio took from his desk two more of his drawings, an almost life-size study of a head and the baptism of a man within the choir of a Roman basilica, done with a beauty of composition.

"Magnificent!" breathed Michelangelo, reaching for the sheets. "You've learned everything that the great artist Masaccio has to teach."

The blood drained from Ghirlandaio's dark face; had he been insulted, judged a copier? But the boy's voice was full of pride. Ghirlandaio was amused: the rawest apprentice was complimenting the master. He took the drawings from him.

"Sketches are nothing, only the finished fresco counts. I shall destroy these."

They heard the voices of Cieco and Baldinelli outside the studio. Ghirlandaio got up from the desk, Michelangelo picked up his paper and new pen, quickly reassembled the bundle of the Slaughter of the Innocents, had it tied and back in its corner by the time the boys came into the room.

Locked in the big drawer of his desk, Ghirlandaio kept a folio from which he studied and sketched while he was conceiving a new panel. Granacci told Michelangelo that it had taken Ghirlandaio years to assemble these drawings of men he considered masters: Taddeo Gaddi, Lorenzo Monaco, Fra Angelico, Paolo Uccello, Pollaiuolo, Fra Filippo Lippi and many others. Michelangelo had spent enthralled hours gazing at their altars and frescoes with which the city was lavishly endowed, but he had never seen any of the working studies.

"Certainly not," replied Ghirlandaio brusquely when Michelangelo asked him if he might see the portfolio.

"But why not?" cried Michelangelo desperately. Here was a golden opportunity to study the thinking and techniques of Florence's finest draftsmen.

"Every artist assembles his own portfolio," said Ghirlandaio, "according to his own tastes and judgment. I have made my collection over a period of twenty-five years. You build your own."

A few days later Ghirlandaio was studying a sketch of a youth with a spear, when a committee of three men called for him to accompany them to a neighboring town.

He failed to put the drawing back into the locked drawer.

Waiting until the others had left for dinner, Michelangelo went to the desk, took up the sketch. After a dozen attempts he made what he considered a faithful copy; and an errant idea popped into his mind. Could he fool Ghirlandaio with it? The sketch was thirty years old, the paper soiled and yellowing with age. He took some scraps into the back yard, ran his finger over the earth, experimented with rubbing the dirt along the grain of the paper. After a while he brought his copy out to the yard, and slowly began discoloring his own sheet.

Old drawing paper had a smoky quality around the edges. He returned to the studio where a fire burned in the hearth, held his discolored scraps over the smoke for testing, and after a moment his copy of the youth. Then he put the imitation on Ghirlandaio's desk and secreted the original.

During the weeks he watched Ghirlandaio's every move; whenever the teacher failed to return a sketch to the portfolio, the boy remained behind to make a reproduction. If it was late afternoon he would take the sheet home and, when the rest of the family was asleep, make a fire in the downstairs hearth and stain the paper the proper color. At the end of a month he had assembled a portfolio of a dozen fine sketches. At this rate his folio of master sketches would become as thick as Ghirlandaio's.

Ghirlandaio still came in early from dinner occasionally to give his apprentice an hour of instruction: in the use of black chalk; how to work in silver point, and then to intensify the effect with white chalk. Michelangelo asked if they might sometimes draw from nude models.

"Why should you want to learn to draw the nude when we must always paint it under drapes?" demanded Ghirlandaio. "There aren't enough nudes in the Bible to make it profitable."

"There are the saints," replied the boy; "they have to be nude, nearly, when they are being shot with arrows or burned on a grill."

"True, but who wants anatomy in saints? It gets in the way of spirit."

"Couldn't it help portray character?"

"No. All of character that's necessary to show can be done through the face . . . and perhaps the hands. No one has worked in nudes since the pagan Greeks. We have to paint for Christians. Besides, our bodies are ugly, misproportioned. A garden of palms and cypresses, oranges in bloom, an architectural design of a straight stone wall with steps running down to the sea . . . that is beauty. And non-controversial. Painting should be charming, refreshing, lovely. Who can say that the human body is any of these things? I like to draw figures walking delicately under their gowns . . ."

". . . and I would like to draw them the way God made Adam."

With June the summer heat clamped down on Florence. The boy packed away his long hose, and stuck his bare feet into sandals. He wore a light cotton shirt. The back doors of the studio were thrown open and the tables moved into the yard under the green-leafed trees.

For the festival of San Giovanni the studio was locked tight. Michelangelo rose early, and with his brothers walked down to the Arno, the river which flowed through the city, to swim and play in the mud-brown waters before he met his fellow apprentices at the rear of the Duomo.

The piazza was covered by a broad blue awning sown with golden lilies to represent heaven. Each Guild had built its own cloud, high up in which sat its patron saint on a wooden frame thickly covered by wool, surrounded by lights and cherubs and sprinkled with tinsel stars. On lower iron branches were children dressed as angels, strapped on by waistbands.

At the head of the procession came the cross of Santa Maria del Fiore, and behind it singing companies of wool shearers, shoemakers, bands of boys dressed in white, then giants on stilts six cubits high, hooded with fantastic masks, then twenty-two towers mounted on carts and carrying actors who gave tableaux out of Scripture: the Tower of St. Michael depicting the Battle of the Angels showed Lucifer being cast out of heaven; the Tower of Adam presented God Creating Adam and Eve, with the serpent making its entrance; the Tower of Moses acted out the Delivery of the Law.

To Michelangelo the tableaux seemed endless. He had never liked biblical plays and wanted to leave. Granacci, enchanted with the painted scenery, insisted on staying to the very end. Just as high mass was beginning in the Duomo a Bolognese was caught stealing purses and gold belt buckles from the worshipers jammed before the pulpit. The crowd in the church and piazza turned into an angry mob shouting, "Hang him! Hang him!" carrying the apprentices along with them to the quarters of the captain of the guard, where the thief was promptly hanged from a window.

Later that day a tremendous wind and hailstorm struck the city, destroying the colorful tents, turning the racecourse for the horse race into a marsh. Bugiardini, Cieco, Baldinelli, Michelangelo huddled inside the Baptistery doors.

"This storm came because that wretched Bolognese stole in the Duomo on a holy day," cried Cieco.

"No, no, it's the other way round," protested Bugiardini.

"God sent the storm as punishment for our hanging a man on a religious holiday."

They turned to Michelangelo, who was studying the pure gold sculptures of Ghiberti's second set of doors, their ten glorious panels populated layer upon layer by all the peoples, animals, cities, mountains, palaces of the Old Testament.

"What do I think?" Michelangelo said. "I think these doors are the gates of paradise."

At Ghirlandaio's the Birth of St. John was ready to be transferred to the wall of Santa Maria Novella. Early as he arrived at the studio, Michelangelo found himself to be the last. His eyes opened wide at the excitement, with everyone bustling about, collecting cartoons, bundles of sketches, brushes, pots and bottles of color, buckets, sacks of sand and lime, pointing sticks. The materials were loaded on a small cart behind an even smaller donkey, and off went the entire studio with Ghirlandaio at its head like a commanding general and Michelangelo, as the newest apprentice, driving the cart. He guided the donkey to the right and found himself in the Piazza Santa Maria Novella, one of the oldest and most beautiful in the city.

He pulled the donkey up short in front of the church.

Gangling Tedesco was the unloading foreman, gustily bossing the thirteen-year-olds in his moment of command. Michelangelo entered the bronze doors, a roll of sketches in his arms, and stood breathing the cool, incense-heavy air. The church stretched before him in the form of an Egyptian cross over three hundred feet long.

He walked slowly up the main aisle, savoring every step, thinking of Giotto—painter, sculptor, architect who, legend said, had been discovered by Cimabue as a shepherd boy drawing on a rock, and brought to his studio—and his successors.

Across the nave to the left he saw the Rucellai chapel, built by his own mother's family in the middle of the thirteenth century.

Michelangelo had never been able to get himself to mount the few stairs leading to the Rucellai chapel. A grudging family loyalty had kept him out. Now that he had made his break from the family and was going to work here in Santa Maria Novella, had he not earned the right to enter? Enter without feeling an intruder on that side of the family which after his mother's death had cut all communication, caring nothing of what happened to the five sons of Francesca Rucellai del Sera, daughter of Maria Bonda Rucellai?

He put down the package he was carrying and walked up the stairs, slowly. Once inside the chapel with its Cimabue Madonna and marble Virgin and Child by Nino Pisano, he fell to his knees; for this was the very chapel where his mother's mother had worshiped all through her youth, and where his mother had worshiped on those feast days of family reunion.

Tears burned his eyes. Prayers sprang to his lips unbidden. Was he praying to the beautiful Madonnas or to his mother? Was there truly a difference? Had she not been very like the Madonnas above him? Whatever vague memories he had of her melted into those of the Lady.

He rose, walked to the Pisano Virgin and ran his long, bony fingers sentiently over the marble drapery. Then he turned and left the chapel. For a moment he stood on top of the stairs thinking of the contrast between his two families. The Rucellai had built this chapel around 1265, at the same time that the Buonarroti had come into their wealth. Michelangelo could not remember having seen a painting or sculpture of the simplest nature in a Buonarroti house.

A shout from Bugiardini on the scaffolding called him. He found the entire studio moving in harmony. Bugiardini had put a heavy coat of plaster on the panel the day before. With Cieco, Baldinelli and Tedesco he took up the cartoon, which they held over the wet panel. Ghirlandaio pounced the lines of the figures onto the fresh plaster with a pointed ivory stick, then gave the signal for it to be taken away. The young apprentices scrambled down the scaffolding, but Michelangelo remained to watch Ghirlandaio mix his mineral-earth colors in little jars of water, squeeze his brush between his fingers and commence his painting.

He had to work surely and swiftly, for his task had to be completed before the plaster dried that night. If he had failed to gauge accurately how much he could do that day, the remaining dry plaster would have to be cut away the following morning, leaving a discernible seam.

Michelangelo stood on the scaffolding with a bucket of water, sprinkling the area just ahead of Ghirlandaio's flying brush to keep it moist. He alone was not permitted to apply paint. He was torn: part of him felt that though he had been in the studio for only three months he was as qualified to work the wall as the other thirteen-year-olds. At the same time an inner voice kept telling him that all of this feverish activity had nothing to do with him. Even when he felt most unhappy about being excluded, he wanted to run out of the choir and the studio to a world of his own.

Toward the end of the week the plaster began to dry. The burnt lime recovered its carbonic acid from the air, fixing the colors. Michelangelo saw that his belief that the pigments sank into the wet plaster was a mistake; they remained on the surface, covered by a crystalline coating of carbonate of lime which fitted them the way the skin of a young athlete contains his flesh and blood. The entire panel now had a metallic luster which would protect the colors from heat, cold and moisture. But the amazing fact was that each day's segment was drying slowly to the very colors Ghirlandaio had created in his studio.

And yet, when he went alone to Santa Maria Novella the following Sunday during mass, weaving his way through the worshiping Florentines in their short velvet *farsetti,* doublets, voluminous cloaks of camlet trimmed in miniver, and high-crowned hats, he felt let down: so much of the freshness and vigor had leaked out from the drawings.

He drifted over to the Duomo, where young men gathered on the cool marble steps to make laughter and view the passing pageant. Every day in Florence was a fair. On Sundays the slender Florentine girls carried their heads high, wore colorful coverings on their blond hair and long-sleeved gowns, high-necked, with overlapping skirts. The older men were in somber cloaks, but the young men of the prominent families created the great splash between the Duomo steps and the Baptistery by wearing their tights with each leg dyed differently and patterned according to the family blazon.

Jacopo was sitting on top of an old Roman sarcophagus. Michelangelo went to his side, ran his hand caressingly over the sarcophagus, his fingers tracing out in its low relief the funeral procession of fighting men and horses.

"Feel how these marble figures are still alive and breathing!"

His voice carried such exultation that his friends turned to stare at him. Now his secret had burst into the open.

"God was the first sculptor; He made the first figure: man. And when He wanted to give His laws, what material did He use? Stone. What were the first tools that men carved for themselves? Stone. Look at all us painters lolling on the Duomo steps. How many sculptors are there?"

He told them why he thought there were no more

sculptors: the strength expended in carving with hammer and chisel exhausted mind and body alike, in contrast to the brushes, pens and charcoal which the painter used so lightly.

Jacopo hooted. Granacci answered his young friend.

"If extreme fatigue is the criterion of art, then the quarryman taking the marble out of the mountain with his wedges and heavy levers has to be considered nobler than the sculptor, the blacksmith greater than the goldsmith and the mason more important than the architect."

"But you have to agree that the work of art becomes noble in the degree to which it represents the truth? Then sculpture will come closer to true form, for when you work the marble the figure emerges on all four sides. . . ."

Jacopo jumped down from his perch on the lid of the sarcophagus. "Sculpture is a bore. What can they make? A man, a woman, a lion, a horse. Then all over again. Monotonous. But the painter can portray the whole universe: the sky, the sun, the moon and the stars, clouds and rain, mountains, trees, rivers, seas. The sculptors have all perished of boredom."

Sebastiano Mainardi joined the group and stood listening. There were spots of color on his usually pale cheeks.

"That's true! The sculptor needs only a strong arm and an empty mind. But the painter has to think of a thousand things every moment, to relate all the integral parts of a painting. Creating the illusion of a third dimension is craftsmanship. That's why a painter's life is exciting, and a sculptor's dull."

Tears of frustration welled in Michelangelo's eyes. He cursed himself for his inability to carve out in words the stone forms that he felt in his innards.

"Painting is perishable: a fire in the chapel, too much cold, and the paint begins to fade, crack. But stone is eternal! Look at this Roman marble sarcophagus; as clear and strong as the day it was carved."

Mainardi raised his arm for attention.

"Michelangelo," he began gently, "has it ever occurred to you that the reason there are no sculptors left is because of the cost of marble and bronze? Who would provide you with the stone, who would support you while you practiced on it? Paint is cheap, commissions are abundant; that's why we take on apprentices."

But Michelangelo refused to compromise. Without another word he walked down the cool marble steps, away from the Duomo, over the cobbled streets to home.

The night was sleepless. He rolled and tossed. Buonarroto, who shared the bed, was placid in sleep. In the bed closer to the door Lionardo, who spent his days yearning to be a saint; and Giovansimone, lazy, rude to his parents, who had once set fire to Lucrezia's kitchen because she had disciplined him. Sigismondo, the youngest, still slept in a trundle at the foot of Michelangelo's bed.

Quietly he sprang out of bed, slipped into his loincloth, short drawers, shirt and sandals, and left the house. He climbed the cart road into the hills, then left it where it turned off for the quarry at Maiano. For four years after his mother died he had been left to roam this countryside, though it was the proper age for him to be in school. There was no master at Settignano, and his father had been too withdrawn to care. Now he climbed through land of which he knew every jutting boulder and tree and furrow.

His upward push brought him to the settlement of Settignano, a dozen houses collected around a gray stone church. This was the heart of the stonemason country, having bred the greatest stonecutters in the world, the generations that had built Florence. It was only two miles from the city, on the first rise above the valley floor, and an easy haul to town.

Down the winding road a few hundred yards was the Buonarroti villa in the midst of a five-acre farm, now leased to strangers. He had not been here for months. As always he was surprised by the beauty and spaciousness of the house, hewn two hundred years before of the best serene stone, graceful in its austere lines, and with broad porches overlooking the valley, the river gleaming below like a silversmith's decoration.

He could remember his mother moving in the rooms, weaving on the broad downstairs porch, kissing him good night in his big corner room overlooking the Buonarroti fields, the creek at the bottom, and the Topolino family of stonemasons on the opposite ridge.

He scampered down the hill between the wheat on one side and the ripening grapes on the other and climbed to the opposite ridge.

He paused when he came in sight of the yard. This was the picture he loved, one which meant home and security for him: the father working with tempered iron chisels to round a fluted column, the youngest son beveling a set of steps, one of the older two carving a delicate window frame, the other graining a door panel, the grandfather polishing a column on a pumice wheelstone with thin river sand. Behind them were three arches, and under them scurrying chickens, ducks, pigs.

In the boy's mind there was no difference between a stonecutter and a sculptor, for the *scalpellini* were fine craftsmen. There might be a difference in the degree of artistry, but not in kind.

The father heard Michelangelo's footsteps.

"Good day Michelangelo."

"Good day, Topolino."

"How goes it?"

Learning Resource Center
Syracuse Junior High School
Syracuse, Indiana

"Not bad. And you?"

"Not bad. The honorable Lodovico?"

"He is well."

Topolino did not really care how things went with Lodovico: he had forbidden Michelangelo to come here. No one got up, for the stonemason rarely breaks his rhythm; the two older boys and the one exactly Michelangelo's age called out with welcoming warmth.

"Welcome, Michelangelo. Welcome."

"Good health, Bruno. Good health, Gilberto. Good health, Enrico."

Topolino spoke. "You're apprenticed to Ghirlandaio?"

"Yes."

"You do not like it?"

"Not greatly."

"Too bad."

"Who does somebody else's trade makes soup in a basket," said the old grandfather.

"Why do you stay?" It was the middle brother asking.

"Where else is there to go?"

"We could use a cutter." This was from Bruno.

Michelangelo looked from the oldest son to the father.

"Is it true?"

"Yes."

"You will take me as apprentice?"

"With stone you're no apprentice. You earn a share."

His heart leaped. Everyone chipped in silence while Michelangelo stood above the father who had just offered him a portion of the food that went into the family belly.

"My father would not permit . . ."

"There you are!"

"Can I cut?"

The grandfather, turning his wheel, replied, "Every little bit helps."

Michelangelo sat before a roughed-out column, a hammer in one hand, a chisel in the other. He liked the heft of them.

He had a natural skill. Under his blows the stone cut like cake. There was a natural rhythm between the inward and outward movement of his breath and the up-and-down movement of his hammer arm as he slid the chisel across a cutting groove. The contact with the stone made him feel that the world was right again.

The stone they were working was warm, an alive blue-gray. It had durability, yet it was manageable. The Topolinos had taught him to work the stone with friendliness, never to grow angry or unsympathetic toward the material.

"Stone works with you. It reveals itself. But you must strike it right. Stone does not resent the chisel. It is not being violated. Its nature is to change. Each stone has its own character. It must be understood. Handle it carefully, or it will shatter. Never let stone destroy itself.

"Stone gives itself to skill and to love."

If a mason beat his stone as an ignorant farmer might beat his beasts, the rich, warm, glowing, breathing material became dull, colorless, ugly; died under his hand. To sympathy, it yielded: grew even more luminous and sparkling.

Stone had a mystique: it had to be covered at night because it would crack if the full moon shone on it. Ice was its enemy.

"Stone will speak to you. Listen as you strike with the side of your hammer."

Stone was called after the most precious of foods: meat.

Monna Margherita, a formless woman who worked the animals and fields as well as the stove and tub, had come out of the house and stood under the arch, listening. Michelangelo felt for her much as he did for Monna Alessandra, his grandmother: affection and security.

He kissed her on both cheeks.

"Patience," she counseled. "Ghirlandaio is a good master. Who has an art, has always a part."

The father had risen.

"I must choose the stone at Cave Maiano. Will you help load?"

"Willingly. Good-by, Grandfather, Bruno, Gilberto, Enrico."

"Good-by, Michelangelo."

They rode on the high seat behind two beautiful-faced white oxen. In the fields the olive pickers were mounted on ladders made of slender tree stalks. They held the branches with their left hands, stripping down the little black olives.

As they rounded a bend, Michelangelo saw the gorge in the mountain with its alternating blue and gray stone and iron-stained streaks. High on the cliff several men were outlining a block to be quarried with a point driven against the grain to loosen the hold from the main mass. He could see the point marks in successive layers through the stone formation, layers of stone peeled off as though stripped from a pile of parchment sheets.

The level work area where the strata fell after they were loosed was shimmering with heat and dust from the cutting, splitting, shaping; by men wet with perspiration—small, lean, sinewy men who worked the rock from dawn to dark without fatigue and who could cut as straight a line with hammer and chisel as a draftsman with pen and ruler; as concentrated in their hardness and durability as the rock itself. He had known these men since he was six and began riding behind the white oxen with Topolino. They greeted him, asked how things went.

Topolino inspected the newly quarried stone with the running commentary Michelangelo knew so well:

"That one has knots. Too much iron in this. This one will be hollow."

Until finally, climbing over the rocks and making his way toward the cliff, he let out his breath sharply:

"Ah! Here is a beautiful piece of meat."

Michelangelo planted his legs wide, swung his weight from the hips; Topolino opened the first crack between the stone and the ground with an iron bar. They moved the stone over the boulders to open ground, then with the help of the quarrymen the block was fulcrumed upward through the open tail of the cart.

Michelangelo wiped the sweat away from his face with his shirt. He bade Topolino good-by.

"Until tomorrow," replied Topolino, flicking the lines for the oxen to move off.

Until tomorrow, Michelangelo thought, tomorrow being the next time I take my place with the family, be it a week or a year.

He made his way down the mountain, feeling fifteen feet tall.

The following week the studio moved to Santa Maria Novella to start the Death of the Virgin. Michelangelo stood irresolutely beneath the scaffolding, unnoticed, then began to walk the long center nave toward the bright sunlight. He turned to take a final look at the scaffolding rising tier upon tier in front of the stained-glass windows, the Ghirlandaio artists, tiny figures weaving before the walls, the sacks of plaster and sand, the plank table of painting materials, all bathed in a soft glow.

At the center of the church were a few wooden benches. He pulled one in place, took drawing paper and charcoal out of his shirt and began drawing the scene before him.

Some time later he felt someone staring holes through him from behind, turned to find Ghirlandaio standing there.

Ghirlandaio whispered hoarsely, "There are some things you know more about than I do, and I have been working for over thirty years! Come to the studio early tomorrow. Perhaps we can make things more interesting for you from now on."

Michelangelo walked home in ecstasy.

The next morning Ghirlandaio was at his table when Michelangelo arrived.

"Sleep is the greatest of all bores. Draw up a stool."

The boy sat before Ghirlandaio, who pulled aside the curtain behind him so that the north light fell on them.

"Turn your head. A little more. I'm going to sketch you

as young John leaving the city to go to the desert. I hadn't found a satisfactory model until I saw you working in Santa Maria Novella yesterday."

Michelangelo swallowed hard. After his sleepless night's dream of originating whole cartoons with which to fill the still empty panels—

Ghirlandaio had not meant to deceive his apprentice. He summoned Michelangelo, showed him the over-all plan for the Death of the Virgin, added casually:

"I want you to collaborate with Granacci on this scene of the apostles. Then we'll let you try your hand at the figures on the left, together with the little angel beside them."

Granacci had not a jealous bone in him. Together they sketched the apostles, the one bald-headed, the other supporting the weeping John.

It was autumn by the time he completed his own drawing for the Death of the Virgin and was ready to create his first fresco. He climbed the scaffolding with Granacci, both of them loaded with buckets of plaster, water, brushes, mixing spoons, the cartoon and colored sketches. Michelangelo laid a modest area of plaster, then held the cartoon of the white-haired and bearded near saint with the enormous eyes. He outlined the figure, then mixed his paints and applied them with a soft brush. He picked up a finely pointed brush and with terra verde sketched the outstanding features, and turned to Granacci with big eyes.

"I can't be any more help to you, *Michelagnolo,*" responded Granacci; "The rest is between you and God. Good luck."

With which he scrambled down the scaffolding.

Michelangelo found himself alone at the top of the choir, alone on his perch above the church and the world. For a moment he suffered vertigo. How different the church looked from up here—so vastly hollow and empty. In his nostrils was the dampness of the fresh plaster and the pungence of paint. His hand clamped the brush and he began to paint.

Only once did he go to the master of the studio for help.

"How do I mix the exact shade I had yesterday?"

"By the weight on your knife of the amount you cut off the pigment cake. The hand can judge more accurately than the eye."

For a week he worked alone. The studio stood by to assist if called, but no one intruded. This was his baptism.

By the third day everyone knew he was not following the rules. He was drawing anatomical nude bodies of male figures, using for models two men he had sketched unloading in the Old Market, then draping them with robes, the reverse of the practice of suggesting a man's bones by the folds of a cloak.

Late that afternoon Ghirlandaio called him aside. He had said no word to Michelangelo about his fresco, either of praise or criticism; it was as though he had never mounted the scaffold at all. He looked up from his desk, his eyes dark.

"They are saying I am jealous. It is true. Oh, not of those two figures, they're immature and crude. But let there be no mistake, I am jealous of what will ultimately be your ability to draw."

Michelangelo suffered a rare moment of humility. He returned to the studio late that night, took his copies of Ghirlandaio's drawings out of the desk and put back the originals. The next morning Ghirlandaio murmured as Michelangelo went by:

"Thank you for returning my drawings. I hope they have been helpful."

The valley of the Arno had the worst winter weather in

Italy. The skies overhead were leaden; the cold had a creeping quality that permeated stone and wool and bit at the flesh within. After the cold came the rain and the cobbled streets were running rivers. Anything not cobbled was a bog of mud.

But by March the north wind had stopped blowing, the sun's rays had a little warmth in them again, and the skies were blue. On the second of these days Granacci burst into the studio.

"Come with me. I have something to show you."

Granacci guided Michelangelo across town toward the Piazza San Marco. Opposite the church was a gate.

"We go in here."

He pushed the gate open. Michelangelo entered, stood confounded.

It was an enormous oblong garden with a small building, or casino, in the center; in front, and directly at the end of a straight path, was a pool, a fountain, and on a pedestal a marble statue of a boy removing a thorn from his foot. On the wide porch of the casino a group of young men were working on stone.

All four walls of the garden were open loggias displaying antique marble busts. There was a straight path lined with cypresses leading to the casino.

Michelangelo turned to Granacci, stuttered:

"Who . . . what . . . is this?"

"A sculpture garden."

"But . . . what for?"

"A school."

". . . school?"

"To train sculptors."

His knees sagged.

"What sculptors?"

"Last July Lorenzo de' Medici started a school for sculptors. He has brought in Bertoldo to teach."

"But Bertoldo is dead!"

"No, he was only dying. Lorenzo had him carried here on a litter, showed him the garden, and told Bertoldo he must restore Florence to its days of greatness in sculpture. Bertoldo got off the litter and promised Lorenzo that the era of Ghiberti and Donatello would be re-created. That's Bertoldo now on the porch," said Granacci. "I met him once. Shall I present you?"

Michelangelo shook his head up and down savagely.

They walked down the gravel path, circled the pool and fountain. Half a dozen men from fifteen to thirty years old were working at broad tables. Bertoldo, so slight he seemed all spirit and no body, had his white hair wrapped in a turban.

"Maestro Bertoldo, may I present my friend Michelangelo?"

Bertoldo looked up. He had light blue eyes and a soft voice that carried over the blows of the hammer. He looked at Michelangelo.

"Who is your father?"

"Lodovico di Lionardo Buonarroti-Simoni."

"I have heard the name. Do you work stone?"

Michelangelo's brain stood numb. Someone called to Bertoldo. He excused himself and went to the other end of the loggia.

Granacci led Michelangelo down the path to the gate and out into the street. Michelangelo sat on a bench in the Piazza San Marco with pigeons thronging about his feet and the heel of his palm pressing his forehead bruisingly. When he looked up at Granacci his eyes were feverish.

"Who are the apprentices? How did they get in?"

"Lorenzo and Bertoldo chose them."

Michelangelo groaned.

"And I have more than two years left at Ghirlandaio's. I have destroyed myself!"

"Patience!" consoled Granacci. "You are not an old man yet. When you've completed your apprenticeship—"

"Patience!" exploded Michelangelo. "Granacci, I've got to get in! Now! I don't want to be a painter, I want to be a marble carver. Now! How can I get admitted?"

"You have to be invited."

"How do I get invited?"

"I don't know."

"Then who does? Someone must!"

"Stop pushing. You'll shove me clear off this bench."

Michelangelo quieted. Tears of frustration came to his eyes.

"Oh, Granacci, have you ever wanted anything so hard you couldn't bear it?"

". . . no. Everything has always been there."

"How fortunate you are."

Granacci gazed at the naked longing on his friend's face.

"Perhaps."

BOOK TWO

THE SCULPTURE GARDEN

He was drawn to the garden on the Piazza San Marco as though the ancient stone statues had magnets buried within them. Sometimes he did not know that his feet were carrying him there. He would find himself inside the gate, lurking in the shadow of the loggia. He did not speak to anyone, did not venture down the path through the meadow to the casino where Bertoldo and the apprentices were working. He just stood motionless, a hunger in his eyes.

"Two whole years? How will I endure it?"

Returning from dinner one spring day Granacci announced to the apprentices' table:

"It's just a year ago today that Michelangelo started. I've ordered a bottle of wine brought in at sundown; we'll have a celebration."

The studio was crackling with tension. Ghirlandaio was sitting at his desk, his scowl blacker than the base of his beard.

"*Il Magnifico* has summoned me and asked if I would like to send my two best apprentices to his new Medici school," he declared.

Michelangelo stood riveted to the planks of the studio floor.

"No, I would not like to send my two best apprentices," cried Ghirlandaio. "To have my studio raided. But who dares say 'No' to *Il Magnifico?* You, Buonarroti. You would like to go?"

"I have been hanging around that garden like a starved dog in front of a butcher stall," pleaded Michelangelo.

"Enough!" It was the angriest Michelangelo had ever seen him. "Granacci, you and Buonarroti are released from your apprenticeship. Now back to work, all of you!"

Joy drenched Michelangelo to the skin. Granacci stood glum.

"Granacci, my friend, what is it?"

"I like paint. I can't work with stone. It's too hard."

"No, no, my friend, you will be a fine sculptor. I will help you. Just wait and see."

Granacci achieved a wistful smile.

"Oh, I will come with you, Michelangelo. But whatever will I do with a hammer and chisel? I'll cut myself off at the knees!"

That night Lodovico demanded, "How long is the apprenticeship? How large the wage?"

"I don't know. I didn't ask."

"You didn't ask!" sneered Lodovico. "Do you think we have the wealth of the Granacci, that we can support you in your follies?"

The Medici sculpture garden was unlike Ghirlandaio's studio; it did not have to earn its living.

It was a warm April day when Michelangelo began his apprenticeship to Lorenzo the Magnificent and Bertoldo.

The first person to greet him was Pietro Torrigiani, a powerfully built blond green-eyed beauty. He said with a flashing white-toothed smile:

"So you're the lurker. The Ghost of the Garden. You haunted these porticoes."

"I didn't think you noticed me."

"Noticed!" replied Torrigiani. "We were devoured by your eyes."

Bertoldo loved only two things as well as sculpture: laughter and cooking. He had written a cookbook, and his one complaint at having moved into the Medici palace was that he had no chance to use his recipes.

He linked his thin arms through those of the new apprentices.

"Not all skill is communicable," he declared. "Donatello made me his heir, but he could never make me his peer. Try as he would he couldn't put his finger on my fist. I will show you everything Ghiberti taught Donatello, and Donatello taught me; how much you absorb depends on your capacity. And now to work. If you have any talent, it will come out."

Michelangelo thought, "Just let them put a hammer and *subbia* in my hands and they will see the chips fly!"

Bertoldo had no intention of putting these tools into the hands of a beginner. He assigned Michelangelo a drawing desk on the portico between seventeen-year-old Torrigiani and twenty-nine-year-old Andrea Sansovino.

The apprentice to whom he became closest was Torrigiani, who looked to Michelangelo more like a soldier than a sculptor. He fascinated Michelangelo. Torrigiani came from an ancient family of wine merchants, long since noble. He could be quarrelsome. He gave Michelangelo a quick, warm friendship.

To Michelangelo's question whether Granacci did not think Torrigiani magnificent, Granacci replied guardedly:

"I have known him all my life. Our families are associated."

"You haven't answered my question, Granacci."

"Before you make a friend, eat a peck of salt with him."

He had been in the garden for a week when Lorenzo de' Medici entered. Michelangelo now saw close up for the first time the man who, without office or rank, ruled Florence and had made her a mighty republic, wealthy not only in trade but in art, literature, scholarship. Lorenzo de' Medici, forty years old, had a roughhewn face that appeared to have been carved out of dark mountain rock; not at all handsome, with muddy skin, a jutting jaw, lower lip which protruded beyond the upper, a turned-up nose, large dark eyes, and a mass of dark hair. He was dressed in a long, sienna-colored robe with purple sleeves, the tip of a white collar showing at the neck. He was just over medium height, with a sturdy physique which he kept in condition by days of hard riding and hawking.

He was also a trained classical student, an omnivorous reader of Greek and Latin manuscripts, a poet and the builder of Europe's first public library, for which he had assembled ten thousand manuscripts and books. He was acknowledged to be "the greatest patron of literature and art that any prince has ever been," with a collection of sculptures, paintings, drawings, carved gems open to all artists and students for study and inspiration. For the scholars who had gathered in Florence to make it the scholastic heart of Europe, he had provided villas on the slope of Fiesole, where they translated newly found Greek and Hebraic manuscripts, wrote poetry, philosophic and religious books, helped create what Lorenzo called "the revolution of humanism."

Lorenzo had an open, lovable nature and a total lack of arrogance. Ruler of the Republic, he had no army, no guard, walked the streets of Florence unattended, speaking to all citizens as true equals, living a simple family life, romping on the floor with his children and holding open house to the artists, literary men and scholars of the world.

Lodovico had never given his consent to Michelangelo's entering the garden. The family rarely saw him; he left at dawn when all were asleep, came home promptly at twelve for dinner, and worked at the garden until dark, loitering as long as possible on the way home so the family would be in bed and there would be only his brother Buonarroto lying awake to ask the news of the day, or his grandmother waiting in the kitchen to give him a light supper.

He found himself plunged into drawing. Live models were drawn from every quarter of Florence: scholars in black velvet; soldiers with bull necks, square heads and thick, arching eyebrows; swashbuckling toughs; farmers off their carts; bald-headed old men with hooked noses and nutcracker chins; monks in black cloaks, black caps with their flaps turned up over their gray hair; the gay blades of Florence, handsome, with Greek noses running straight from the brow, curly hair worn low on their necks, round empty eyes; the wool dyers with stained arms; the calloused ironmongers; the burly porters; plump house servants; nobles in red and white silk hemmed with pearls; slender boys in violet; chubby children to serve as models for cupids.

Michelangelo grumbled at Bertoldo's harsh criticism of a torso he had drawn:

"How can we draw only from the outside? All we see is what pushes against the skin. If we could follow the inside of a body: the bone, muscle . . . Never have I seen the inside of a man."

Bertoldo swore softly. "Doctors are allowed to dissect one body on a special day of the year, in front of the City Council. Other than this, it is the worst crime in Florence. Put it out of your mind."

"My mouth, yes; my mind, no. I'll never sculpture accurately until I can see how a human body works."

"Not even the Greeks dissected. Do you need to be better than Phidias?"

"Better, no. Different, yes."

Michelangelo had never seen Bertoldo so agitated. He reached a hand to the old man's thin arm, patted it quietingly.

To his surprise Michelangelo also acquired the devotion of Torrigiani, who now moved his workbench closer to Michelangelo's. Torrigiani had an overwhelming personality; he swept Michelangelo off his feet with his charm, his attentions, his vivacity. He was a dandy who garbed himself in colorful silk shirts and a broad belt with gold buckles; he stopped at the barber in the straw market every morning before coming to work to be shaved and have his hair combed with a perfumed oil. Michelangelo was a messy worker: he got charcoal on his hands, which he then forgetfully rubbed into his face; he spilled paint on his shirt, ink on his stockings.

When the apprentices walked in the morning or in the afternoon Torrigiani slipped his arm through Michelangelo's, kept him a captive though enchanted audience.

"Ah, to be a soldier, Michelangelo. To fight in mortal combat, to kill the enemy with sword and lance, conquer new lands and all their women. That is the life! An artist? Bah! It is work for the sultan's eunuchs. You and I must travel the world together, my friend, find combat and danger and treasure."

Michelangelo felt a deep affection for Torrigiani. He felt himself to be simple, to have won the admiration of Torrigiani . . . it was heady wine to one who never drank.

With the first intense locked-in heat of the garden came the first casualty: the student, Soggi. His enthusiasm had been withering like the grass of the meadow. He had won no prizes or commissions, and although Bertoldo had been paying him a few coins, his earnings were higher only than Michelangelo's, which were non-existent. For this reason Soggi thought that Michelangelo might join with him.

One breathless evening late in August he waited until everyone had left, then flung down his tools and came to the newest apprentice.

"Michelangelo, let's you and I get out of here. All this stuff is so . . . so impractical. Let's save ourselves while there is still time."

"Save ourselves, Soggi? From what?"

"Look, don't be blind. They're never going to give us any commissions or money. Who really needs sculpture in order to live?"

"I do."

"Where are we going to find work? If Lorenzo should die . . ."

"But he's a young man, only forty."

". . . then we would have no more patron, no more garden. Are we to wander about Italy like beggars with hats in our hands? Do you need a marble cutter? Could you use a Madonna? A Pietà? I can make you one, if only you'll give me a roof and victuals."

Soggi swept his few personal possessions into a bag.

"Not me! I want to be in a trade where folks come to me. Every day! For *pasta* or pork, for wine or *calzoni*. People can't live without these things, every day they must buy. So every day I must sell. What do you say, Michelangelo? They haven't paid you a single scudo. Look how ragged your clothes are. Do you want to live like a pauper all your life? Quit now, with me. We'll find jobs together . . ."

Soggi's outburst was deeply felt; it had been building up for weeks, perhaps months. Yet at the back of his mind Michelangelo was a little amused.

"Sculpture is at the top of my list, Soggi. In fact, there is no list. I say, 'Sculpture,' and I'm finished."

The next morning when Bertoldo heard of Soggi's departure he shrugged.

"The casualties of sculpture. Everyone is born with a little talent; but with most people, how quickly the flame flickers out."

He ran a hand resignedly through his thin white hair.

Granacci, having completed a painting for Lorenzo, had shown so much talent at organization that Lorenzo had asked him to become the manager of the garden. He enjoyed being an executive, spending his days making sure that the proper stone, iron or bronze arrived, setting up contests for the apprentices, getting modest commissions from the guilds.

"Granacci, you mustn't," protested Michelangelo. "You have as much talent as anybody in this garden."

"But I enjoy it," replied Granacci mildly.

"Then stop enjoying it. If we need charcoal, or a model, let us get them for ourselves. Why should you give up your work to help us get ours done?"

Granacci was not insensible to the compliment embedded in Michelangelo's fury.

"There's time for everything, my friend," he replied. "I have painted. I will paint again."

But when Granacci returned to painting Michelangelo was angrier than ever, for Lorenzo had pressed him into service to design stage settings for a morality play, banners and arches for a pageant.

"Granacci, idiot, how can you stand here singing so happily, painting carnival decorations that will be thrown out the day after the pageant?"

"But I like doing what you call trivia. Everything doesn't have to be profound and eternal. Pageants and parties are important because people get pleasure from them, and pleasure is one of the most important things in life, as important as food or drink or art."

"You—you—Florentine!"

As the days of fall deepened, so did Michelangelo's friendships. But Bertoldo was pushing him hard, never pleased, crying: "No, no, you can do it better. Again! Again." Making him redraw models from a ladder above them, the floor beneath, obliging him to come in on a holiday to create a theme that would embrace all the figures he had sketched during the week.

Walking home with Granacci at night, Michelangelo cried in anguish:

"Why am I discriminated against?"

"You're not," replied Granacci.

"But anyone can see it. I am not permitted to enter any of the competitions for Lorenzo's prize money, or work on any of the commissions. I'm not permitted to visit the palace and see the art works. You're manager of the garden now. Speak to Bertoldo. Help me!"

"When Bertoldo considers you ready to enter contests, he'll say so. Until then . . ."

In his loneliness he turned to Torrigiani. They became inseparable. Michelangelo raved about Torrigiani: of his wit, his flair, his physique . . .

Granacci raised an eyebrow.

"Michelangelo, I am in a difficult position: I can't say too much without appearing jealous and hurt. But I must warn you. Torrigiani has done this before."

"Done what?"

"Won someone over completely, only to fly into a rage and break off the relationship when there is someone new. Torrigiani needs an audience; you are providing him with that audience. Do not confuse this use with loving you."

Bertoldo was not so gentle. When he saw a drawing of Michelangelo's in which he had imitated one that Torrigiani had just completed, he tore it into a hundred shreds.

"Walk with a cripple for a year and at the end you will limp. Move your desk back where it belongs!"

Bertoldo knew that Michelangelo had reached a boundary of patience. He put an arm as brittle as an autumn leaf about the boy's shoulder.

"And so: on to sculpture."

Michelangelo buried his head in his hands; his amber-colored eyes were intense with feeling, sweat broke out on his forehead. His heart bounded and his hands trembled.

"Now what is sculpture?" demanded Bertoldo in a mentor's tone. "It is the art which, by removing all that is superfluous from the material under treatment, reduces it to that form designed in the artist's mind . . ."

"With hammer and chisel," exclaimed Michelangelo, recovering his calm.

". . . or by successive additions," persisted Bertoldo, "as in modeling in clay or wax."

Michelangelo shook his head vigorously.

"Not for me. I want to work directly on the marble. I want to work as the Greeks did, carving straight from the stone."

"A noble ambition. But first you must learn to model in clay and wax."

Bertoldo showed him how to make an armature, using sticks of wood or iron wires. Once the framework was up, Michelangelo started applying the wax to see how close he could come to creating a three-dimensional figure from a two-dimensional drawing.

"It must be perfect, not only from the front but from every angle," said Bertoldo. "Which means that every piece has to be sculptured not once but three hundred and sixty times, because at each change of degree it becomes a different piece."

Michelangelo was fascinated.

After he had massed his wax on the skeletal frame he followed Bertoldo's orders to work it with tools of iron and bone, refine it with his strong fingers. The results had raw power.

"But no grace," criticized Bertoldo; "and not the slightest facial resemblance."

"The devil with portraiture. I never will like it."

"Never is longer at your age than mine. When you're hungry and the Duke of Milan asks you to do his portrait—"

Michelangelo glowered. "I don't get that hungry."

April was only a couple of months away. Lodovico told Michelangelo he would take him out of the garden if he were not paid by then. Bertoldo, when he came wrapped in heavy robes, was a pale wraith; but Michelangelo knew that he must speak. He showed Bertoldo the clay figures he had been modeling, asked permission to copy them in stone.

"No, my son," croaked Bertoldo hoarsely, "you are not ready."

"The others are; I am not?"

"You have much to learn. Patience! God shapes the back to the burden."

Michelangelo still had not been invited to the palace, and when Lorenzo invited the newest apprentice, Michelangelo grew angry. He felt exclusion implied rejection.

Then, on a cold March day, Bertoldo said, "There's a newly discovered Faun at the palace: pagan Greek, beyond doubt. About the fifth century before Christ. You must see it. Right now."

The Medici palace was large enough to house a numerous family of three generations, the government of a republic, a world-wide business, a center for artists and scholars. It was austere, with a majestic simplicity that characterized the taste of the Medici.

They entered through the massive gate into the square courtyard. Michelangelo's eye moved to two of the great sculptures of the city: the Davids of Donatello and of Verrocchio. He rushed with a cry of joy to touch the pieces. He gazed openmouthed at Donatello's David, so young and soft, with long curls of hair, the slender arm holding a gigantic sword, the left leg curved so gracefully to put the open-sandaled foot on Goliath's decapitated head.

Then as Bertoldo led him from room to room his head began to spin: for here was a veritable forest of sculptures and gallery of paintings. No good Italian artist since Giotto was unrepresented.

They reached Lorenzo's *studiolo,* a small writing room.

"Here is the Faun," Bertoldo said. "Now I will leave you for a few minutes while I get something from my room."

Michelangelo went close to the Faun. He found himself looking into gleaming, gloating eyes. He took drawing paper and red crayon from inside his shirt, sat at the far side of the room and sketched the Faun.

That night he tossed and turned. Into his mind there flashed the picture of a modest-sized piece of white marble, lying in the grass in the garden, exactly the right size for a Faun like the one in Lorenzo's *studiolo*.

Before daybreak he went to the marble block in the garden and picked it up in his arms and struggled under its weight down the path. He knew he had no right to touch this marble, that at least by implication he had rebelled against the authority of the garden, overthrown Bertoldo's iron-edged discipline. Well, he was on his way out anyway if his father had his say.

His hands caressed the stone, searched out its contours. For him the marble was a living, breathing substance. Marble was the hero of his life; and his fate. Not until this very moment, with his hands on the marble, had he come fully alive.

For this was what he wanted to be all his life: a white-marble sculptor, nothing more, nothing less.

He picked up Torrigiani's tools and set to work, in his mind the clearly etched image of the Faun in the palace.

He placed his chisel on the block, struck the first blow with his hammer. This was where he belonged. He, the marble, the hammer and chisel, were one.

The Faun was completed. For three nights he had worked behind the casino; for three days he had hidden it beneath a wool cloth. Now he was willing for Bertoldo to see it. He was polishing the top of the head when Lorenzo came down the walk. He stopped in front of the workbench.

"Ah, the Faun from my study," said Lorenzo.

"Yes."

"You left out his beard. Isn't the job of the copyist to copy?"

"The sculptor is not a copyist."

"Not even an apprentice?"

"No. The student must create something new from something old."

"And where does the new come from?"

"From where all art comes. Inside himself."

He thought he saw a flicker in Lorenzo's eye. It was quickly suppressed.

"Your Faun is old, but you left him all his teeth."

When he left, Michelangelo took up his chisel and went to work on the Faun's mouth. Lorenzo returned the next day. He stopped in front of the workbench.

"Your Faun seems to have matured twenty years in a day."

"The sculptor is master of time: he can age his subjects forward or back."

Lorenzo seemed pleased.

"I see you have removed an upper tooth. And two lower ones in the other corner."

"For balance."

"It was perceptive of you to rework the entire mouth. Someone else might have been content just to hammer out the few teeth."

"It followed logically."

Lorenzo said, "I'm pleased to see that we have not been making soup in a basket."

The next morning a page in varicolored stockings and scarlet coat appeared in the garden. Bertoldo called out:

"Michelangelo, you are wanted at the palace."

"You've gotten yourself sacked!" exclaimed one of the students. "For stealing that marble."

Michelangelo looked at Bertoldo. His expression told nothing. He went with the page.

Lorenzo was seated behind his desk in the library. Michelangelo bowed stiffly from the waist.

"How old are you, Michelangelo?" Lorenzo asked.

"Fifteen."

Lorenzo opened his desk, took out a parchment folio. From it he spread out dozens of drawings. Michelanglo could not believe what he saw.

"But . . . those are mine. . . ."

"Just so. We have put many obstacles in your path, Michelangelo. Bertoldo has borne down hard, with harsh criticism and little praise or promise of reward. We knew you had a real talent but did not know your character. If you had left us for lack of praise or money awards . . ."

There was a silence in the beautiful room.

Lorenzo came to the boy's side.

"Michelangelo, you have the makings of a sculptor. Bertoldo and I are convinced that you could become heir to Ghiberti, Donatello. I should like you to come and live in the palace. As a member of my family. From now on you need concern yourself only with sculpture."

"I like best to work in marble."

Lorenzo chuckled.

"No thanks, no expression of pleasure at coming to live in the palace of a Medici. Only your feeling for marble. Will you bring your father to me?"

"Tomorrow."

In the palace, standing before Lorenzo, Michelangelo found his father humble, almost pathetic. And he felt sorry for him.

"Buonarroti-Simoni, we would like Michelangelo to live with us here, and become a sculptor. Everything will be provided for him. Will you concede the boy?"

"*Magnifico messere,* I know not how to deny you," replied Lodovico, bowing deeply. "All of us are at the pleasure of Your Magnificence."

"Good. What do you do?"

"I have never followed any craft or trade. I have lived on my meager income, attending to the few possessions left to me by my ancestors."

"Then make use of me. See if there is in Florence something I can do for you. I will favor your interest to the utmost of my power."

Lodovico glanced at his son, then looked away.

"I know not how to do anything but read and write. The companion of Marco Pucci in the customhouse has just died, and I should be pleased to have his place."

"I had expected you would request something much grander. But if you desire to become the companion of Pucci, you can do so."

He turned back to Michelangelo. A warm smile lighted the dark, homely face.

"It is sixty years since my grandfather Cosimo invited Donatello into his home to execute the bronze statue of David."

BOOK THREE

THE PALACE

A page escorted him up the grand staircase and along the corridor to an apartment opposite the central courtyard. Bertoldo opened the door.

"Welcome, Michelangelo, to my home. *Il Magnifico* thinks I have so little time left, he wants me to teach you in my sleep."

There were two wooden beds in the L-shaped room, each with a coffer at its foot.

"This arrangement will give us privacy," said Bertoldo. "Put your things in the coffer at the foot of your bed."

The next day Michelangelo returned to his room to find that the palace tailor had left a new outfit on his bed. It was amazing how much more attractive the new clothes made him look, the crimson cap sending color into his cheeks, the cowl collar of the violet cloak making his head seem better proportioned, the golden shirt and stockings adding a sheen of gaiety.

In his absorption, he did not see Bertoldo enter.

"You fancy yourself in that raiment?"

"I didn't know I could look like this."

"You can't. They're for special occasions only."

"Isn't Sunday dinner a holiday?"

"Put on this blouse and tunic. Come the Day of the Virgin, you can show off."

Michelangelo sighed, took off the violet cloak and unlaced the fine yellow linen blouse, then glanced mischievously at his teacher.

"Ah well, put not an embroidered crupper on a plow horse."

They made their way to the dining room filled with notables. Piero de' Medici, oldest son of Lorenzo, and his elegantly gowned wife Alfonsina Orsini came in late and had to take places at the foot of one of the long tables. Michelangelo saw that they were offended. Giovanni, Lorenzo's second son, and his cousin Giulio entered. Giovanni had his mother's light brown hair and fair complexion, was tall and corpulent, with a heavy face and plump underchin. Giulio was dark, handsome, saturnine. His eyes slashed through the assemblage. He missed nothing that could be useful to him.

Waiters passed among the diners with heavy silver trays of fresh-water fish. A youngish man in a multicolored shirt picked up a small fish, put it to his ear, then to his mouth as though talking to it, and after a moment burst into tears.

"Why are you crying?" asked Lorenzo.

"My father was drowned some years ago. I asked this little fish whether he ever saw him anywhere. He said he was too young to have met him and suggested that I ask those bigger fish who may know more about the matter."

Lorenzo, amused, said, "Give the lad some of the big fishes so that he may interrogate them."

The laughter had an annealing quality; strangers at Lorenzo's table who had never met began talking with the people around them.

The fish dish was removed and he was served with *fritto misto.* Michelangelo was too fascinated watching Lorenzo as he spoke in turn to some thirty or forty guests to more than taste the food.

The servants brought young suckling pigs roasted on a spit, with rosemary in their mouths. An improviser upon the lyre entertained by singing the news and gossip of the week accompanied by satiric comments in rhymed and cadenced verse.

After dessert the guests promenaded in the wide foyer.

Watching them, Michelangelo thought, "Everyone is a friend to the Medici . . . and no one."

The following morning he and Bertoldo went to the far end of the garden, to the collection of marble blocks.

Bertoldo turned to his protégé.

"I am not a great marble carver. But with you perhaps I can become a great teacher." And he began Michelangelo's teaching by telling him about air bubbles, the spots in the marble that fall out or become hollow after weathering. They cannot be seen from the outside, and one must learn to know when they are inside.

Bertoldo demonstrated that even when he was tearing out marble to get rid of what he did not want he must work with rhythmical strokes so that he achieved circular lines around the block. Did he understand?

"I will, after you turn me loose among these marbles. I learn through my hands, not my ears."

"Then take the wax out! That Faun wasn't too bad, but you arrived at your results through blind intuition. For consistent results you have to know why you are doing what."

The outdoor sculpture workshop was a combination forge, carpenter's and blacksmith's shop. Standing alongside the forge were newly arrived rods of Swedish iron that

Granacci had bought the day before so that Michelangelo could make himself a full set of nine chisels.

Bertoldo told him to start a fire in the forge; chestnut wood made the best charcoal and produced a slow, intense, even heat.

"I already know how to temper tools," said Michelangelo. "The Topolinos taught me."

The next morning Michelangelo rose in the dark, in order to be in the garden at dawn. He knew that it was the first rays of the sun that revealed the truth about marble. Quality that could survive the earliest sun would be intact when night fell.

He went from block to block, tapping with his hammer. The solid blocks gave out a bell-like sound, the defective ones a dull thud. One small piece that had been exposed to the weather for a long time had developed a tough skin. With hammer and chisel he cut away the membranous coating to get to the pure milky substance below. Wanting to learn the direction of the vein, he held his hammer tightly and fractured off the high corners.

He liked what he saw; took a piece of charcoal and drew the head and beard of an old man on the marble. Then he pulled up a bench, straddled the block, gripping it with both knees, picked up hammer and chisel. Tensions within him fell away with each falling chip. His arm grew lighter and stronger with the passing of the hours. These metal tools clothed him in their own armor. They made him robust.

Bertoldo entered the shop, saw Michelangelo at work, cried out, "No, no, that's wrong. Stop! That's the amateur way to carve."

Michelangelo heard the voice over the pounding of his hammer, turned to flash recognition, but without ceasing the gouging-out movement of his *ugnetto*.

"Michelangelo! You're beginning at the wrong end."

Michelangelo did not hear him. Bertoldo turned away from the sight of his apprentice cutting a furrow through the stone as though it were quince jelly. He shook his head in amused despair.

"As well try to keep Vesuvius from erupting."

The following week he found three gold coins on his washstand, which Bertoldo said would be left for him each week.

He went to the outdoor market and purchased gifts for the Topolinos, then arranged with one of the grooms in the basement of the palace to borrow a horse and saddlebag. Sunday morning after attending mass in the palace chapel he packed the bag and set out for Settignano.

The Topolinos were so surprised to see him come riding up the road on a silver-gray stallion, sitting on a silver saddle, that they forgot to say hello. He got down from the horse, tied him to a tree, took off the saddlebag and emptied it onto the rough board table. After a moment of silence the father asked what the packages were. Michelangelo replied, "Gifts."

"Gifts?" The father gazed at his three sons in turn, for except to children, Tuscans do not give presents.

"For four years I ate your bread and drank your wine."

The father replied roughly, "You cut stone for your soup."

"Each week Lorenzo gives me three gold coins."

"What for?"

"Pleasure."

"Pleasure? What manner of pleasure?"

Michelangelo thought about that.

"It is to bring things to your friends."

Slowly, amidst a deep silence, he began distributing his gifts.

"To my mother, a lace scarf for mass. For Bruno, a

leather belt with silver buckle. For Gilberto, a yellow shirt and stockings. For grandfather, a wool scarf for your throat in winter. For Father Topolino, high boots for when you work in Cave Maiano. Enrico, you said that when you grew up you would own a gold ring. Here."

For a long moment they gazed at him, speechless. Then the father pulled on the high boots; Bruno clasped the belt about his waist; Gilberto donned the new gold shirt; the grandfather stood wrapping and unwrapping the soft wool scarf around his neck. Enrico mounted the horse, the better to admire his ring in privacy.

Then the father spoke.

"All of these . . . Lorenzo gives you this money to buy us gifts."

"Yes."

"He is truly The Magnificent One."

The time had come to choose a theme. What should it be?

"I feel close to the Madonna," he thought. "She is the only image I have of my mother. I will take the Madonna and Child for my theme."

But he had still to decide how he would present them.

He haunted the rooms of the palace, drawing after the masters, sometimes with Giuliano de' Medici keeping him company, and went into the poorer parts of town where the women worked on the sidewalks before their houses with their babes on their laps. He went into the countryside to the farmers around Settignano who had known him since he was a child.

He drew the mother and child in every position he found. For a few scudi he persuaded the women to move, change, shift themselves and the child to give him different angles.

He decided that he would carve Mary with the child on her lap, his face buried in his mother's breast, but his back fully turned on his viewers.

As far as he knew, no one had shown Jesus with his back turned. Yet his drama would not be begun for some thirty years. This was the mother's time, and the mother's portrait.

He reviewed the hundreds of sketches of mother and child he had made in the past months, put the drawings aside. Was it possible to conceive a piece of sculpture without knowing the marble from which it would draw its sustenance? He sought out Granacci and asked if they could visit the stone shops of the city.

In one yard he saw a piece that captivated him at once. It was of modest size, but its crystals were gleaming white. He poured water on it to look for cracks, struck its ends with a hammer to listen for its sounds, tested for flaws, bubbles, stains.

"This is the one, Granacci," he cried with glee. "It will hold the Madonna and Child. But I'll have to see it by the first rays of sunlight."

"If you think I'm going to sit on the ground worshiping your marble until dawn . . ."

"No, no, you settle the price and go home."

Michelangelo was standing over his marble when the fingers of dawn came over the hills. The block had no perceptible flaw: no crack or hollow, no discoloration, the crystals flickering brilliantly on its surface.

"You are a noble block," he said aloud.

"Marble" was derived from the Greek word meaning "shining stone." How his block glistened in the early morning sunlight as he set it up vertically on the wooden bench. He had lived with this block for several months now, studied it in every light, from every angle, in every degree of heat and cold.

He picked up his hammer and chisel and began cutting. He was not working from his drawings or clay models. He was carving from the images in his mind.

Marble would not yield to exterior force without accenting its own essence: stoniness. He had not realized to what extent marble had to be battled. His respect for his material grew blow by blow.

Bringing out the live figures involved long hours and longer days, a slow peeling off, layer by layer. After each series of blows he stepped back to inspect his progress.

On the left-hand side of his design there descended the flight of heavy stone steps. Mary was seated in profile on a bench to the right, the broad stone balustrade giving the illusion of ending in her lap, just under her child's knee. He saw that if Mary's strong hand, holding the child's legs securely, were to open more widely, it could be holding firmly not only her son but also the bottom of the balustrade, which would become an upright beam. Mary would then be supporting on her lap both the weight of Jesus and the cross on which her son would be crucified.

Now he had the upright, but where was the transverse bar? He studied his drawings to find a way to complete the imagery. He looked at the boy, John, playing on top of the steps. If he threw the plump arm across the balustrade at a right angle, the boy's body and right arm formed the living crossbeam.

With the carving of images of two other small children playing above the stairs, his Madonna and Child was finished. He began under Bertoldo's rigorous instruction the one task in which he had no training: polishing.

Slowly the highlights emerged: sunlight on the Madonna's face, on the curls, left cheek and shoulder of the child. On the foredrapery covering the Madonna's leg, on the back of John as he straddled the balustrade, on the inside of the balustrade itself to accent its importance in the structure. All the rest—the block-seat, stairs, walls—was in quiet shadow.

Lorenzo summoned the scholars of the Plato Academy. When Michelangelo entered the room with Bertoldo they found that the block had been mounted on a high flat altar covered with black velvet. The scholars ignored him as though he were not in the room, while they considered his work from every angle. He felt them searching, pondering. Then, slowly, one by one, they turned back to him; pride was in their eyes.

When he returned to his apartment he found a leather pouch on his washstand. It was filled with bright gold florins.

"What is this?" he asked Bertoldo.

"A purse from Lorenzo."

Michelangelo picked up the pouch and walked to Lorenzo's bedroom. Lorenzo was sitting at a small table.

"Lorenzo, I can't understand why . . ."

"Gently, gently. Sit down here. Now, start at the beginning."

Michelangelo gulped.

"It's this money. You should not have to buy the marble. It is yours already. I've lived in the palace while carving it, you've given me everything . . ."

"I was not buying the piece, Michelangelo. It belongs to you. The purse is a completion prize. I thought you might like to travel and see other art works. I will give you letters of introduction."

2. The Madonna of the Stairs, about 1491. Florence, Casa Buonarroti.

Michelangelo rushed home, spilled out the golden coins across his father's desk.

"But . . . what . . . what . . . ?" Lodovico stumbled.

"My prize money."

"How much?"

"I haven't stopped to count," replied Michelangelo loftily.

". . . thirty, forty, fifty," counted his father. "Enough to support a family in ease for half a year. Michelangelo, you must start on another piece immediately, tomorrow morning, since they are so well paid."

Michelangelo was amused. No word of thanks. Only joy at running his hands through this pile of gold pieces.

"We're going to look for another farm," cried Lodovico. "Land is the only safe investment. Then with the extra income . . ."

"I'm not sure I can let you do that, Father. *Il Magnifico* is giving me the florins for travel: to see all the sculptures . . ."

"Travel to see sculptures!" Lodovico was aghast. "You look, you leave, the money is gone. But with farms . . ."

His brother Buonarroto asked, "Are you really going traveling, Michelangelo?"

"No," said Michelangelo laughingly. "I want only to work." He turned to Lodovico. "They're yours, Father."

Several times a week Bertoldo insisted that they go to the churches to continue drawing from the masters. They were sketching in the Brancacci chapel. Torrigiani set his stool so close to Michelanglo's that his shoulder pressed against Michelangelo's arm. Michelangelo moved his stool a little. Torrigiani was offended.

"I can't draw without a free arm," said Michelangelo.

"Why are you so cranky?"

"I want to concentrate."

"I'm bored. We've drawn these frescoes fifty times. What more is there to learn?"

"How to draw like Masaccio."

Torrigiani said with a crooked smile, "I'm surprised the favorite student still has to submit to these schoolboy exercises."

"Copying Masaccio is not a schoolboy exercise, except to a schoolboy mind."

"Oh, so now your mind is better than mine. It's as they say: little man, little life; big man, big life."

"Big man, big wind."

Torrigiani was furious. "You meant that as an insult!"

He sprang up from his stool, put his massive hand on Michelangelo's shoulder and yanked him to his feet. Michelangelo had time to see Torrigiani's grim expression, but he had no chance to duck or avoid the blow. Torrigiani's fist exploded on the bridge of his nose with the sound of powder exploding. He tasted blood and crushed bone in his mouth, and then, as from a distance, heard Bertoldo's anguished cry.

While stars burst in a black heaven, he slipped to his knees and lost consciousness.

He awakened in his bed in the palace. His head was a mass of pain. Bending over him was Pier Leoni, Lorenzo's physician, Lorenzo and Bertoldo. He heard someone say:

"Torrigiani has fled the city, Excellency."

"Send our fastest riders after him. I'll lock him in the stocks."

The doctor began exploring his face with his fingers.

"The bridge of his nose is crushed. The bone splinters may take a year to work their way out. The passage is completely closed now. Later, if he's lucky, he'll be able to breath through it again."

He slipped an arm under Michelangelo's and pressed a cup to his lips.

"Drink. It will put you to sleep. When you wake the pain will be less."

When he awakened he was alone in the room. The pain had localized now, and he felt the throbbing behind his eyes and nose. He got out of bed, reeled, caught the side of the wash table to steady himself. Then, summoning courage, looked up into the mirror. He could barely recognize his own face in the glass. Both of his eyes were swollen the size of blue goose eggs. Torrigiani's big fist had thrown his face out of focus. He crawled on hands and knees back into his bed. And he was sick at heart.

The swelling receded, the discoloration faded; but he was still unable to present himself to the world in this changed form. He slipped out late at night and walked the silent streets for hours, working off his caged energies.

Finally Bertoldo said, "I'll take you to Pisa and show you whole new themes for narrative, like my riding warrior."

Bertoldo ordered horses that night. At dawn they were riding down the Arno to the sea. That night Michelangelo pulled off his shirt and britches and stretched himself under the red coverlet, his hands behind his head. He realized that he had been out all day, among people, and had not once thought of his nose.

"Glory be to God," he thought, "I'm cured."

He returned next day to the garden.

He received a message from his father. The family was concerned about Lionardo, who had been reported ill in the monastery at San Marco.

"Could you use your Medici connections to get in to see Lionardo?" asked Lodovico, when he went to see them.

"No outsider is allowed in the monks' quarters."

After a number of days he learned that the reforming monk, Savonarola, would preach in San Marco the following Sunday.

He would take up a position at the side door leading in from the cloister. Lionardo would have to pass close to him. But the monks' cowls were pulled so far forward that it was impossible for Michelangelo to see whether Lionardo was in the group.

When a murmur announced the entrance of Savonarola, he slipped into a pew close to the pulpit. Savonarola slowly climbed the pulpit stairs. His head and face were deep in his Dominican cowl. Michelangelo could see little but the tip of his nose and a pair of dark veiled eyes. His voice took on a commanding tone as he preached on the corruption of the priesthood. The priests were put into the Church by their families for worldly gain; they were guilty of bribery, selling of relics, accumulation of benefices.

Savonarola pushed back the cowl and Michelangelo saw his face, the upper lip thin and ascetic, the lower lip fleshy and voluptuous. Black eyes were sunken under high-boned, hollow cheeks; his nose jutted out with wide, flaring nostrils. His voice filled the church.

"O Italy, O Rome, O Florence, give up your pomps and shows. The whole of Italy will feel God's wrath. Blood will run in the streets. Unless ye repent! repent! repent!"

The cry of "Repent!" echoed a hundredfold while Savonarola, masking his face, came down the pulpit stairs and out the cloister door, leaving Michelangelo deeply moved, a little exalted, a little sick. He received a note from Lionardo asking him to come to San Marco. The cloister was beautiful at dusk, tranquil and secluded from the world.

Lionardo seemed to Michelangelo as cadaverous as Savonarola.

"The family has been worried about your health."

Lionardo's head shrank deeper into the cowl. "My family is the family of God." He went on with affection, "I called for you because I know you are not evil. You have not been corrupted by the palace."

Amused, Michelangelo asked, "How do you know these things?"

"We know everything that goes on in Florence. Fra Savonarola has had a vision. The Medici, the palace, all the godless art works within its walls will be destroyed. They cannot save themselves; but you can. Repent, and forsake them while there is still time. There are to be nineteen sermons. By the end of them, Florence and the Medici will be in flames."

They stood side by side in the airless corridor along one side of the cloister. Michelangelo was shocked into silence.

"You won't save yourself?" implored Lionardo.

"If my soul is to be saved, it can only be through sculpture. That is my faith, and my discipline. We both serve Him equally."

Lionardo's eyes burned into Michelangelo's for a moment. Then he was gone.

Savonarola's sermons in San Marco attracted such large crowds that he transferred his activities to the cathedral. Ten thousand Florentines stood packed together to hear the friar who, because of his fasting and constant prayer, could barely summon the strength to mount the pulpit stairs. He had assumed a complete identification of himself with Christ.

"As ye can see and hear, I do not speak with my own tongue but that of God. I am His voice on earth."

A cold shiver ran through the congregation.

Michelangelo gazed up at the marble carvings of children singing, dancing, laughing. They seemed to cry out,

"People are good!" while Savonarola was thundering, "Humanity is evil!"

Who was right? The sculptors? Or Savonarola?

Worse was to come. Already Savonarola had gone beyond attacking the sins of the city and had turned his thunders against its politics. And, in Florence, politics meant Lorenzo de' Medici.

Now Savonarola charged that Lorenzo had confiscated money in the city treasury and used it to buy sacrilegious manuscripts and evil works of art. Lorenzo, the corrupt tyrant, must go. The dishonest Signoria must go. The judges, the officials, must go. A new government must be installed to render Florence a City of God.

Who was to govern Florence? Revise its laws and execute them?

Savonarola.

God had ordered it.

The continuing prophecies of doom brought mounting hysteria to the city. Students refused to attend their classes, printers to print anything Savonarola disapproved. Artists deserted to him and publicly burned their works, declaring them immoral. Even some men who had been most loyal to Lorenzo gave in to the madness let loose by the fanatic preacher.

Ever since he had returned to the garden after his smashed nose had healed and his visit with Bertoldo to Pisa, Michelangelo had been working on a sculpture in high relief showing the battle between the centaurs and people of Thessaly. The theme, taken from Ovid's *Metamorphoses,* was a pagan one suggested to him by one of the scholars of Lorenzo's Plato Academy. Now, torn between approval of Savonarola's crusade for reform and his disapproval of the friar's attacks upon the Medici and the arts, Michelangelo shut himself away from everything and,

3. The Battle of the Centaurs, about 1492. Florence, Casa Buonarroti.

for a month, eating and sleeping little, tackled the twenty figures on his marble block.

One day his brother Lionardo, in cloak and cowl, came to the garden.

"Welcome to my workshop, Lionardo."

Lionardo gazed at the Battle.

"It is your sculpture I have come about. We want you to offer it up to God."

"How do I do that?"

"By destroying it in Savonarola's first fire in the purifying of Florence."

"You consider my marble obscene?"

"It is sacrilegious. Bring it to San Marco and fling it on the flames yourself."

Michelangelo took him by the elbow, escorted him to the rear gate and put him into the street.

He had planned to do weeks of polishing. Instead he

asked Granacci to help him move the block into the palace that night.

They carried the block to Lorenzo's sitting room. Lorenzo had not seen the piece for a month. He came into the room with the aid of a cane, hobbling painfully from an attack of gout. "Ah!" he exclaimed, and dropped into a chair. He sat for a long time in silence. Finally Lorenzo turned and looked up at Michelangelo.

"You were right not to polish. I can feel every body, every crushed bone. It's unlike any marble I've seen."

"We've already had an offer for the piece."

"A patron? Someone wants to buy?"

"Not exactly. They want it as a contribution. From Savonarola, through my brother Lionardo, to offer it up to God on their bonfire."

There was an almost imperceptible pause before Lorenzo said, "And you answered?"

"That I was not free to give it. The piece belonged to Lorenzo de' Medici."

"The marble is yours."

"Even to give to Savonarola for burning?"

"If that is your wish."

"But suppose, Excellency, that I had already offered the piece to God? The God who created man in His own image of goodness and strength and beauty? Savonarola says that man is vile. Would God have created us in hate?"

Lorenzo rose abruptly, walked about the room with only the barest indication of a limp.

"Come with me," he said. "There is something I must show you."

They went to the family church of the Medici. Its principal façade was obviously uncompleted.

"Michelangelo, this is the last great work of art I must complete for my family, a marble façade with some twenty sculptured figures in its niches."

"Twenty sculptures! I will do it, Lorenzo, I promise. But I will need time, I still have so much to learn . . . I have not yet tried my first free-standing figure."

When he reached his apartment he found Bertoldo wrapped in a blanket, sitting over a live-coal brazier, his eyes red and his face a pasty white. Michelangelo went to his side.

"Are you all right, Bertoldo? Let me put you to bed."

He settled Bertoldo under the feather-bed quilt, went down to the basement kitchen and ordered a mug of wine heated on the dying embers. He held the silver cup to Bertoldo's lips.

Bertoldo closed his eyes and dropped off to sleep.

In a few moments there was a change in his breathing. Michelangelo sent a groom for Lorenzo's doctor.

Michelangelo spent the night holding Bertoldo so that he could breathe a little more easily. The doctor confessed that he could think of nothing to do.

Bertoldo died in the late afternoon of the second day. He uttered his last words with a little smile.

"Michelangelo . . . you are my heir . . . as I was Donatello's."

"Yes, Bertoldo. And I am proud."

"I want you to have my estate. It will make you . . . rich . . . famous. My cookbook."

"I shall always treasure it."

Bertoldo smiled again, as though they shared a secret joke, and closed his eyes for the last time. Michelangelo had lost his master. There would never be another.

The disorganization of the garden was now complete. All work stopped. The group broke up. The garden was lonely.

Michelangelo was an artist without ideas, a mendicant begging among the hours. He had no desire to draw. His broken nose began to pain him; one nostril was closed completely, making it difficult for him to breathe.

Lorenzo decided to take a cure in one of his villas, with six months away from the palace and its duties. There he could not only eradicate his gout but lay his plans to come to grips with Savonarola. Fra Savonarola seemed to have the upper hand. Florentines were still flocking to his side.

Michelangelo was troubled by the thought of Lorenzo's departure. Lorenzo's oldest son, Piero, never friendly to Michelangelo, would be in command and what would life be like for him here? Piero could order him out of the palace. For that matter, what was his status, now that the sculpture garden had virtually closed down?

Then Lorenzo sent for him.

"Would you like to come to Fiesole with us?" *Il Magnifico* asked. "In the morning Giovanni is to be made a Cardinal of the Church. It would be well for you to witness the ceremony. Later, when he is in Rome, Giovanni will remember you attended."

He was awakened two hours before morning light, dressed himself and joined the procession going down the hill to the church, where Giovanni had spent his night in prayer. His heart sank when he saw that Lorenzo was being carried on a litter.

The little church sparkled in the light of a hundred candles. Giovanni knelt before the altar to receive the sacrament. High mass was sung, the superior of the abbey blessed the insignia of Giovanni's new rank: his mantle, broad-brimmed hat with the long tassle. The Papal Brief was read, ordering the investment, after which a sapphire ring, emblematic of the Church's celestial foundation, was slipped onto Giovanni's finger by Canon Bosso.

Michelangelo left the church and walked down the road to Florence.

Two days later he stood in a reception line to bid fare-

well to the new cardinal and his cousin Giulio, who was accompanying him. Giovanni blessed Michelangelo and invited him to visit if he should ever come to Rome.

Lorenzo had been away two weeks when a rumor came that he was failing. A new doctor had administered a mixture of diamonds and pearls. It failed to help.

Michelangelo paced the corridors in an agony of apprehension. At daylight he threw a saddle over a horse and rode the four miles to Lorenzo's villa.

He went around the far side of the estate and made his way to Lorenzo's bedchamber. He slipped behind the hanging next to the door, as Lorenzo's confessor motioned everyone from the bedside. He took Lorenzo's confession, gave him absolution.

After a moment Piero came in, his head bowed. Lorenzo began to speak.

"Piero, my son, you will possess the same authority in the state that I have had. Florence is a republic. It will not be possible for you to please everyone. Pursue that course of conduct which strict integrity prescribes. Consult the interests of the whole community. If you will do so, you will protect Florence and the Medici."

Piero kissed his father on the forehead.

There was a hurried movement from the outside hall. To Michelangelo's amazement Savonarola brushed past him, went to Lorenzo and dropped his hood. The others fell back.

"You sent for me, Lorenzo de' Medici?"

"I did, Fra Savonarola."

"How can I serve you?"

"I wish to die in charity with all men."

"Then I exhort you to hold the faith."

"I have always held it firmly. Give me your blessing, Father."

Savonarola lowered his head, recited the prayers for the dying, and departed.

Lorenzo sent for his servants. When they surrounded his bed he bade them farewell, asking their forgiveness if he had ever offended them.

Michelangelo strove with all his might not to run to Lorenzo's side, drop to his knees and cry out, "I, too, have loved you! Bid me farewell." He had not been summoned here. He was an intruder, his presence unknown. And so he buried his face in the rough undersurface of the velvet, even as Lorenzo fell back on his pillow.

Michelangelo slipped out of the open door, ran down the stairs and into the garden.

Lorenzo was dead! He had lost his greatest friend.

BOOK FOUR

THE FLIGHT

He shared his former bed with Buonarroto. Piero did not want him. After two years in a comfortable apartment it was not easy for him to live in this small room with his three brothers.

For three months he could not work. He had never gone so long without drawing. Ghirlandaio urged him to come back to his studio and finish his apprenticeship, but Michelangelo knew he had to go forward, and returning to fresco painting would be to lose all he had learned of sculpture over the past three years.

A chance encounter with his old friend Father Nicola Bichiellini, prior of the Order of Hermits of Santo Spirito, indirectly brought him back to work.

At the palace he had learned to love books from the scholars of the Plato Academy, who had taken pains to teach him the pleasures of study. Now he asked Father Bichiellini's permission to read in the library of Santo Spirito, the oldest library in Florence. Later the prior arranged for him to move freely about the monastery, not ordinarily open to any except the silent hermit-monks who lived there, so that Michelangelo might study and copy the frescoes of many of Italy's greatest artists. For weeks he spent his days in the hermitage copying or reading, speaking to no one except Father Bichiellini, who sensed Michelangelo's need to talk and gave freely of his time.

"Buonarroto, how much money are you holding for me?" demanded Michelangelo one evening.

Buonarroto consulted his account book, told his brother how many florins were left from the palace savings.

"Good. It is enough to buy a piece of marble, and leave some over for rent."

The single desire of his heart rose out of love and sorrow: to do something for Lorenzo. Lorenzo had often spoken of Hercules, suggesting that the twelve labors were not to be taken literally, but were meant as symbols for all the varied and near impossible tasks with which each new generation of man was faced.

He must find a way to represent Hercules so that he became Lorenzo. In the meanwhile he had to get out of the house, into his own workshop.

He remembered the workshop of the Duomo which had been headquarters for materials while the Cathedral was being built. The foreman, bald as a slab of marble, came to ask if he could be of service. Michelangelo introduced himself.

"I was an apprentice in the Medici garden. I need a large marble, but I have little money. I thought the city might be willing to sell something it did not need."

"Call me Beppe. What interests you?"

Michelangelo took a deep breath.

"First, Beppe, this big column. The one that has been worked on."

"That's called the 'Duccio block.' Stands seventeen, eighteen feet high. Board of Works bought it for Duccio to carve a Hercules. It reached here ruined."

Michelangelo ran his fingers exploringly over it.

"Beppe, would the Board of Works sell it?"

"Not possible. They speak of using it one day."

"Then what about this smaller one?"

Beppe examined the nine-foot block Michelangelo indicated.

"I could ask. Come back tomorrow."

"And would you plead price for me?"

Beppe did a job for him.

"She's yours. They told me to set a fair price. How about five florins?"

Now that he had his marble he had to find a workshop. Beppe again came to his rescue.

"I tell the Board I can use part-time man, that you offer to work for no pay. Set up your shop along the far wall."

He set up an armature, bought a supply of pure beeswax, began modeling . . . and was dissatisfied.

"How can I establish a figure if I don't know what I'm doing? How can I achieve anything but surface skin sculpture, exterior curves, outlines of bones, a few muscles brought into play? What do I know of the causes? How can I know what creates, from within, the shapes I see from without?"

Learn anatomy he must! But the only way he could learn it was by dissecting, and the penalty for violating a corpse was—death. But there must be a way and he must find it.

Where could he find available corpses? Which dead in Florence were unwatched and unwanted? Only the very poor, the mendicants who filled the roads of Italy. These people were taken to church hospitals when they were sick. And the church with the largest charity hospital was in Santo Spirito!

Could he ask Prior Bichiellini for his unclaimed corpses? If the prior were caught, he would be put out of his order, excommunicated. Yet this was a courageous man who feared no force on earth so long as he did not personally offend God.

He wandered through Santo Spirito, checking entrances to the dead room where the bodies were kept overnight until burial in the morning.

The prior let him recite only a part of his proposal. "Enough! I comprehend fully. Let us never mention this subject again. You have not brought it up. It has vanished like smoke, leaving no trace."

Stunned by the rapid rejection, Michelangelo walked through the blustery streets. He was desolate.

He had no intention of abandoning the search. Somehow he would find a way to learn what lay under the skin of men's bodies. Meantime he returned to the library of Santo Spirito to look among its books for new clues on how the ancients had conceived of Hercules.

Again the prior offered his assistance, finding him a heavy leather volume on one of the higher shelves, scanning through it, exclaiming, "Ah yes, here is some material," laying a heavy bronze key across the pages.

It was not until the fourth or fifth session that Michelangelo began to notice the key. The prior used it not only to keep books open but as a place marker when he closed a volume, a pointer when he was underscoring lines.

Always the key. Always the same key. But never when he was in the study with others.

"It must mean something. But what? What are keys for? Obviously to open doors. How many doors are there in which I am interested? Only one. The dead-room door." He would try the key in the door of the dead room. If it fitted . . .

It was midnight when he reached the monastery, having slipped out of his house noiselessly and taken a circuitous route to the hospital. An oil lamp stood in a niche beside the dead room. He took a candle out of a canvas bag he carried, lighted it, shielded it under his cape.

He inserted the big key, felt the lock slip. In an instant he had opened the door, darted into the room, closed and locked it behind him. He did not know whether he dared face the task ahead.

The dead room was small, about eight feet by ten, windowless. The stone walls were whitewashed, the floor of rough blocks. In the center of the room, on narrow planks mounted on two wooden horses, and wrapped from head to foot in a burial sheet, was a corpse.

He stood leaning against the door, breathing hard, the candle shaking in his hand like a tree in a storm. It was the first time he had been alone in a room with death, let alone locked in, and on a sacrilegious errand. He was more frightened than he had ever been in his life.

"What kind of nonsense is this?" he demanded of himself.

He put down his bag and looked for a place to set his candle, of importance to him not only for light but as a clock as well. It had taken much experimenting to ascertain with accuracy how long each type of candle would burn. This one would last three hours. When it began its first sputtering he would have to leave.

He emptied his bag of its scissors and kitchen knife, took off his cape, uttered a jumbled prayer, and approached the corpse.

He caught an odor, something like very old flowers dying in water. It was not strong but it remained in his nostrils inescapably.

It was a considerable time before he could pick up the knife, recall what he had read about the human body, the few illustrations he had seen. Swallowing hard, he brought the knife down and made his first incision.

The smell was growing heavier. Nausea started within him. But as he worked, his initial emotion of disgust was overcome by excitement.

Suddenly the candle began to splutter. Three hours already! He could not believe it. Yet he did not dare ignore the warning. He set his green bag and candle on the floor, picked up the winding sheet from the corner, and began to rewind the corpse.

The perspiration ran down into his eyes, his heart pounded so loud he thought it would wake the monastery as he used the last vestige of his strength to lift the corpse from the table with one arm while he pulled the winding sheet under and around the necessary five times. He barely had a moment to make sure that the corpse was stretched

out upon the planks as he had found it, to check the floor for possible stains or wax, before the candle gave its last flickering sputter and went out.

He took a wandering route home, stopping a dozen times to retch. When he reached home he washed his hands with harsh lye soap.

His body, as he got into bed, was icy. He huddled against his brother, but not even Buonarroto's warmth could help him.

He had chills and fever all day. He lay there feeling as clammy as the corpse. Nothing was able to remove the smell of death from his nostrils.

About eleven o'clock he rose and, with his legs rickety beneath him, made his way to Santo Spirito.

There was no corpse in the dead room. Neither was there one on the following night. The two days gave him a chance to recover. On the third night he again found a body in its winding sheet on the planked table.

This time he used his knife with more authority, opening the abdomen with a clean cut, then using his left hand to pry apart the rib cage, which made a noise like crackling wood.

Experimentally, he pressed the lung; a hissing noise came out of the mouth of the corpse. He dropped the candle in fright. When he regained his calm and had picked up the candle, he realized that in touching the lung he had forced out the residual air; and for the first time he understood what breathing was, because he could see and feel and hear the communication between the lungs and the mouth, realized what it did to the whole figure.

He felt that night a sense of triumph, the happiness that arises out of knowledge, but when the candle began to splutter he was emotionally exhausted and next day he could not eat.

That night he was back again in the dead room.

He lost count of the number of corpses he dissected, working night after night until his candle warned him to leave the dead room. He was often revolted, sometimes afraid, sometimes doubtful of his right to do what he must for sculpture's sake. But in the end he knew the structure of man, knew the functioning of the stomach and bowels and kidney and intestines; knew them and held in his mind pictures so clear he could transfer them accurately to the paper upon his drawing board. Now he was ready to go to work on the Hercules.

He went to visit Prior Bichiellini, casually laid the bronze key over the pages of the book the prior was reading, and said, "I should like to carve something for the church."

The prior was pleased.

"I have long felt the need of a crucifix for the central altar. I've always envisioned it in wood."

For once he had the good sense not to say, "Wood is not my trade." If the prior wanted a Crucifixion in wood, then wood it must be, though he had never even whittled.

"May I work in the monastery carpenter shop?"

"The brothers would be pleased to have you."

The lay brothers in the carpenter shop treated him as another carpenter. This suited Michelangelo; he felt at home working in the comfortable silence framed by the pleasant sounds of saw, plane and hammer. He worked on the various woods to get the knack of carving in this material.

He carved his figure in the hardest wood available in Tuscany, walnut, and when he had finished with hammer and chisel, sandpapered it down and rubbed the surface with stainless oil and wax. His fellow carpenters stopped by his bench to observe progress. The prior said simply:

"It is what I envisioned for the altar. Thank you."

A heavy snowstorm left Florence a white city. Michelangelo was huddled over a brazier in the Duomo workshop when a groom came looking for him.

"His Excellency, Piero de' Medici, asks if you could come to the palace."

He found the Medici children and grandchildren assembled in Lorenzo's study, a bright fire burning.

It was the birthday of the youngest of Lorenzo's children, Giuliano. Cardinal Giovanni, who had settled in a small but exquisite palace when a hostile Borgia had been elected Pope, looked plumper than ever sitting in Lorenzo's chair, hovered over by his cousin Giulio. They were dressed in their gayest brocades, jeweled satins and cut velvets.

Piero stood with his back to the fire. He smiled. "Michelangelo, it is our pleasure to welcome you back to the palace.

Today we must do everything that pleases Giuliano."

"I should like to help make Giuliano happy today."

"Good. The first thing he said this morning was, 'I should like to have the greatest snowman ever made.' And since you were our father's favorite sculptor, what would be more natural than that we should think of you?"

Something within him sank like a stone.

"Please do it for me, Michelangelo," cried Giuliano. "It would be the most wonderful snowman ever made. We'll all serve as your assistants."

And he knew he would agree.

Late that afternoon, when the last of the Florentine crowds had thronged through the palace grounds to see the hilariously grotesque giant snowman, Piero sat at his father's desk in the big office, under the maps of Italy.

"Why not move back into the palace, Michelangelo? You would have the same privileges as when my father was alive."

Michelangelo gulped; he had been fifteen when he had come to live in the palace. He was almost eighteen now. Hardly an age to receive spending money left on his washstand. Yet it was a chance to get out of the drear Buonarroti house, to earn some money, perhaps to carve something good for the Medici.

A groom moved him back into his old apartment, with Bertoldo's sculptures still untouched on the catercornered shelves. A palace tailor came with fabrics and measuring tapes; and on the following Sunday, Piero's secretary deposited three gold florins on the washstand.

The Topolinos rode into the city behind their white oxen on Sunday after mass and hoisted the Hercules block onto their cart. They drove in through the back entrance of the garden, unloaded and propped the marble next to his old sculpture shed.

Comfortably settled, he designed his Hercules. He was working with Seravezza marble, quarried high in the Alps. He attacked it with fury and the marble began to match his clay model: the powerful chest, magnificent forearms, the head focusing enormous power. Hammer and chisel in hand, he stood back from the galvanic male figure before him, thinking that the marble had yielded to love.

Monna Alessandra went to bed one night feeling tired and never awoke. For Michelangelo the loss was poignant; since the death of his own mother thirteen years before, Monna Alessandra had been the only woman to whom he could turn for love and understanding. Without his grandmother the Buonarroti house seemed gloomier than ever.

The palace, by contrast, was in an uproar. The last of Lorenzo's daughters was about to be married, and Piero was preparing to spend fifty thousand florins to give Florence the greatest celebration in its history.

That marriage proved to be a turning point: for Michelangelo; for Florence. The people murmured against Piero. Savonarola demanded that Piero be prosecuted for violation of the city's sumptuary laws. The wedding celebration was a signal to the Medici cousins to begin their political campaign against Piero.

Granacci came into the garden at dusk to tell him that someone had seen his Hercules and would like to speak to him about a commission. Michelangelo hid his surprise when he found the new patrons to be the Medici cousins, Lorenzo and Giovanni. Lorenzo was the spokesman.

"Michelangelo, we saw the two marble pieces you sculptured for our uncle Lorenzo, and should like you to carve a piece for us."

Michelangelo was silent. The younger brother continued.

"We've always wanted a young St. John. In white marble. Would the theme interest you?"

Michelangelo shifted awkwardly from foot to foot. He needed the money. It would put marble in his hands. Yet he wondered why they had not asked him at some time in the two years since Lorenzo's death. Prior Bichiellini had said the cousins aimed to drive Piero out of Florence. And Piero was *Il Magnifico's* son. He could not be disloyal to Lorenzo.

"We are prepared to pay a good price," said Lorenzo, while his brother added, "And there is a place at the back of our garden for a workshop. What do you say?"

"To be wanted is always good. May I think it over?"

"Of course," replied Lorenzo heartily. "We have no desire to rush you. Give us the pleasure of your company at Sunday dinner."

By Sunday he knew his mind. When, after dinner, he stammered that he appreciated their offer but could not at the moment accept, Lorenzo replied easily:

"We are in no hurry. The offer stands."

At the palace he found an urgent message from his father. Lodovico led him into the boys' bedroom, lifted a stack of clothing from the top of his brother's locker, and scooped out a pile of jewelry, gold and silver buckles, medallions.

"What does this mean?" he asked Michelangelo. "Has your brother, Giovansimone, been burglarizing people's homes at night?"

"Nothing quite so illegal, Father. Giovansimone is a captain in Savonarola's Army of Boys. They strip women in the streets who violate the padre's orders against wearing jewelry in public. If they hear of a family violating the sumptuary laws, they strip it bare. If they meet opposition, they stone people half to death."

"But is Giovansimone allowed to keep these things? They must be worth hundreds of florins."

"He is supposed to bring them all to San Marco. But he has converted his old gang of hoodlums into what Savonarola calls his 'white-shirted angels.' The Council is powerless to stop them."

With the fall, Florence became embroiled in an international dispute that could lead to the city-state's destruction. Charles VIII, King of France, had built the first permanent army since Caesar, some twenty thousand trained and heavily armed men. He was now bringing that army across the Alps and into Italy to claim the Kingdom of Naples through inheritance. The Medici cousins assured the king that Florence awaited his triumphal entry. But Piero refused Charles safe passage. The citizens of Florence who would have fought for Lorenzo were ready to welcome the French because they would help drive out Piero. Savonarola too invited Charles to enter Florence.

A dozen times Michelangelo vowed he would flee the palace. Loyal to Lorenzo, Giuliano, and even to Cardinal Giovanni, he had no feeling for Piero. But he could not bring himself to join the deserters.

On September 21 Fra Savonarola, in a final effort to drive Piero out, preached a sermon in the Duomo. Never before had the friar had such power, and never had his voice rung out with such a clap of doom. The hair of the Florentines stood on end as they cried and lamented while Savonarola portrayed the destruction of Florence and every living creature in it. People left the church half dead with fright, speechless, their eyes glassy.

The web closed tighter each day: it could be only a few days before the French army entered Florence.

One morning Michelangelo rose to find the palace abandoned. Piero had rushed out to treat with Charles. Alfonsina had left with her children and Giuliano for refuge in a hillside villa. Aside from a few old servants, Michelangelo seemed alone. The magnificent palace was frightening in its hollow silence, as he walked the echoing corridors and looked into the big empty rooms.

Piero offered Charles the coast fortresses, Pisa and Leghorn and two hundred thousand florins if he "would continue down the coast and avoid Florence." Outraged at this humiliating capitulation, the City Council summoned the people and castigated Piero for his "cowardice, foolishness, ineptitude, surrender."

Piero dashed back to Florence to reassert his rights. The crowd yelled, "Go away! Do not disturb the Signoria!" The people hissed and threw stones. Piero drew his sword. The crowds chased him through the streets. He disappeared into the palace and diverted the throngs momentarily by having the remaining servants bring out wine and cake.

Then couriers came down the street crying, "The Signoria has banished the Medici! For life! There is a price of four thousand florins on Piero's head. Down with Piero!"

Entering the palace, Michelangelo found that Piero had escaped through the rear garden and fled. Cardinal Giovanni, his fat face red with perspiration from the armload of manuscripts he was carrying, behind him two of his house servants also loaded down with fine bindings, was cutting through the garden and out the rear gate to safety. His apprehensive face lit up when he saw Michelangelo.

"Buonarroti! I've saved some of Father's rarest manuscripts, the ones he loved best."

Florence was only a moment behind.

Into the courtyard surged the mob. Cries of "The Medici are banished!" were followed with "Everything in the palace is ours!" Rioters poured in to sack the palace.

Michelangelo stood defensively before the Donatello

David. The crowd still poured through the main gate, jamming the courtyard, individual faces that he had seen all his life on the streets and in the piazzas, quiet, good-natured people suddenly inflamed, bent on destruction, with the faceless irresponsibility of the mob. What had caused the change? Was it the sense of being within the Medici palace for the first time as masters rather than outsiders?

He was knocked very hard against the David and a lump was raised on his head. The Donatello Judith and Holofernes was picked up base and all, and carried out through the rear garden. What was too big to move was shattered with smashes of pikes and poles.

He raced up the main staircase to the study, slammed the door behind him. He looked about at the priceless treasures. What could be done to protect them?

His eyes fell upon the dumbwaiter. He opened the door, pulled on the ropes and, when the lift was level, began piling in the small paintings, objects: cups of jasper, glass vases by Ghirlandaio. The old toothless Faun that he had copied for his own first piece of sculpture he stuffed inside his shirt. Then he pulled the opposite rope, sent the box down a way and closed the door. A mass of humanity reached the study at that moment and began looting the room. He fought his way to his own apartment, where he threw Bertoldo's models and a few of the bronzes under the beds.

Hundreds of rioters were sweeping through the palace and into the great rooms. He watched helplessly as they cut paintings out of their frames, ripped sculptures off their bases, smashing the chairs and tables, what was too large to be moved, destroying chests.

He made his way down the rear staircase, found pen

and ink, wrote Giuliano a brief note: *When it is safe . . . send someone to your father's study . . . I loaded the food lift as full as I could.* He signed it *M.B.*

When the city at last slept he slipped past the quiet houses to the Medici stables. Two of the grooms had stayed with the horses. They knew he had the right to take out horses whenever he desired. They helped him saddle up. There was no guard at the gate he rode out on the way that would take him to Venice.

By afternoon of the second day he had crossed the Apennines and dropped down into Bologna, enclosed by orange brick walls, turrets and almost two hundred towers. He entered the city toward the river side. The narrow, tortuous streets, covered over by the protruding second floor of the houses, were airless. Each Bolognese family had built a tower for protection against its neighbors, a Florentine custom that had been abolished by Cosimo, who had obliged the Florentines to saw off their towers at roof height. The wider streets and the piazzas were lined with arches of orange brick to protect the people from snow, rain and the intense summer heat, so that the Bolognese could traverse his town from any direction and never be exposed.

Michelangelo reached the main square, dismounted and was promptly surrounded by Bolognese police.

"You are a stranger in Bologna?"

"Florentine," Michelangelo replied.

"Your thumb, if you please."

"Thumb? What do you want with my thumb?"

"To see the mark of the red wax."

"I don't carry red wax."

"Then you will have to come with us. You are under arrest."

He was led to the customs office where the officer in charge explained that every stranger coming into Bologna had to register and be thumbprinted as he came through one of the city's sixteen gates.

"How could I know?" demanded Michelangelo. "I've never been here before."

"Ignorance of the law excuses no one. You are fined fifty Bolognese pounds."

"Fifty Bolognese . . . I don't have that much money."

"Too bad. Fifty days in jail."

Michelangelo stared. Before he could recover his wits a man stepped forward.

"May I speak with the young man, Officer?"

"Certainly, Excellency."

"Is not your name Buonarroti?"

"It is."

"Is not your father an officer of the Florentine customs?"

"Yes, sir."

The Bolognese turned to the customs official.

"Our young man comes of a fine Florentine family; his father has charge of a branch of their customs office, as you have. Do you not think the important families of our two sister cities might exchange hospitality?"

Flattered, the officer replied, "Assuredly, Excellency."

Back in the brittle winter sun of the piazza, Michelangelo studied his benefactor. He might be in his mid-forties, with a broad, pleasant face.

"You are most kind, and I am stupid: you remembered my unmemorable face, while I, though I knew we had met . . . ?"

"We sat next to each other at one of Lorenzo de' Medici's dinners," explained the man.

"Of course! You are Signor Aldovrandi. You told me about the work of a great sculptor which is here in Bologna."

"Won't you give me the pleasure of your company at supper?"

"The pleasure will be mine. I haven't delighted my stomach since I lost sight of the Duomo."

"Then you have come to the right city," replied Aldovrandi. "Bologna is known as The Fat. Here we eat better than anywhere in Europe."

The Aldovrandi palace was a graceful building of brick, three stories high. Aldovrandi took Michelangelo to see his wood-paneled library, of which he was enormously proud.

"Lorenzo de' Medici helped me assemble the volumes. Tell me, Michelangelo, what brings you to Bologna?"

Michelangelo explained that he was on his way to Venice.

"How does it happen that you do not have fifty Bolognese pounds if you are traveling so far?"

"I hope to find work in Venice."

"Then why not remain in Bologna? We may even discover a sculpture commission for you."

Michelangelo's eyes gleamed. "I'll look for lodgings at once."

"Unthinkable!" replied Aldovrandi. "No friend and protégé of Lorenzo de' Medici may live in a Bolognese inn. You will be our guest."

He had been invited into a joyful house. He heard voices and laughter ringing through this wing of the palace which housed Aldovrandi's six sons. Signora Aldovrandi was a pleasant woman who welcomed Michelangelo as warmly as though he were a seventh son. His host, Gianfrancesco, belonged to the branch of the Aldovrandi which had prospered so greatly that he was free to spend his time in the arts. He invited Michelangelo for a tour of the city.

They walked under the arches where the shops displayed the most delicious foods of Italy: exquisite cheeses, the whitest of breads, rarest of wines, deer, quail, hare, pheasant; and in every block of the city their world-famous salami. Everywhere Michelangelo passed students from the university, who did their studying at the little cafés under the orange-colored porticoes, playing dice and cards between pages of their assignments.

"There is one thing I miss, Messer Aldovrandi. I have seen no stone sculpture."

"Because we have no stone quarries. Our own sculpture is of terra cotta."

A few moments later they came upon a young man making terra-cotta busts. He was powerfully built, with enormous shoulders and biceps, his skin was burnt the precise orange of Bologna's brick. Aldovrandi called him Vincenzo.

"This is my friend Buonarroti," he said, "the best young sculptor in Florence."

"Ah, then it is proper that we meet," replied Vincenzo, "for I am Bologna's best young sculptor. I am Dell'Arca's successor. I am to finish the great Pisano tomb in San Domenico."

"You have received the commission?" asked Aldovrandi sharply.

"Not yet, Excellency, but it must come to me."

As they walked on Aldovrandi said:

"Successor to Dell'Arca indeed! He is the successor to his grandfather and father, who are the finest brickmakers in Bologna. Let him stick to his trade."

They made their way to the church of San Domenico. The interior had three naves and a sarcophagus of St. Dominic to which Aldovrandi led him. He pointed out the work that had been continued by Niccolò dell'Arca.

"There are three figures left to be sculptured: an angel, St. Petronius, and a St. Proculus. These are the marbles that Vincenzo said he was going to carve."

He went everywhere with Aldovrandi: to palaces for dinner, to friends' for intimate suppers. The Bolognese were a hospitable people who loved to entertain.

And then it was Christmas. The symbolic "good wish" log burned in the drawing-room fireplace. The poor children sang carols outside for their gifts. Signora Aldovrandi presided over the game of "fortune extracting" from a sack.

Aldovrandi turned to Michelangelo:

"Now you must try your fortune."

He put his hand into the hemp bag. There was one package left. From the broad smiles all about him it was apparent that everyone was in on the joke. He pulled, and out came a terra-cotta replica of the Dell'Arca San Domenico tomb. In the three empty places, where the angel, St. Petronius and St. Proculus were missing, were oversized caricatures of himself, broken nose and all.

"I . . . I have the commission?"

Aldovrandi smiled at him happily. "The Council awarded it to you last week."

He had been working only a few days at a workshop near the church when a massive shape loomed before him. He looked up, saw that it was Vincenzo, the terra-cotta sculptor. His face was raw from the cold, his eyes were intense.

"Buonarroti, you got the work I been after. You take bread out of the mouths of us native sculptors."

Placatingly Michelangelo replied, "I understand. I lost some carving at Santo Spirito last year to silver workers."

"It's good you understand. Go to the Council, tell them you decide against it. Or you'll be sorry."

When Michelangelo told Aldovrandi of the encounter, he replied:

"He can't carve marble. Forget him."

"I'll never let you forget me," said Vincenzo the following day when Michelangelo reported that there was nothing he could do to help him.

Michelangelo looked at the enormous bony hands of Vincenzo, twice the size of his own. He thought of Torrigiani, could see Torrigiani's powerful fist coming through the air, hitting him, could taste the blood and feel the crushed bone. He became a little faint.

"What's the matter, Buonarroti? You don't look good. Afraid I make life miserable for you?"

"You already have."

But no more miserable than he would be to have to relinquish the opportunity to carve three beautiful blocks of white Carrara marble. If this were the price . . .

Once a week business associates of Aldovrandi made the trip to Florence and brought back news.

A week after Michelangelo had fled, Charles VIII had entered the city, collected a hundred and twenty thousand florins, received the right to maintain two fortresses in Florence until his war with Naples was over, and had taken his army away. Yet the wheels of the city-state had creaked to a painful halt. The city was torn by factions. By mid-December news reached Bologna that Savonarola had backed the democratic government.

With the coming of the new year, Piero de' Medici returned to Bologna to set up headquarters. Coming home from his workshop, Michelangelo found Piero and Giuliano.

When they met at the entrance to the dining room, Michelangelo exclaimed, "Excellency, how good to see you again. Though I could wish it were at the Medici palace."

"We'll be back there soon enough," growled Piero. "The Signoria drove me out by force. I am assembling an army and shall drive them out by force."

Giuliano had bowed formally to Michelangelo, but when

Piero took Signora Aldovrandi in to dinner, the two young men hugged each other.

At the Aldovrandi table, Piero immediately outlined his plan for the reconquest of Florence. All he required was sufficient money, hired mercenaries, weapons, horses. Piero expected Aldovrandi to contribute two thousand florins to his campaign.

"Excellency, are you sure this is the best way?" asked Aldovrandi respectfully. "When your great-grandfather Cosimo was exiled he waited until the city found it needed him and called him back. Wait for that hour, Excellency."

"I am not as forgiving as my grandfather. Florence wants me back right now. It is just Savonarola and my cousins who have schemed against me."

He turned to Michelangelo.

"You shall enter my army as an engineer, help design the wall fortifications after we have conquered the city."

"But if the city were bombarded it could be destroyed . . ."

"What then? Florence is a pile of stones. If we knock them down, we will put them together again."

"But the art . . ."

"What is art? We can replace all the paint and marble in a year. And it will be a Florence that I will command!"

Aldovrandi turned to Piero.

"In the name of my friend, *Il Magnifico,* I must decline. Lorenzo would have been the first to stop you, were he alive."

Piero turned to Michelangelo.

"And you, Buonarroti?"

"I too, Excellency, must decline. I will serve you in any way you ask, but not to wage war against Florence."

Piero pushed his chair back, rose to his feet, and left the room.

Michelangelo said, "Forgive me, Giuliano."

Giuliano had also risen, turned to leave.

"I too shall refuse to wage war. That would only make Florence hate us the more. *A rivederci,* Michelangelo."

He was at work on the figure of St. Petronius when he acquired a neighbor in the stall opposite. It was Vincenzo, whose father had a contract for making new brick and tile for a cathedral repair job. A crew of mechanics came in to fill the stalls for the repairs, and Vincenzo afforded the workyard running entertainment by taunting Michelangelo throughout the workday.

The laughter of the workmen made him a little ill. He suffered through the days and weeks, but St. Petronius emerged holding in his arms a model of the city. As a craftsman Michelangelo knew he had done a good job. As a creative artist he felt that he had contributed little.

"It is very fine," said Aldovrandi when he saw the polished piece. "Dell'Arca could not have surpassed it."

"But I am determined to give you something more," said Michelangelo doggedly. "I must not leave Bologna without carving something exciting and original."

"Very well, you disciplined yourself to give us the St. Petronius we wanted. I will discipline Bologna to accept the St. Proculus that you want."

After May Day he completed the drawing of his virile St. Proculus, who had been martyred before the gates of Bologna in 303, while in the full flower of his youth. Quite unabashedly, he modeled his own portrait: the punched-in bridge of the nose, the flat spread of the cheekbones and wide spread of the eyes, the thatch of hair worn halfway down his forehead, the steadfast gaze, resolved to triumph.

The hot summer months passed in fulfillment. Vincenzo had disappeared. The Aldovrandi family departed for their summer villa in the mountains. He stayed alone in the pal-

4. St. Proculus, 1494–95. Bologna, San Domenico.

ace and saw his host only when Aldovrandi rode in for a day to take care of his affairs. Once he brought startling news from Florence.

"Your Fra Savonarola has come out into the open. He has declared war on the Pope!"

Michelangelo was not as shocked as Aldovrandi expected, for Prior Bichiellini had predicted long ago that the Pope was Savonarola's ultimate target.

"How has the Pope replied?"

"He summoned Savonarola to Rome. But Savonarola has declined, declaring, 'It is not the will of God that I should leave this place at present.' "

The summer was over and the St. Proculus was finished. Michelangelo was exhausted, but happy with it. So was Aldovrandi.

"We could honor you in San Domenico."

"My work is done, and I have grown homesick for Florence," said Michelangelo quietly. "You have been a good friend."

"When will you return?"

"I don't know. Perhaps never."

"Everyone returns to Bologna. It's on the road to everywhere."

"Then I'll be back."

He had been away a year and the family was genuinely glad to have him home. Lodovico was delighted with the twenty-five ducats Michelangelo brought. Buonarroto had grown a full foot; Sigismondo was apprenticed to the Wine Guild; and Giovansimone had left the house entirely, maintaining himself regally in a flat across the Arno as one of the leaders in Savonarola's Army of Boys.

Granacci reported, "The Popolano family wants you to sculpture something for them."

"Popolano? I don't know any Popolanos."

"Yes, you do." Granacci's voice had an edge to it. "It's the Medici cousins, Lorenzo and Giovanni. They have changed their names to coincide with the People's Party, and are now helping to rule Florence. They asked me to bring you around when you returned."

The brothers received him in a drawing room.

Giovanni ordered sweet wine and cake and Lorenzo said they were still interested in having a young St. John. If he cared to move into the palace, for convenience' sake, he would be welcome.

He went to see Beppe in the Duomo workyard and heard of a small, quite good piece of marble in a neighboring yard which he could buy at a reasonable price. The rest of the money advanced to him for the St. John he turned over to his father.

He could not bring himself to live in the renamed "Popolano palace," but he did set up his workbench in the garden. The cousins treated him as a friend, frequently inviting him inside, to see a new piece of art or illuminated manuscript.

He carved a fifteen-year-old boy, a vital portrait of a youth. The Medici cousins were well pleased. They paid him the balance of the florins and told him he was welcome to continue using their garden as his workshop.

But not a word about another commission.

"Nor can I blame them," Michelangelo commented to Granacci. "I have carved six pieces in four years but only the St. Proculus has something original in it."

On his birthday he walked disconsolately into the workshop in the Popolano garden. He found a block of white marble sitting on his workbench. Across it, scrawled in charcoal in Granacci's handwriting, was the greeting:

"Try again!"

He did, an infant, robust, lusty, pagan, carved in the Roman tradition. He never imagined he was doing a serious piece, it was something he got fun out of. Out of the block emerged a delightful child of six, sleeping with his right arm under his head, his legs spread comfortably apart. He intended to return the marble to Granacci with a note which would read:

"Only a little the worse for wear."

When Lorenzo Popolano saw the completed piece his face flushed with pleasure.

"If you were to treat it so that it seemed to have been buried in the earth, I would send it to Rome, and it would pass for an antique Cupid. You would sell it for a far better price. I have a shrewd dealer there, Baldassare del Milanese. He will handle it."

He rubbed garden dirt into the crystals and stained the outside edges heavily with earth tans and rust, as amused at the idea of the fraud as he had been at the carving itself.

The Bambino was sold to the first customer to whom Baldassare offered it: Cardinal Riario di San Giorgio, for a pouch of gold florins, thirty of them. Michelangelo had thought an antique Cupid in Rome would bring at least a hundred florins. Even so, it was twice what it would have brought in Florence.

In June a groom came from Giovanni Popolano asking Michelangelo if he would come to the palace to meet a Roman nobleman, Leo Baglioni.

He said, "Would you be so kind as to make a simple drawing for me? A child's hand, for example. I am particularly interested in drawings."

Michelangelo drew rapidly, a number of memories of children in various poses. After a time Baglioni said:

"There can be no question about it. You are the one."

"The one?"

"Who carved the Cupid. Forgive me for dissembling, but I was sent to Florence by Cardinal Riario di San Giorgio, to see if I could find the sculptor of the Cupid."

"It was I. Baldassare del Milanese sent me thirty florins for the piece."

"Thirty! But the cardinal paid two hundred . . ."

"Two hundred! Why, that . . . that thief . . ."

"Precisely what the cardinal said," declared Leo Baglioni with a mischievous gleam in his eye. "He suspected it was a fraud. Why not return to Rome with me? You can settle your account with Baldassare. The cardinal would be pleased to offer you hospitality. He said that anyone who could make such an excellent fake should be able to make even better authentic carvings."

"A few articles of clothing from my home, sir, and I shall be ready for the journey."

BOOK FIVE

THE CITY

He stood on a rise just north of the city. Rome lay below in its bed of hills, destroyed, as though sacked by vandals. Leo Baglioni traced the outlines of the Leonine Wall, the fortress of Sant'Angelo.

They rode through a small piazza that stank from piled garbage, and followed narrow lanes with broken cobbles underfoot. The noise of carts passing over the stones was deafening. Shops were huddled between ancient palaces that looked as though they would topple at any moment. Michelangelo felt sick to his stomach: the Mother City of Christendom was a waste heap and a dunghill.

His host led him into the Campo dei Fiori, a vegetable, flower, cheese, fish and meat market, crowded with row upon row of clean colorful stalls, with cooks and housewives of Rome shopping for their dinner. For the first time since they had descended into Rome he was able to look at his host and tender him a wisp of a smile.

"Several times I almost turned my horse and made a run for Florence," Michelangelo said.

"Rome is pitiful. Pope Sixtus IV made a real effort to widen the streets and repair some of the buildings; but under the Borgias the city has fallen into a worse condition than before. Here's my home."

Michelangelo was given a corner room in Baglioni's house. Late in the afternoon they strolled to Cardinal Riario's palace. He received Michelangelo, read Lorenzo Popolano's letter of introduction, bade Michelangelo welcome to Rome.

"Your Bambino was well sculptured, Buonarroti, even though it was not an antique. I have the impression that you can carve something quite fine for us."

"Thank you, Excellency."

"I should like you to go out this afternoon and see our best marble antique Greek and Roman statues. Start with the arch of Domitian, then go to . . ."

By the time the cardinal finished he had named some twenty pieces of sculpture in a dozen different collections and parts of the city.

Baglioni guided him from sculpture to sculpture, until at last Michelangelo cried:

"Please, no more. I'm quivering inside. I must lock myself in my room and try to digest what I've already seen."

The cardinal sent for him next day.

"Tell me, Buonarroti, what do you think of the marbles you have seen? Can you do something equally beautiful?"

"I may not carve anything as beautiful. But we will see what I can do."

"I like that answer, Buonarroti, it shows humility."

He did not feel humble, all he had meant was that his pieces would be different from anything he had seen.

"We had best start at once," continued Riario. "My carriage is outside. It can take us to the stoneyard."

In the stoneyard Michelangelo wandered among the blocks, wondering how large a piece he dared select. He stopped before a white Carrara column over seven feet tall and four feet thick. His eyes lighted with excitement. He assured the cardinal that there could be a fine statue contained in it. Cardinal Riario quickly paid out thirty-seven ducats from the purse on his belt.

When the block had been delivered to a workshop near the cardinal's palace, Riario sent for him and said, "Now that you are about to undertake a prolonged piece of work, you had better move into the palace."

"On what terms am I to live in the palace, Excellency?"

"Let us just say that your address is the palace of the Cardinal Riario. And now we must leave you."

No word about what the cardinal wanted sculptured. Or what the price would be. Or whether he was to have regular payments during his year of work. The palace would be his address; he knew nothing more.

But he learned. He was not to live here as a son, or as a close friend. A chamberlain directed him to a narrow cell at the rear of the ground floor where he unpacked his few possessions. When he went looking for his first meal he found himself relegated to what was known as the "third category" dining room, in which he found his companions to be the cardinal's scriveners, the head bookkeeper, the purchasing agent for the palace, the managers of his lands.

The Cardinal Riario had made himself clear; Michelangelo Buonarroti was to live in the palace as one of the crew of skilled workmen. Nothing more.

Early the next morning he went to see Baldassare the art dealer, who had just been obliged to return Cardinal Riario's two hundred ducats for the Bambino. Baldassare was a swarthy fat man with an enormous stomach which he pushed ahead of him.

"I am Michelangelo Buonarroti, sculptor of Florence. I want you to return my Bambino. I will repay the thirty florins you sent me."

"Certainly not!" the dealer cried.

"You defrauded me."

"On the contrary, it is you who are the fraud. You sent me a false antique."

Michelangelo walked fuming out of the yard. Then he burst into laughter.

"Baldassare is right. It is I who was the cheat. I falsified the Bambino." He heard someone behind him exclaim:

"Michelangelo Buonarroti! Do you always talk to yourself?"

He turned, recognized a chap of his own age who had been apprenticed to the Money Changers Guild. In Florence they had never become friends, but here they fell on each other's necks.

"Balducci. What are you doing in Rome?"

"Working for Jacopo Galli's bank. Head bookkeeper. The dumbest Florentine is smarter than the smartest Roman. That's why I'm moving up so fast. How about having dinner together? I'll take you to a restaurant in the Florentine section. Wait till you taste the *tortellini* and beefsteak, you'll think you're back in sight of the Duomo."

That evening Balducci took him to the home of Paolo Rucellai, Michelangelo's distant cousin. Rucellai lived in the district of Ponte, known as "a little Florence, walled within itself." Here the Florentines in Rome lived close together, with their own markets, which imported their *pasta,* meats, vegetables, fruits and sweets from Tuscany.

In the midst of the chaos and filth of Rome the prosperous Florentines swept and washed down their streets every day at dawn, put their houses in a good state of repair. There were fines against dumping refuse in the streets or hanging laundry from the front windows instead of the back. Armed guards policed the quarter at night; it was the only section where one was sure not to stumble over a corpse on one's stoop at daybreak. At the Rucellai house he was presented to the leading families of the community, who accepted him at once.

He set up his seven-foot block and waited for the cardinal to present him with a subject.

"Exercise extreme care," Leo Baglioni warned him, "not to touch that column until Cardinal Riario gives you permission to do so. He is adamant about his properties."

He was humiliated at being cautioned like a laborer not to manhandle the property of his employer. Yet he had to promise not to chip a single crystal off the block.

A chance meeting with a fellow Florentine provided a needed diversion. Giuliano da Sangallo was a friend of Lorenzo. He was an architect, the first man to instruct Michelangelo in that art. He asked Michelangelo how things were going and listened carefully to the younger man's frustrations.

"You are in the service of the wrong cardinal," Sangallo concluded. "When Cardinal Rovere returns to Rome, I shall introduce you, and tomorrow I will come for you and show you the Rome I like best; not this stinking shambles of today."

He was as good as his word. Next day he handed Michelangelo a block of architectural paper, exclaimed, "Now we recreate Rome as Augustus saw it," and led the way from building to ancient, magnificent building. By nightfall Michelangelo was exhausted from trying to keep up with Sangallo's flying hands and his stream of verbal descriptions of Rome's grandeur.

Two more months passed before he could get another appointment with Cardinal Riario.

"What have you got for me today?" he asked in good

humor. "Something vigorously pagan, to match those fine antiques in the Cardinal Rovere's garden?"

Michelangelo lied quickly. "Yes, Your Grace."

He searched his mind for the most totally joyous pleasure-giving Greek god he could find, "A Bacchus?"

Bacchus was also Dionysus, a nature god, symbolizing fruitfulness, who brought strange and wondrous gifts to man. He would design a Bacchus for the cardinal.

His work was his only reward: on Good Friday violence broke out in Rome, moved on to revolt in the Florentine quarter when the Pope excommunicated Savonarola and ended in the grisly murder of Juan Borgia, brother of the Pope.

Cardinal Riario went into mourning with his Pope. The palace was closed to all but the most compelling business. Sculpture was far from compelling business.

Once more Michelangelo was desperate. And his purse was nearly empty, for he had used almost the last of his savings for marble to make a Cupid commissioned by Piero de' Medici and never paid for.

Michelangelo decided to go to Cardinal Riario and make him take some action.

The cardinal listened, playing quietly with the long gold chain around his neck.

"I would not expect you to have given this time for nothing."

"Thank you, Excellency; I knew you would be generous."

"Indeed I shall. I relinquish all right and title to the marble block and the thirty-seven ducats it cost me. The marble is yours, in return for patient waiting."

And then his luck changed. He finished polishing his Cupid, a lovely child just awakened from sleep and holding up its arms to be taken by his mother. Balducci was enchanted with its lighthearted warmth. He asked if they could carry it to the Galli house to show to his boss, Jacopo Galli.

Jacopo Galli was the tallest man Michelangelo had ever seen, hunched over at the shoulders from a lifetime of stooping to the short-statured Romans. He greeted Michelangelo cordially.

"Ah, you come with a marble in your arms. That is the sight I like best in my garden."

Galli removed a torso from a pedestal on the low wall next to the steps and replaced it with the Cupid. His eyes were twinkling. "I feel as though your Cupid has been sitting there since the day I was born. Would you sell it to me? What price shall we set?"

Humbly, Michelangelo murmured, "That is up to you."

"First, tell me your circumstances."

Michelangelo related the story of his year with Riario.

"So you end up without a scudo of pay, and a seven-foot marble block? Shall we say the Cupid is worth fifty ducats? Because I know you need money I will allow my cupidity to knock the price down to twenty-five ducats. Then, because I detest shrewdness in dealing with the arts, I will take the twenty-five ducats I was going to underpay you, and add them to my original estimate. Do you approve my formula?"

Michelangelo's amber eyes shone.

"Signor Galli, for a year I have been thinking bad things about the Romans. In your name, I apologize to the whole city."

Galli bowed. "Now tell me about this seven-foot marble block. What do you think might be carved from that?"

Michelangelo told him about his drawings for a Bacchus. Galli was intrigued.

"Would you be willing to move your block here, and carve this Bacchus for me? You could have a room to live in. I would pay you three hundred ducats for the completed statue."

Michelangelo bowed his head so that the candle gleam would not betray him. He had been saved from an ignominious return to Florence, from defeat.

He moved into the Galli house next day and set up his workshop in a shed at the edge of a fig orchard. Here he began his drawings for the Bacchus, using as model a young, self-indulgent nobleman, for he did not intend to portray Bacchus as the customary old man. Later Jacopo Galli found him a big-eyed, seven-year-old boy with golden curling hair as a model for a small Satyr.

One Sunday morning he invited Galli to see the drawing. Galli was delighted. "I don't know how to thank you," he said.

The weeks and months of uninterrupted carving flowed by. He took no time off for friends or rest or social life. The gold ducats Jacopo Galli paid him as he went along he sent home to his father.

The winter was mild: on the few sharp days he wore his wool hat with its earmuffs and a warm tunic. One day Galli asked permission to bring his friend Cardinal Groslaye to see the Bacchus.

The cardinal was enchanted. "How do you achieve in a half-finished figure this sense of throbbing vitality? I can feel the blood and muscle under the marble." His fading eyes gleamed as he added, "You know, my son, I am growing old. I must leave something behind me, something of singular beauty. I have secured permission from the Pope to dedicate a sculpture in the Chapel of the Kings of France in St. Peter's. There is a niche that will take a life-size sculpture."

A sculpture for St. Peter's, the oldest and most sacred basilica in Christendom, built over the tomb of St. Peter!

Could it be possible that the French cardinal would choose him?

That Sunday Michelangelo went to mass in St. Peter's to see the Chapel of the Kings of France and the niche about which the cardinal had talked. He measured with his eye the vacant niche on the opposite wall, disappointed to find it so deep that a statue would be seen only from the front.

He knew very soon that his theme would be a Pietà: Pity, Sorrow. He had wanted to do a Pietà ever since he had completed his Madonna and Child.

Galli took him to the cardinal's palace, where they waited for him to complete the five daily hours of prayer and offices required of every Benedictine. When the cardinal heard about the Pietà his eyes sparkled.

"What about the marble, Michelangelo? Could you find such a perfect piece as you speak of, here in Rome?"

"I think not, Your Grace. A column, yes; but an oblong

block that is wider than it is tall, and cut deep, that I have not seen."

"Then you must go yourself to the quarries in Carrara and find our marble."

On the way home Galli said, "You must go at once. I will advance the expenses for your trip."

"I can't."

"Why not?"

"I must finish the Bacchus," he replied.

"The Bacchus can wait. The cardinal can't. One day soon God will rest His hand just a trifle more heavily on his shoulder, and Groslaye will go to heaven. From heaven he cannot commission a Pietà."

"That is true. But I cannot stop work now," Michelangelo insisted stubbornly.

"I release you from our agreement. When you have finished the Pietà you will come back to the Bacchus."

"For me there is no coming back. The sculpture is growing complete in my mind. I must finish it now to get it perfect."

Toward the end of March, Michelangelo, eager to hear news of Florence, went to dine with the Rucellai. He learned that the city had turned against Savonarola after seven years of wrangling. The voters elected a new council, arrested the friar, and appointed a Commission of Seventeen to examine him and secure a confession that his words were not divinely inspired.

Savonarola refused to recant. The commission tortured him. Savonarola agreed to write a confession. He was released from his cell. What he wrote was not satisfactory to the Signoria. He was tortured again, and again, signed a confession written by a notary.

The commission declared Savonarola guilty of heresy and he was sentenced to death.

The throng began filling the piazza during the night,

pushing up against the gibbet. By dawn the square and all the streets leading into it were a seething mass.

Savonarola was led out onto the Signoria steps and stripped of his vestments. He mounted the scaffold, praying silently. Ropes and chains were put about his neck. Within an instant his neck was broken.

The pyre under the gibbet was lighted. The flames rose. His body was held aloft by the chains after the ropes had burned. The half-consumed corpse was stoned. The ashes were dumped into the Arno.

The martyrdom of Savonarola shook Michelangelo profoundly. He hardly knew what to think or feel: except pity.

He turned to his work. With marble in his hands, the world was good.

By the end of summer the Bacchus was finished. Galli was overjoyed with his statue.

"I feel as though Bacchus is fully alive, and will drop his cup at any moment. The Satyr is innocent and naughty at the same time. You have made for me the finest sculpture in all Italy."

It was Giuliano da Sangallo's opinion Michelangelo valued most. Sangallo said, "You've built this Bacchus the way we build a temple. It was a courageous experiment in construction. This fellow will stand erect as long as there is space for him to displace."

The following night Galli brought home a contract between Michelangelo and the Cardinal of San Dionigi, and which the cardinal had signed. In it Michelangelo found himself called *maestro* for the first time. For the sum of four hundred and fifty ducats he agreed to make a Pietà of marble, to be completed by the end of a year. In addition to guaranteeing the cardinal's payments to Michelangelo, Galli had written:

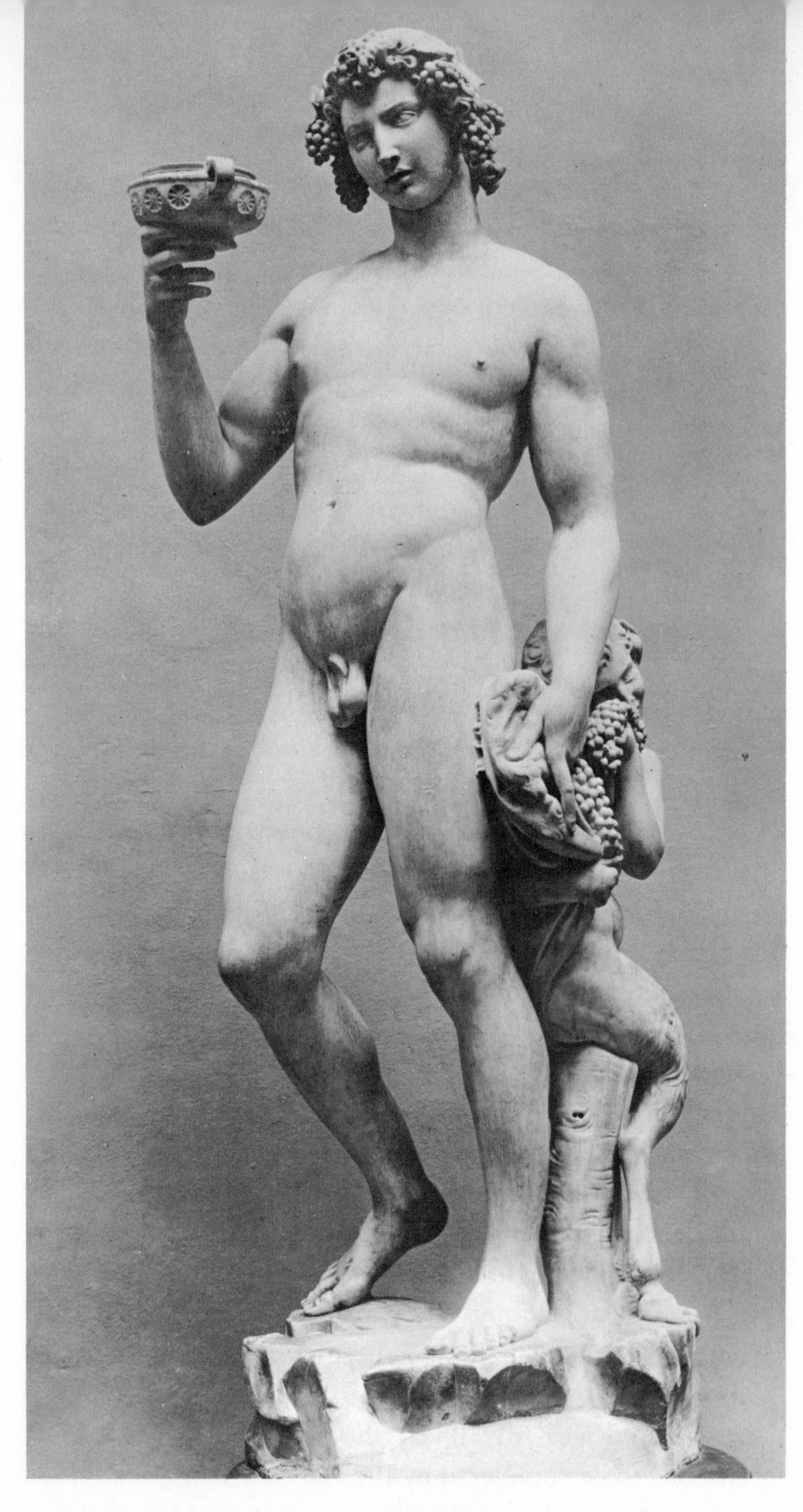

5. Bacchus, 1496–97. Florence, Bargello.

I, Jacopo Galli, do promise that the work will be more beautiful than any work in marble to be seen in Rome today, and such that no master of our own time will be able to produce a better.

Michelangelo gazed at Galli with affection.

"You have taken quite a gamble. Suppose when I finish the cardinal says, 'I have seen better marbles in Rome.' What happens then?"

"I give His Grace back his papal ducats."

"And you are stuck with the carving!"

Galli's eyes twinkled. "I could endure it."

He settled down to the Pietà. But the Bacchus, set up in Galli's garden, had made him famous. Many people came to see it and him and he realized that if he were to finish the Pietà he must leave the Galli household and establish his own quarters. He had grown up. He was on his own. He could see no other way.

He set out to find a suitable place and on the third day of searching discovered what he wanted, a big corner room with two windows and a smaller room with a fireplace. It was in bad repair but that could be remedied. He paid two months' rent, put the key in his pocket and returned to the Galli house where he found his brother Buonarroto come from Florence as a guard on a mule train.

Michelangelo gazed with pleasure at the stubby features. It had been a year since they had seen each other.

"You couldn't have come at a better time," he cried. "I need help in setting up my new home."

He bought plaster, whitewash and lye and the two brothers set to work to make the new quarters clean and habitable.

Balducci knew a secondhand furniture dealer, where he bargained shrilly for the best prices on a bed, rope mattress, kitchen table, two cane chairs, chest of drawers, a few pots, dishes and knives.

Buonarroto settled Michelangelo in, shopped and cooked the food, cleaned the rooms. The housekeeping went downhill the moment he left. Michelangelo took no time off to cook, to go out to a restaurant. He lost weight, even as his rooms lost their tidy appearance. He knew by the end of a month that this system was not going to work.

Buonarroto solved his problem. Michelangelo answered to a knock late one afternoon to see a plain-faced lad of about thirteen, holding out a letter on which Michelangelo recognized his brother's handwriting. The note introduced Piero Argiento, who wanted to be apprenticed to a sculptor. He had made the long trip on foot to Rome.

Michelangelo invited him in, studied the boy. His manner was quiet, his voice plain.

"Can you read and write, Argiento?"

"The Ingesuati fathers in Ferrara taught me to write. Now I want a three-year apprenticeship. With a Guild contract."

Michelangelo was impressed by the forthrightness. He gazed into the brown eyes of the lad before him, at the soiled shirt, worn-out sandals, the thin, hungry cheeks.

"I live simply, Argiento. You can expect no luxury."

"I am of farmers. What is to eat, we eat."

"Since you need a home, and I need a helper, suppose we try it for a few days? If it doesn't work out, we part as friends. I'll pay your way back to Florence."

"Agreed. Thanks."

"Take this coin, and go to the market for food."

"I make a good soup-of-the-country."

They established a simple routine. After their one-dish midday dinner, Argiento cleaned the rooms while Michelangelo took an hour's walk along the Tiber to the docks to listen to the Sicilians sing as they unloaded the boats. By the time he returned home Argiento was taking his *riposo* on the truckle bed in the kitchen under the wooden sink. Michelangelo had two more hours of quiet at his workbench before Argiento woke, washed his face noisily in a basin, and came to the worktable for his daily instruction. These few hours in the afternoon appeared to be all the teaching Argiento wanted. At dusk he was back in the kitchen, boiling water. By the time dark settled in he was asleep on his truckle bed. Michelangelo then lit his oil lamps and returned to his workbench.

Work on the Pietà progressed steadily. Michelangelo walked the streets searching for models, made hundreds of sketches, proceeded to create a three-dimensional figure in clay.

He had designed the Madonna gazing down in anguish upon her dead son held on her lap. It was unusual to combine two life-size figures in the same sculpture, to put a full-grown man onto the lap of a woman. How was he to prevent his statue from seeming ungainly?

He hurried to Sangallo's house and asked the architect to design a stand which would simulate the seated Mary. Then he brought some scrap lumber, and he and Argiento built the trestle, covering the structure with folds of cheesecloth dipped in river mud, which would simulate the draperies of the Madonna's gown.

Now he was ready to pose his models and complete his clay.

The arrangement with Argiento was working well, except that sometimes Michelangelo could not figure who was master and who apprentice. Argiento had been trained so rigorously by the Jesuits that Michelangelo was unable to change his habits: up before dawn to scrub the floors, whether they were dirty or not; water boiling on the fire for washing laundry every day, the pots scoured with river sand after each meal.

"Argiento, this is senseless," he complained, not liking to work on the wet floors, particularly in cold weather. "You're too clean. Scrub the studio once a week. That's enough."

"No," said Argiento stolidly. "Every day. Before dawn. I was taught."

"And God help anyone who tries to unteach you!" grumbled Michelangelo.

It took a piece of bad luck to show Michelangelo that the boy was devoted to him. He was crouched over his anvil in the courtyard sharpening his chisels, when a splinter of steel flew into his eye and imbedded itself in his pupil. He stumbled into the house, his eye burning like fire. Argiento made him lie down on the bed, brought a pan of hot water, dipped some clean white linen cloth and applied it to extract the splinter. Though the pain was considerable Michelangelo was not too concerned. He assumed he could blink the splinter out. But it would not come. Argiento never left his side, keeping the water boiled, applying hot compresses throughout the night.

By the second night Michelangelo was in a state of panic: he could see nothing out of the eye. At dawn Argiento went to Jacopo Galli. Galli arrived with his family surgeon, Maestro Lippi. The surgeon carried a cage of live pigeons. He told Argiento to take a bird out of the cage, cut a large vein under its wing, let the blood gush into Michelangelo's injured eye.

The surgeon came back at dusk, cut the vein of a second pigeon, again washed out the eye. All the next day Michelangelo could feel the splinter moving, pushing. By nightfall it was out.

Argiento had not slept for some seventy hours.

"You're tired," said Michelangelo. "Why don't you take a few days off?"

Argiento's stubborn features lit up with pleasure. "I go visit the horses."

The next day Michelangelo began work on the marble.

Winter came down like a clap of thunder: cold, wet, raw. As Buonarroto had predicted, there were leaks. Michelangelo and Argiento moved his workbench and bed to dry sections of the room, brought the forge in from the courtyard. He wore his Bologna cap over his head and ears. His nostrils swelled, giving him constant pain, making breathing difficult. When his fingers were blue he tried to carve while wearing woolen mittens.

One Sunday Argiento returned from an outing feeling hot and strange. By midnight he had a high fever. Michelangelo picked him up off his truckle bed and put him into his own. By morning Argiento was in a delirium, sweating profusely.

At dawn Michelangelo summoned a passer-by and sent him for a doctor. The doctor stood in the doorway, cried, "It's the plague! Burn everything he has touched since he came in here!" and fled.

Michelangelo sent a message to Galli. Maestro Lippi took one look, said scoffingly:

"Nonsense, it is not the plague. Quartan fever."

The illness took three weeks to pass. Michelangelo began to worry that he could not finish his statue within the stipulated year's time.

Winter was mercifully short in Rome. By March the country was flooded with a bright, brittle sunlight. And with the warmer weather came the Cardinal of San Dionigi to see how his Pietà was faring.

"Tell me, my son," he said softly, "how does the Madonna's face remain so young, younger than her son's?"

"Your Grace, it seemed to me that the Virgin Mary would not age. She was pure; and so she would have kept her freshness of youth."

The answer was satisfactory to the cardinal.

"I hope you will finish in August. It is my dearest wish to hold services in St. Peter's for the installation."

He carved in a fury from first light to dark, then threw himself across his bed, without supper and fully clothed, like a dead man. He awoke around midnight, refreshed, nibbled at a heel of bread, lit the lamp, and tried to see the area he was carving. The light was too diffused.

He bought some heavy paper, made a hat with a peak, tied a wire around the outside and in the center fashioned a loop big enough to hold a candle. The light, as he held his face a few inches from the marble, was bright and steady. The candles burned quickly, the soft wax running over the peak of his paper cap and onto his forehead, but he was delighted with his invention.

He made rapid progress, refusing all invitations. On a summer morning Paolo Rucellai sent for him to come as soon as possible. Michelangelo wondered what news it could be that Paolo considered urgent.

"Michelangelo, you look so thin."

"The sculpture grows fat, I grow thin. That is the natural order of things."

Rucellai regarded him in wonderment. "On yesterday's post I received a letter from my cousin Bernardo. Florence is planning a sculpture competition."

Michelangelo's right hand began to tremble; he put his left hand over it to quiet it.

"To compete for what . . . ?"

"Bernardo's letter says: *'To bring to perfection the mar-*

ble column already blocked out by Agostino di Duccio, and now stored in the workshop of the cathedral'!"

"The Duccio block!"

"You know it?"

"I tried to buy it from the Signoria for my Hercules. I can see it before my eyes."

"Can you make something good of it?"

Michelangelo's eyes shone. *"Dio mio."*

"Then you want to try for the competition?"

"More than anything in my whole life! Tell me, what must the theme be: political, religious? Is it for Florentine sculptors only? Must I be there to compete? Will they . . ."

"Whoa, whoa," cried Rucellai, "I have no further information. But I will ask Bernardo to send me full particulars."

Rucellai sent for him three weeks later. The theme for the competition had still not been determined. The date was set for the year 1500.

"But this is already summer of '99. I have so much work left on the Pietà." His face was anguished. "I cannot rush, it is too important."

Paolo put an arm about his trembling shoulders.

"I will bring you information steadily. It will take many months before the terms are set."

It was the cardinal who lost the race with time. He died quietly in the midst of his offices. Jacopo Galli attended the funeral with Michelangelo, standing below a catafalque sixteen feet long and nine feet wide between the columns of the church, with singers behind the main altar. Returning to the Galli home, Michelangelo asked:

"Who decides whether or not the Pietà is 'more beautiful than any work in marble to be seen in Rome today'?"

"The cardinal already decided that. After his visit with

you in May. He said you were fulfilling the contract. That's enough for me. When do you think it will be finished?"

"I have still six to eight months of work."

"In time for the Centennial Year, then. That will give you an audience from all over Europe."

Michelangelo shifted uneasily.

"Would you send that last hundred ducats to my family? They are in some kind of trouble again."

Galli looked at him sharply. "That was your last payment. You say you have six to eight months of work left, and I have sent almost all of the cardinal's ducats to Florence. It begins to look like a bottomless well."

"This money I want to invest in buying a shop for my brothers, Buonarroto and Giovansimone. Buonarroto cannot seem to find a place for himself. Giovansimone, since Savonarola's death, takes jobs, then disappears for days. If they could find a good shop, and I shared in the profits . . ."

"Michelangelo, if neither of them is a good businessman, how are they going to make a profit?" Galli was exasperated; but when he spoke again his voice was solicitous. "I can't let you pour your last money down a hole. You must be practical and protect yourself against the future. Eighty per cent of your money from the Bacchus and the Pietà has gone to your family. I ought to know, I'm your banker."

Michelangelo hung his head, whispered, "Buonarroto won't work for anyone else, so I must set him up in business. And if I don't get Giovansimone in a straight path now, I may never have another chance."

The money was transferred to Florence, Michelangelo keeping a few ducats for himself.

By the next spring the Pietà was finished. The white marble, polished and gleaming, lighted up the dingy room as though it were a stained-glass chapel.

Jacopo Galli came to the studio and studied the Pietà

6. Pietà, 1498–1500. Rome, St. Peter's.

in silence. After a time he said softly, "I have fulfilled my contract with the cardinal: this is the most beautiful work in marble to be seen in Rome today."

"I'm nervous about the installation," said Michelangelo. "Our contract doesn't say that we have the right to put the Pietà in St. Peter's. With the cardinal dead . . ."

"We won't ask any questions. We'll install it without a sound. What no one knows, no one can object to."

Michelangelo was aghast. "You mean, sneak my sculpture in?"

"Nothing furtive. Just discreet. Once the Pietà is sitting in its niche, no one will bother to have it removed. Suppose you hire those stoneyard friends of yours to help you. Tomorrow, after dinner, while the city is resting."

He asked Guffatti, the owner of a stoneyard near Santo Spirito, to come to the workshop. Guffatti stood in front of the sculpture in silence, then said:

"I bring the family."

The family turned out to include not merely three husky sons but a variety of cousins. They wrapped it in a half-dozen mangy blankets and carried it to the doors of the basilica, lifted it from their wagon and began the heavy labor of carrying it through the church. Three times they had to set it down to rest and wipe the perspiration from their brows. Only the fact that the marble was sacred kept them from cursing. Finally they lowered their bundle carefully before the empty niche in the Chapel of the Kings of France, unwrapped the blankets, wiped their hands clean of sweat, raised the Pietà reverentially to its place. Michelangelo straightened it to the position he wanted. The Guffatti family bought candles, lit them before the statue.

They refused to take one scudo for their hours of back-breaking labor.

"We take our pay in heaven," said the father.

It was the best tribute Michelangelo could receive. It was also the only tribute he received.

The following night, green sailcloth bag in hand, Michelangelo entered St. Peter's. He took a candle from the bag, put it in the wire loop of his hat, reached into the bag for hammer and chisel. He raised his tools and onto the band going tightly between the Madonna's breasts he cut in swift, decorative letters:

MICHELANGELO BUONARROTI OF FLORENCE MADE THIS.

He returned to his rooms, packed his things. Just before dawn, Michelangelo and Argiento made their way to the Porta del Popolo. Michelangelo rented two mules, joined the pack train, and at first light set out for Florence.

BOOK SIX

THE GIANT

Returning to Florence with no commissions and no funds, he had been obliged to send Argiento back to his family's farm and himself return to his father's board.

The city itself had undergone many perceivable changes in the almost five years he had been gone. The people bowed their heads in shame when they passed the spot where Savonarola's body had been burned; at the same time they were trying to replace what Savonarola had destroyed, spending large sums with the gold- and silversmiths, the gem cutters, the costume makers, the embroiderers, designers of terra-cotta and wood mosaics, the makers of musical instruments, the manuscript illuminators.

He had left for Rome a boy, returned a man, ready to carve mountains of marble; but as he turned to gaze sightlessly at the Madonna and Child and Centaurs he had carved for Lorenzo de' Medici and which he had affixed on nails to the side wall of his combination workroom and bedroom, he thought unhappily that as far as Florence knew he might never have carved the Bacchus or Pietà.

At night he read by candlelight in Dante and in the Old Testament, looking for a mood and heroic theme for the sculpture competition.

Then he learned that the members of the Wool Guild and the Board of Works of the cathedral had been unable to make up their minds about the carving of the giant block. It was just as well, thought Michelangelo, for he also had heard that many favored giving the commission to Leonardo da Vinci, recently returned to Florence.

Michelangelo had never met Leonardo, who had abandoned Florence eighteen years before; but Florentine artists were saying that he was the greatest draftsman in Italy. Curious, Michelangelo had gone to Santissima Annunziata when the cartoon for Leonardo's Virgin and Child and St. Anne was on exhibition. He had stood before the cartoon with his heart beating like a hammer. Never had he seen such power or authenticity of drawing, such forceful truth about the figure, except, of course, in his own work.

Leonardo rejected the commission. On the grounds that he despised marble sculpture as an inferior art, good only for artisans. Michelangelo heard the news in a state of turmoil. He was glad to have the Duccio block free, and Leonardo da Vinci out of the running; but he felt a resentment against the man for his belittling statement, which all Florence took up and was repeating.

One darkness before dawn he rose, dressed hurriedly, ran to the Duomo workshop, and stood at the corner of the column. The diagonal beams of first sunlight streamed across the marble, projecting his shadow upward the full seventeen-foot length of the column, magnifying his silhouette and turning him into a giant. He caught his breath, thought of David as he knew his story from the Bible. "This is how David must have felt," he told himself, "on that morning when he stepped forth to face Goliath." A Giant for the symbol of Florence!

Galli wrote him from Rome saying Cardinal Piccolomini was willing to commission Michelangelo to create an altarpiece in the cathedral in Siena, fifteen small figures, all of them fully clothed, to be completed in three years.

Michelangelo's face dropped. Three years of carving draperies and never a figure of his own choosing. Yet he needed the money and his father, who thought of little else, pressed him to accept the commission.

He went to the Council Hall, to see Gonfaloniere Soderini, the Head of the Council.

"Welcome," Soderini murmured, "what brings you here?"

"Troubles, Gonfaloniere," replied Michelangelo, "but I suppose no one comes up here to unburden his pleasures?"

"That's why I sit behind such a capacious desk; so that it can hold all the problems of Florence."

"It is your shoulders that are broad."

Soderini ducked his head deprecatingly.

Michelangelo told Piero Soderini about the proposed Piccolomini contract.

"I don't want this commission, Gonfaloniere. I'm on fire to carve the Giant! Can't you force the Boards of the Duomo and the Wool Guild to decide about the competition? If I don't get it, at least it will be out of my range of possibility. I could go on to this Piccolomini contract as something I can't escape."

He was breathing hard. Soderini gazed at him.

"This is not a good time to force things. We're exhausted from our war with Pisa. Caesar Borgia is threatening to conquer Florence. Last night the Signoria bought him off. Thirty-six thousand gold florins a year for three years, his salary for serving as captain general of the Florentine forces."

"Blackmail," said Michelangelo.

Soderini's face turned red. "Many do kiss the hand they wish to see cut off. The guilds have to provide this money. So the Wool Guild is not in the mood to discuss a sculpture competition. Hadn't you better be more receptive to the Piccolomini offer?" suggested Soderini.

Michelangelo groaned. "Cardinal Piccolomini wants to choose all fifteen subjects. I cannot carve until he approves the designs. And what wages: thirty-three and a third ducats for each figure, enough to pay rent, buy supplies . . ."

"How long since you've carved marble?"

"More than a year."

"Or been paid?"

"More than two."

"Do today what you must do today," said Soderini. "Tomorrow you will be free to do what you must do tomorrow. We bought off Caesar Borgia. For you as an artist it is the same as with us as a city-state; only one law prevails: survival."

At Santo Spirito, Prior Bichiellini, sitting behind the desk in his manuscript-lined office, pushed his papers aside, his eyes blazing behind the spectacles.

"Survival on what plane? To stay alive as an animal stays alive? For shame! The Michelangelo I knew six years ago could never think, 'Better mediocre work than no work at all.' This is opportunism, fit for mediocre talent. Don't take the commission. Do the best that is in you, or nothing at all. There is only a God-given number of years in which to work to fulfill yourself. Don't squander them."

Michelangelo hung his head in shame.

"If I sound like a moralist," said the prior quietly, "please remember that it is my job to be concerned with your character."

Michelangelo went out into the bright sunlight, sat on the edge of the fountain in the Piazza Santo Spirito and splashed cold water on his face, even as he had on those nights when he had emerged from the dead room. He groaned aloud, "Three years! *Dio mio!*"

Back in his studio, Granacci barely listened to him.

"Without work Michelangelo, you are the most wretched creature alive. What does it matter if you have to carve dull statues? Your worst will be better than anybody else's best. Do as many figures as you have time for. Everybody in Florence will help you outwit Siena."

"Outwit a cardinal?"

Granacci grew serious. "I'm trying to face reality. You want to carve, ergo, take the Piccolomini contract and do the best you can. When something better comes along, you'll sculpture better."

He returned to the drawing board, to sketches, attempts to capture saints for the Piccolomini contract. But he could think of nothing but the Duccio column and the Giant-David.

The weeks passed. He learned that half a dozen sculptors had walked away from the damaged marble, saying it would certainly break in two at the point where it had been gouged. But Michelangelo was not discouraged. He had calculated to a hairsbreadth the deepest point of the gouging and knew it was possible to design a David to fit the marble.

He gathered up an armful of new sketches and went again to plead with Piero Soderini. The commission must come to him if only the Gonfaloniere could force the Wool Guild to act.

"Yes, I might force it through," agreed Soderini. "But then the Boards would have acted against their will. They would resent you. They must want this piece carved and must choose you as their sculptor. You perceive the difference?"

"Yes," replied Michelangelo sadly, "it makes sense. Only I can't wait any longer."

He accepted the Piccolomini contract, sent for Argiento, found a workshop and two blocks of marble and without clay or wax models, carved two of the fifteen figures; one a St. Paul, the other St. Peter.

He kept the whereabouts of his workshop a secret from everyone except Granacci, who came one day to see the work.

"I can't believe it! You signed the contract on June 19; here it is only the middle of July, and you have two of the statues completed. They're quite good, in spite of all your moaning that you could carve nothing worth while. At this rate, you'll be finished with the fifteen statues in seven months."

Michelangelo gazed at his St. Peter and St. Paul, replied soberly: "These first two figures are not bad, they contain my hunger to carve. But once they're shoved into those narrow niches, they'll die a quick death."

"Why don't you go to Siena," Granacci interrupted, "and see the tomb? You'll feel better."

He left that day.

As he entered Siena he thought of the most galling part of the contract he had undertaken. Cardinal Piccolomini had required him to complete a figure of St. Francis begun by his old enemy Torrigiani, who had smashed his nose.

Michelangelo swallowed hard at the sight of Torrigiani's sculpture: wooden, lifeless, rigid, stylized expressionless face.

He vowed to give this poor marred St. Francis, whom

7. St. Francis from the Piccolomini Altar in the Siena Cathedral, 1501–4.

even the birds would not recognize, all of the love and skill at his command.

The next day he made his drawings. By nightfall he was putting new edges on old chisels, balancing them for his hand, getting accustomed to the heft of the hammer. The following dawn he began carving.

He felt an identity with St. Francis, and with this maimed block from which he was emerging. When he came to the head and face he carved his own hair, brushed in a straight line down the forehead, his own caved-in face as he had seen it in the Medici mirror the morning after Torrigiani stove it in.

A mood of sadness pervaded him as he rode home to Florence. He found Argiento wiggling excitedly from one foot to the other, waiting for Michelangelo to look at him.

"Well, Argiento, what are you bursting with?"

"Gonfaloniere Soderini, he wants to see you, he sends a page every hour!"

The Piazza della Signoria was aglow with orange light from the burning oil pots that hung from every window and from the top of the crenelated tower. Soderini met Michelangelo.

"Why the oil pots? What are we celebrating?" Michelangelo asked.

"You."

"Me?"

"In part." Soderini's eyes twinkled wickedly in the orange light. "The directors of the Wool Guild and the Duomo voted you the Giant . . ."

Michelangelo went rigid. The Duccio column was his!

Soderini's voice continued gaily. "When we realized that our best Florentine carver was bound by a Sienese cardinal, we asked, 'Does Siena suppose that Florence does not appreciate its own artists? Or that we can't afford to employ them?' After all, we've spent years at war with the Sienese!"

"But the Piccolomini contract . . ."

"Out of patriotic duty you must postpone the Piccolomini contract, and on September first take over the Duccio block."

Granacci launched a celebration party built around the meeting of the Company of the Cauldron, a select club of artists to which he belonged. To salute Michelangelo's good fortune, eleven members of the Company showed up.

The party lasted until dawn; but before that, two incidents occurred which would affect the pattern of his days.

The first filled him with joy. The ill and aged Rosselli, a rival of Ghirlandaio, gathered the ten members of the Company about him, announced:

"It is not meat and drink, if you will forgive a pun, for a member of this Company of the Cauldron to be carried to these meetings on a litter. Therefore, much as I dislike promoting anyone from the Ghirlandaio studio, I herewith resign from the Company and nominate Michelangelo Buonarroti to succeed me."

He was accepted. He had been no part of any group since the Medici sculpture garden. He remembered again his lonely childhood, how difficult it had been for him to make friends, to be gay. Now all these artists of Florence were applauding his election.

The second incident was to cause him considerable anguish. It was begun, though unwittingly, by Leonardo da Vinci.

Michelangelo was already angry at Leonardo by the first time he had seen him in Florence. Leonardo carried his head thrown back, the broad forehead topped by a haze of reddish hair, softly curled and worn down to his shoulders; a broad nose, rounded, full-blooded lips, the face dominated by cool blue eyes of a piercing penetration and intelligence. He wore a rose-colored cloak, barely covering his shoulders and falling short at the knees, wearing his shirt and stockings tight to the point of bursting.

He had made Michelangelo feel ugly and malformed, conscious that his clothes were inexpensive, ill fitting and worn. The lace about Leonardo's neck and wrists, the jewels, made him feel tattered and dirty by comparison.

When he had spoken of this to Rustici, who was Leonardo's friend, Rustici had reproved him.

"Don't be fooled by an elegant exterior. Leonardo has a magnificent brain. He has been dissecting animals for years, and keeping meticulous notebooks of his anatomical drawings. In his pursuit of geology he has discovered fish-shell fossils on top of the mountains of the upper Arno, proving that they were once under water. He is also an engineer and inventor of unbelievable machines. Even now he is completing experiments for a machine that will fly through the air as the birds do. He is the only man in Florence who works as hard and as long as you do: twenty hours a day. Look for the real Leonardo beneath that defensive elegance."

In the face of this brilliant recital, Michelangelo could not bring himself to mention his anger at the man's outspoken deprecation of sculpture. Leonardo's hearty welcoming of him into the Company of the Cauldron this evening had also assuaged his uneasiness. Then he heard Leonardo's high-pitched voice behind him, declaring:

"I refused to compete for the Duccio block because sculpture is a mechanical art. Sculpture is so much less intellectual than painting; it lacks so many of its natural aspects. I spent years at it, and I tell you from experience that painting is far more difficult, and reaches the greater perfection. Sculpture is for laborers."

Michelangelo felt his spine stiffen and rage rise in him. One day he would make Leonardo eat those words.

Next day, with the help of Beppe and the workmen in the Duomo yard, Michelangelo set up the Duccio block in a far corner under an oak tree. He spent weeks considering how he would represent the figure. He decided to show David at the moment he made his decision to fight Goliath, for Michelangelo was not content to portray the biblical hero as a special individual, as a single man. His David would be Everyman, all those who, from the beginning of time, had faced a decision to strike for freedom. Once he knew what he wanted, he began work on a clay model, eighteen inches high, and the marble came alive in his mind. Even the limitations of the marred block began to appear as assets.

Then Giuliano da Sangallo returned from Savona.

"Tell me about your design for the Giant," he demanded. "And what have you heard of interesting architectural jobs in Florence?"

"There are several of great urgency," said Michelangelo. "A revolving table strong enough to turn a two-thousand-pound column of marble, so I can control the light and sun. A fifteen-foot scaffold, one in which I can change the height and work all around the block."

Sangallo was amused. "Let's get pen and paper. What you need is a series of four towers, with open shelves that take planks from either direction, like this . . . As for your turntable, that's an engineering task. . . ."

Beppe's crew roped the column, attached a block and tackle, slowly raised it to stand upright on Sangallo's turntable. Michelangelo and Argiento built the scaffold towers.

Now the column cried out to him. His tools tore into it, searching for elbows and thighs and chest. The white crystals that had lain dormant for half a century yielded as

his hammer and chisel swept upward from the ankle through the knee and thigh without stopping in a driving "Go!"

This was his most glorious experience in working marble. He could not bring himself to stop for food or change of clothes. He fed his marble hunger twenty hours a day, the acrid dust coagulating in his nostrils, his hair covered white with it, the vibrations of the marble consistency running from the chisels and hammer up his shoulders, then down his chest, throbbing and vibrating through his body and brain long after he had thrown himself across his bed in exultant exhaustion.

Christmas came, he accompanied his family to high mass at Santa Croce. The New Year he ignored. Argiento turned the table to catch the most light, moving the plank-platform up and down the David, forward and back as he worked the four sides simultaneously. The neck was so tremendous he could work it without fear of the head breaking off.

Soderini came into the yard to observe progress. He knew that Michelangelo would have no peace at home until a price was set on the finished David. Toward the middle of February, after Michelangelo had been working for five months, he asked:

"Do you feel you have moved far enough along now for the Boards to see the work? I can have them meet here, and arrange a final contract. . . ."

The Boards were pleased. They awarded Michelangelo four hundred large golden florins provided he completed the work within two years.

"Now I can forget about money until I have finished. That is paradise for an artist."

Sometimes Michelangelo sat at the David's feet and gazed up at him. He thought, "It takes as long for a marble column to bear as it does a fruit tree." Yet each separate form within the sculpture was beginning to mirror the time and love he had lavished on it.

The one thorn in his flesh was Leonardo da Vinci's belittling of the sculptor's art. To Michelangelo it appeared a serious threat. Leonardo's influence in Florence was spreading; if it should convince enough people that marble carving was a second-rate craft, when his David was completed it would be received with indifference. Growing within him was a need to counterattack.

The following Sunday when the Company of the Cauldron was meeting, and Leonardo made light of stone carving, Michelangelo said:

"True, sculpture shares nothing with painting. It exists on its own premises. But primitive man carved in stone for thousands of years before he began to paint on cave walls. Sculpture is the first and original art."

"By that very claim it is condemned," answered Leonardo in his high-pitched voice. "It satisfied only until the fine art of painting was developed. It is now becoming extinct."

Infuriated, Michelangelo struck back with a personal attack.

"Isn't it true, Leonardo," he demanded, "that your equestrian statue in Milan is so colossal that it can never be cast? And hence will never come into existence? No wonder you talk against sculpture, you're not capable of bringing a piece to completion!"

There was an uncomfortable silence in the room.

A few days later Florence learned that, despite its payments to Caesar Borgia, he was helping to incite a rebellion against Florentine rule. Leonardo da Vinci joined Caesar Borgia's army as an engineer, to work alongside Torrigiani and Piero de' Medici. Michelangelo was outraged.

"He's a traitor," he cried angrily. "Caesar Borgia offers him a big salary, and so he will help conquer Florence. After we gave him hospitality . . ."

"It really isn't that bad," said Rustici placatingly. "Leonardo is at loose ends, he can't seem to finish his painting of Monna Lisa del Giocondo. You two stand like the Apennines above the rest of us, yet you hate each other. It doesn't make sense. Or does it?"

Toward the end of April, Soderini asked Michelangelo to accompany him to the Duomo.

"For years Florence has been talking of having the Twelve Apostles in marble for the cathedral. Larger than life size. That would fill the cavernous space, would it not?"

"With the light of a thousand candles."

"I've been speaking to the members of the Boards. They think it a magnificent idea."

Numbly, Michelangelo murmured, "It's a lifetime of work."

"So were Ghiberti's doors."

Soderini linked his arm through Michelangelo's, walked him down the long nave toward the open door.

"It would make you the official sculptor of Florence. The contract I have been discussing with the Boards includes a house we will build for you, and a studio of your own design."

"A home of my own! And a studio."

"I thought that would please you. You could do one Apostle a year. As each was delivered you would own another twelfth of your house."

Michelangelo stopped in the doorway. He was only twenty-eight and he was going to have a home of his own and a sculpture studio adequate to carve heroic pieces. But he was not happy. He hesitated to lock himself into a commission that would consume the next twelve years of his life. He went for advice to Sangallo.

Sangallo said, "It's a lot of years. But can you turn down the Gonfaloniere and the Boards? They are offering you the biggest commission since Ghiberti's doors. The members would be offended. That would put you in a difficult position. Take the contract, build your house and studio, carve as many Apostles as you can do well. When you're through, you're through; you'll pay off the rest of the house in cash."

"Another Piccolomini contract," said Michelangelo mournfully.

He signed the contract.

The first fruit of his contract for the Twelve Apostles was a visit from a neighbor, Agnolo Doni, his own age. Doni had made a fortune and was engaged to Maddalena Strozzi.

"I'll come straight to the point, Buonarroti," he said. "I want you to do a Holy Family as a wedding present for my bride-to-be."

Michelangelo flushed with pleasure; Maddalena had been brought up with his Hercules.

"A Holy Family in white marble . . ." he murmured.

"Who said anything about marble? That would cost a lot of money. All I want is a painting, to be used as an inset in a round table."

"Why should you come to me for a painting? I haven't put color on a brush for fifteen years."

"Pure loyalty. What do you say? A Holy Family. Thirty florins. Ten for each figure. That's a generous sum, isn't it? Shall we call it a bargain?"

"I don't know how much the painters will charge you, Doni, but you can have your choice of half a dozen of the best in Italy."

"Look, Buonarroti, I want you to paint a Holy Family. It is well known that to carve marble is to be only a fraction of an artist."

"Enough," growled Michelangelo, furious at this repetition of Leonardo's denunciation. "I'll paint your Holy Family. For one hundred gold florins."

"One hundred!" screamed Doni. "How can you cheat one of your oldest friends?"

They compromised on seventy florins. By the crafty smile in Doni's shrewd eyes, Michelangelo perceived that Doni had outwitted him and would have paid the hundred.

Yet his interest was piqued. He had dozens of drawings for a Madonna and Child. They were intensely spiritual. Yet a Holy Family should be the opposite in spirit: earthy, a family of simple people.

During the hot summer days he tramped the roads of Tuscany, sketching the farmers in the fields, eating before their door in the cool of evening, the young country mothers nursing their young, a strong-limbed, healthy young girl, a red-cheeked curly-haired child, a bald-headed bearded grandfather, put them together in an affectionate grouping on the grass. To amuse himself he painted a sea on one side of the family, mountains on the other; before the sea and the mountains he drew in five nude youths, creating the effect of a Greek frieze.

Doni's face went the color of his red tunic when he answered Michelangelo's summons to see the finished picture.

"Show me one thing that is holy about this picture of peasants! One sentiment that is religious! You're mocking me! I cannot give this picnic on the grass to my delicate bride."

"Might I remind you that you did not reserve the right of rejection?"

Doni's eyes narrowed to slits as he cried in horror:

"What are those five naked boys doing in my Holy Family?"

"Why, they've just come out from a swim in the sea," replied Michelangelo calmly, "and are drying themselves in the sun. Remember your original offer was thirty florins, ten for each figure. If I wanted to be greedy I could charge you fifty florins extra for the five youths. But I won't, because we are of the same quarter."

Doni stormed out. The next day his servant arrived with a pouch of thirty-five florins, half the price agreed upon, and a release for Michelangelo to sign. Michelangelo sent Argiento back with the pouch. On a scrap of paper he scrawled:

> *The Holy Family will now cost you one hundred and forty florins.*

Florence enjoyed the contest, with bets on who would win. Michelangelo found himself on the short end of the odds because no one had ever bested Doni in a deal. However he had bragged all over town that he was having Florence's official artist paint a wedding gift for his bride. Doni arrived at the Duomo workshed with a leather purse containing seventy florins, crying:

"Here's your money, give me my painting."

"Doni, that wouldn't be fair. You hate the picture, and I release you from your agreement."

"Don't try to outwit me. I'll force you to fulfill your contract."

"I didn't know you loved the painting that much. Now I believe that you're a great art collector. Just hand over the hundred and forty florins . . ."

"You're a swindler! You agreed to paint the picture for seventy . . ."

". . . an agreement you threw open to renegotiation by offering me thirty-five florins. My price is now one hundred and forty."

"Never," screamed Doni. "I'll see you hanged from the Bargello first."

Michelangelo decided he had had his fun. He wrote to Doni:

> *I fully appreciate how expensive my painting must seem to you. As an old and dear friend, I will release you from any financial embarrassment.*

Doni came running on Argiento's heels, flung down a pouch.

"I demand the painting! It is now mine by legal right."

He picked up the leather bag, untied the thong and poured the hundred and forty gold pieces onto the work-table. "Count them! One hundred and forty pieces of gold!"

Michelangelo picked up the painting, handed it to Doni. "My compliments to your wife-to-be."

Doni made his way to the door, grumbling, "Artists! Supposed to be impractical. Ha!"

Michelangelo gathered up the coins. He had enjoyed the whole affair. It was as refreshing as a vacation.

There was rejoicing in August when the Borgia Pope, Alexander VI, died. When Cardinal Piccolomini of Siena was elected to the papacy, Michelangelo was apprehensive. He had done no further work on the Piccolomini statues. One word from the new Pope, and Gonfaloniere Soderini would be obliged to take him off the David until the remaining eleven figures were completed and delivered.

For a month he worked frenziedly. Most of David's body was realized, only the face and head remained. For the first time he realized the weight of the contract for the Twelve Apostles, which would also hang over his head for years.

Cardinal Piccolomini lasted as Pope Pius III for one month, dying suddenly in Rome. Cardinal Rovere was elected Pope Julius II.

Leonardo da Vinci returned from Caesar Borgia's army, was awarded a commission to create a fresco for the wall just behind the platform on which the Signoria sat. The payment was to be ten thousand florins!

Michelangelo was livid. This was the largest and most important painting commission given by Florence in decades. Ten thousand florins to Leonardo for a fresco which was to be completed in two years! And to a man who would have helped Caesar Borgia conquer Florence! Four hundred florins to himself for the Giant-David! For the same amount of work!

He ran in his rage to Soderini's office. Soderini heard him out and allowed a few moments of silence for Michelangelo to hear his angry words echoing off the walls before answering.

"Leonardo da Vinci is a great painter. I have seen the Last Supper in Milan. It is tremendous. I am frankly covetous of Milan's fresco, and I am anxious that he paint one for Florence. If it is as fine, it will enrich us enormously."

Michelangelo, dismissed, went back to the David. There began the final months of work, so highly pleasurable to him now that the two years of labor were coming into focus.

At the end of January, 1504, Soderini called a meeting of artists and artisans of Florence to decide where the Giant-David should be placed. They agreed it should stand before the Signoria, a spot Michelangelo would have chosen.

It was the largest marble statue ever to be carried through the streets of Florence. It was decided to encase

it in a net of ropes inside a big wooden frame. In spite of forty workmen, the statue was moved but a few feet an hour. By nightfall they had gotten it only half a block.

By evening, the fourth day of its journey, the David arrived at its destination at the foot of the palace steps facing the open piazza. Michelangelo drew in his breath sharply. He had not seen the David at such a distance. There it stood in all its majestic grace, lighting up the Signoria with pure white light. He stood below the figure, feeling insignificant, weak and homely, powerless now that the statue was out of his hands, asking himself, "How much of what I wanted to say have I managed to convey?"

He went home and slept more soundly than he had for months. He woke feeling refreshed, bathed in the wooden tub and put on a fresh white linen shirt, stockings and sandals, and returned to the Signoria.

A crowd was standing below the David in silence. Fluttering from the statue were pieces of paper stuck to the marble during the night. He had seen this sight in Rome, when people had pasted up verses derogatory to the Borgia on the door of the Vatican, or affixed their smoldering complaints to a statue nearby.

He walked through the crowd. It fell back to let him pass. He tried to read their expressions, to see what was in the wind.

He came to the David, climbed up on the base, began taking off the papers, reading them one by one. By the end of the third, his eyes began to mist, for they were messages of love and acceptance:

You have given us back our self-respect.
We are proud to be Florentines.
How magnificent is man!
You have made a thing of beauty.
Bravo!

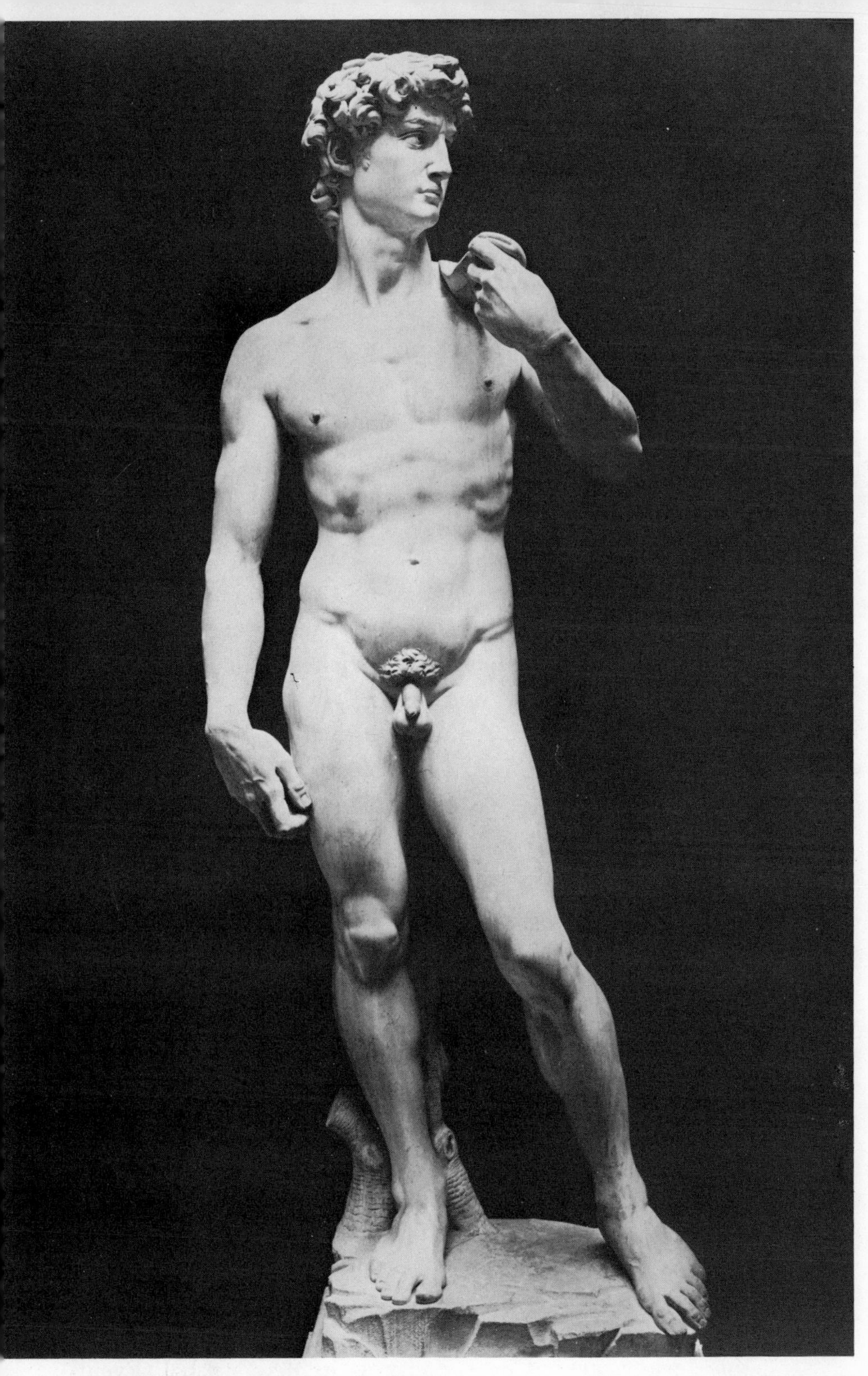

8. David, 1501–4. Florence, Academy.

He turned, stood above the crowd gazing up at him. There was silence in the square. And yet he had never felt such complete communication. It was as though they read each other's thoughts, as though they were one and the same: they were a part of him, every Florentine standing below, eyes turned up to him, and he was a part of them.

An immediate repercussion of the David was a commission to create a Madonna and Child in marble for Bartolommeo Pitti. And the Signoria passed a resolution to get Michelangelo's house and studio built.

The Topolinos were soon cutting stone according to his specifications. When the building blocks were ready the entire family built the house. Michelangelo painted the interior walls the warm blues, rose and orange colors he had evolved for the clothes of the Doni Holy Family.

The furniture money had to come out of his own purse. He could buy only modestly: a wide bed, chest, single chair for his bedroom; for the loggia, chairs and table and a leather chair and bench for the family room. Argiento moved his bed from the workshop in the piazza, putting it in the small downstairs bedroom near the front door. Michelangelo hung his earliest Madonna and Child opposite his bed, put the Centaurs in the family room.

He worked joyfully in the late summer making the sketches for the Pitti Madonna and figures for the Apostle St. Matthew for the Duomo.

Prior Bichiellini came to give the new house the traditional blessing. He bent on his knee, spoke a prayer to the Madonna. Then he rose, put both hands on Michelangelo's shoulder. "Bless you and this workshop."

The months that followed were the happiest he had known. The David, still called the Giant by most Florentines, was accepted by the city as its new symbol. Events

9. Madonna and Child with Little St. John (Pitti Madonna), about 1504. Florence, Bargello.

took a sharp turn for the better: Caesar Borgia, seriously ill, ceased to be a menace. There was a spirit of confidence and energy in the air. Trade was booming; there was work for all, a market for every man's product. The government, with Soderini as its permanent head, was stable and secure. Much of this the city-state attributed to the Giant-David. The date of its installation marked a new era in the minds of the Florentines.

A few months short of thirty, Michelangelo seemed to have reached the full expression and acceptance for which he had yearned.

His period of grace was short-lived.

During the early months of 1504 Leonardo da Vinci had spent his time in a series of mechanical inventions. Rebuked by the Signoria for neglecting his fresco, he had started in May to work on it in earnest. The cartoon became the talk of Florence: artists flocked to Leonardo's workroom. Word went around the city that something wondrous was in the making. Michelangelo began to perceive that he was being superseded. Leonardo da Vinci was the figure of the moment. Florence proudly proclaimed him "the first artist of Tuscany."

This was bitter medicine to Michelangelo. He managed to see the Leonardo cartoon without anyone knowing he was there. The Battle of Anghiari was tremendous! Leonardo had created a masterpiece of the horse at war, ridden by men in ancient Roman armor savagely trying to destroy each other.

Leonardo was a great painter, he could not dispute that; perhaps the greatest the world had yet seen. Instead of reconciling him, this inflamed him the more. Michelangelo was the best draftsman in all Italy. But he would have to prove it. And no proof would serve except a fresco, of the same proportions as Leonardo's.

Leonardo's fresco was going to occupy the right half of the long eastern wall of the Great Hall. He would ask Soderini for the left half. Then Florence could say who was the first artist of the time!

Late that afternoon he presented himself at Gonfaloniere Soderini's office, bathed, barbered, wearing his clean blue shirt, and told Soderini why he had come. Soderini was flabbergasted; it was the first time Michelangelo had ever seen him lose his presence.

"But that is unreasonable!" he cried. "You've told me yourself that you never liked fresco."

"I was wrong." His head was down, his voice dogged. "I can paint fresco. Better than Leonardo da Vinci. It would be a great race that would excite people."

"The Signoria would never approve. You already have a contract with the Wool Guild and Duomo to carve the Twelve Apostles."

"I'll carve them. But the other half of the wall must be mine."

"Why wasn't I content with two months as Gonfaloniere?" Soderini sighed, "Why did I have to take this job for life?"

"Because you are a wise and persuasive Gonfaloniere who is going to get the city to appropriate another ten thousand florins for the painting of the other half of the wall."

To excite the Signoria sufficiently to spend an additional sum, to delight the Wool and Duomo Boards enough to release him from his contract for a year, he would have to paint a scene of glory and pride for the Florentines.

He decided to do a scene of the Battle of Cascina, during the conquest of Pisa. The Florentine forces had made camp on the bank of the Arno on a hot summer day, a number of the soldiers were bathing in the river, others were coming out to dry themselves, while still a third group, having shed their heavy armor, was sun-bathing on the grass. Suddenly a guard burst into the group, crying, "We are lost! The Pisans are about to attack!" The Florentines scrambled out of the river, those on the bank hastily buckled on their armor, others went rushing for weapons . . . in time to beat back three Pisan attacks.

He went to the Street of the Stationers, bought the largest squares of paper he could find, colored inks, chalks, took them back to his workbench. Drawing swiftly, he organized the scene on the Arno, some of the soldiers still in the water, others trying to climb the steep bank, others throwing on a garment while reaching for a weapon.

Three days later he took his sketches to Soderini. The Gonfaloniere studied the drawings in silence. When he looked up, Michelangelo recognized the affectionate regard in which Soderini held him.

"I was wrong to discourage you. This fresco can be as revolutionary as the David. I'm going to get you this commission."

And so he did, for a sum of three thousand florins, less than a third of Leonardo da Vinci's pay.

Worked carefully, the Cascina cartoon, which he called the Bathers, would have taken a full year. By New Year's Day of 1505, three months after he had started, Michelangelo's cartoon was completed. Argiento, Granacci, and Michelangelo stretched and tacked the cartoon to a light frame against the rear wall. It filled the room with fifty to sixty desperately challenged men. In the panel were contained fear, terror, hopelessness; and at the same time all the manly emotions surging upward to overcome surprise and disaster by swift, purposeful action.

Many painters came to see the sketches. Twenty-two-year-old Ridolfo Ghirlandaio asked if he might copy. Andrea del Sarto, a nineteen-year-old Florentine, arrived with drawing materials. Antonio Sangallo brought his nephew. Twenty-one-year-old Raphael Sanzio came too.

Michelangelo liked Raphael immediately. He had a sensitive, patrician face, altogether manly. He turned to the cartoon, spoke no word for the rest of the afternoon. When dark fell, he came to Michelangelo and said, "This makes painting a wholly different art. I shall have to start back at the beginning. Even what I have learned from Leonardo is no longer sufficient."

Without willing it, or even wanting it, Michelangelo found himself at the head of a school of talented young apprentices.

It was at this moment that the summons arrived from Pope Julius II. He wanted Michelangelo to come to Rome.

It was a bad time for him to leave, for it was important that he transfer the cartoon to the Signoria wall while the painting was fresh and glowing in his mind, before there could be any threats to the project. After that, he had to carve the Apostle Matthew, for he had been living in his home for a considerable time and must start to pay for it.

He reported the summons to Gonfaloniere Soderini. Soderini studied Michelangelo's face carefully for what seemed a long time before he spoke.

"One cannot refuse the Pope. If Julius says 'Come!' you must go. His friendship is important to us in Florence. We will hold your contract in abeyance until you learn what the Holy Father wants. But remember that the contracts must be honored!"

"I understand, Gonfaloniere."

Michelangelo had only to enter the Porta del Popolo to see and smell the startling changes. The streets had been washed. Gaping walls and abandoned houses had been torn down so that the streets could be widened. The swine market had been cleaned out of the Roman forum. A number of new buildings were under construction.

He went to the house of Sangallo, who had been recalled to Rome by the Rovere Pope as official architect. Sangallo greeted him warmly, said:

"The Holy Father is eager to see you. I shall go to the Papal palace at once and ask for an appointment for tomorrow morning."

"Not so fast," Michelangelo cried. "I still don't know what it is the Pope wants me to carve!"

"A tomb. Not a tomb, the Tomb. The Tomb of the World."

"A tomb," groaned Michelangelo. "Oh no!"

"You don't understand. This tomb will be important. The Holy Father wants you to carve as many heroic marbles as you can conceive. You'll be the first sculptor to have that many sculptured marbles in one place since Phidias did the frieze on the Parthenon."

Michelangelo saw before him the first pontiff to wear a beard, a spare figure, lean, once handsome in a strong-featured fashion but now with deep lines in his face, his beard showing streaks of white. What Michelangelo felt most was the enormous energy.

Pope Julius II looked up and waved them in. Sangallo knelt, kissed the Pope's ring, introduced Michelangelo, who also knelt and kissed the ring. The Pope said, "I have seen your Pietà in St. Peter's. That is where I wish my tomb to be erected."

"Could Your Holiness stipulate where in St. Peter's?"

"In the center," replied Julius coldly.

"I shall study the basilica. Would you speak, Holy Father, about your wishes for the tomb? I must build on the foundation of Your Holiness's desires."

This answer pleased Julius. He began speaking in his

rough-timbred voice, pouring out plans, ideas, bits of historical data, ambitions for the Church. Michelangelo listened as concentratedly as he could. Then Julius struck terror into him.

"I desire you to design a frieze of bronzes to go around all four sides of the tomb. Bronze is the best medium for storytelling; through it you can relate the most important episodes of my life."

Michelangelo locked his back teeth, wanting to exclaim, "To tell stories is for those who sing ballads."

Early next day he walked to St. Peter's to see his Pietà. Strong morning light was coming in from the high windows in the opposite wall, suffusing the faces of Mary and Jesus. The marble seemed alive and warm. How he had worked to achieve this!

He entered the main basilica, wondering where in this central nave there could be a place for Julius's tomb to join the other ninety-two Popes buried there.

He spent several weeks designing the sketches, massive figures of Moses and St. Paul, of four male Captives for each side of the tomb and of Victors, struggling, hoping, fighting, conquering. The tomb would have the scope of the Bathers in the three-dimensional character of marble. The bronze frieze, too, would be there. But it would be no more than a narrow band, the least part of the structure.

Sangallo was excited when he saw the forty large sketches. "Exactly what the Pope had in mind!" he exclaimed. But Jacopo Galli, old and ill, still Michelangelo's friend and agent in Rome, was furious. He thought the plans were far too elaborate and complicated. "The good figures," he said, "will be surrounded by so much mediocrity they will be lost. You will carve a glorious tomb, Michelangelo, but not this one! How many actual statues do you have indicated here?"

"About forty."

"How long did you carve on the Bacchus?"

"One year."

"The Pietà?"

"Two."

"The David?"

"Three."

"Then by the simplest arithmetic, these forty figures on the tombs will take you between forty and a hundred years."

"No." Stubbornly. "I've learned my craft now. I can work fast. Like lightning."

Jacopo Galli shot him a piercing look.

"Will you? Let's make sure."

He took up a batch of papers.

"Here are the contracts I drew for the Pietà and Piccolomini Altar. We'll write the best clauses from each. Now, if I know the Pope, he will want the tomb completed immediately. Hold out for ten years, more if you can. As for price, he drives a hard bargain. Don't take a scudo less then twenty thousand ducats . . ."

When he came again to the Pope, Michelangelo was taken aback to find the architect, Bramante, there. He felt uneasy; why was Bramante here at this hour appointed for the examination of the tomb drawings?

Julius took the folio of sketches from Michelangelo's hand, spread them eagerly before him.

"It is even more imposing than I had dreamed. Bramante, will it not be the most beautiful mausoleum in Rome?"

"In all Christendom, Holy Father," replied Bramante.

"Buonarroti, Sangallo informs me that you wish to choose the marbles yourself in Carrara. Set out immediately. One thousand ducats will be provided for the purchase of the stones."

There was a moment of silence. Michelangelo asked respectfully, "And for the sculpturing, Your Holiness?"

"The Papal Treasurer shall be instructed to pay you ten thousand ducats when the tomb is satisfactorily completed."

Michelangelo gulped. But how could he demand double what the Pope had offered? The thousand ducats would barely pay for the marble and get it to Rome. But he wanted to carve these marbles!

"You are generous, Holy Father. And now may I speak of the time for completion? If I could have a minimum of ten years . . ."

"Impossible!" thundered Julius. "It is my dearest wish to see the tomb completed. I will grant you five years."

His jaw stiffened. One could no more bargain with the pontiff over time than over money. He would manage . . . he had the power of ten ordinary sculptors. He would complete the tomb in five years, even if it killed him.

"All will be done, Holy Father, as you say. And now, could I presume to ask that the contract be drawn?"

There was a peculiar silence. The Pope glared, then replied:

"Now that everything is arranged, I should like you and Sangallo and Bramante to visit St. Peter's to determine the proper place for the tomb."

There simply was no room in the basilica for the tomb. They went outside, circled toward the rear, where there were a number of ill-assorted buildings, built over the centuries since St. Peter's had first been erected by Constantine in 319.

"For this tomb," said Sangallo, "we must have a completely new building. The architecture of the building must be born of the tomb itself."

Hope revived in Michelangelo.

"I will design it," Sangallo continued. "Here on this eminence there is sufficient space if we clear out these wooden structures and decaying shrines. It would be visible from the city below."

To Michelangelo's surprise, Bramante's eyes were sparkling with approval.

"Then you like the idea, Bramante?" Michelangelo asked.

"Sangallo is right. What is needed here is a beautiful new chapel."

Sangallo beamed with pleasure. But when Michelangelo turned to Bramante to thank him, he found that the architect's eyes had gone opaque, there was a twitching at one corner of his mouth.

BOOK SEVEN

THE POPE

He had no way of knowing, during his stay in the mountains of Carrara, that his years of grace were over. He returned to Rome in time for Julius's New Year's reception of 1506 to find that the war between himself and the Pope had begun. Bramante had persuaded Julius to abandon Sangallo's idea for a separate chapel to house his tomb; instead, a new St. Peter's was to rise on the hill where the chapel was to have gone, the best design to be chosen through public competition. Michelangelo heard of no provision for his tomb. He had spent the Pope's entire thousand ducats for marbles and shipping, but Julius refused to give him more money until he had seen one of the statues carved. When Julius provided him with a house behind the Piazza San Pietro, a papal secretary informed him that he would have to pay several ducats a month for its use.

"Could I wait until I am paid something by the Holy Father before I return his rent money?" he asked caustically.

At Sangallo's his old friend showed him his finished designs for the new St. Peter's, incorporating the Old Basilica.

"You don't think Bramante has a chance to win the competition?"

"He has talent," replied Sangallo. "But he has had no experience in building churches."

Thirty-four wagonloads of Michelangelo's Carrara white marble arrived by boat and were carried by his old friends, the Guffati family, to Michelangelo's house. Since Jacopo Galli had died, Michelangelo borrowed a thousand ducats from Baldassare Balducci, who was now owner-manager of Galli's old bank. He paid the Guffati, bought a tarpaulin to protect the marble and some used furniture from Balducci's loan, and sent for Argiento to look after his house.

In order to buy the other equipment he needed, Michelangelo had to go to his banker friend for a second loan.

"I don't mind making a second loan," said Balducci. "But I do mind your getting deeper into the hole. When do you expect to put this tomb on a businesslike basis?"

"As soon as I have some carving to show Julius."

"But that could take months! What do you intend to live on until then? Be sensible, go to the Pope. From a bad paymaster, get what you can."

Sangallo did not think it a good time to ask the Pope for money.

"The Holy Father is judging the plans for St. Peter's. The winner is to be announced on March first. At that time I will take you to His Holiness."

But on the first of March the Sangallo palace fell silent. Bramante had been awarded the commission!

"How could this have happened?" cried Michelangelo. "You are the Pope's official architect. You are one of his oldest and most loyal friends. I will get the truth from Leo Baglioni."

Baglioni gazed at him in genuine astonishment. "The truth? Don't you know the truth? Come with me."

Bramante had bought an old palace and rebuilt it with simple elegance. The house was jammed with important personages of Rome.

Leo Baglioni steered Michelangelo upstairs to a large workroom. Pinned to the walls and scattered about the worktables were Bramante's drawings for the new St. Peter's. Michelangelo gasped: it was an edifice to dwarf the cathedral of Florence, yet of an elegant, lyrical design, noble in its conception. By comparison Sangallo's Byzantine conception, a dome over a square, seemed ponderous and fortress-like.

Now Michelangelo knew the truth. Bramante's St. Peter's was the more beautiful and modern in every aspect.

That night, as he lay cold and sleepless in his bed, it became obvious to him that Bramante, from the moment the Pope had sent him with them to find a proper spot for the tomb, had laid his plans to see that a special chapel would never be built. He had used Sangallo's idea and Michelangelo's plans for his own purpose: the securing of a commission to build a new cathedral.

St. Peter's would be a glorious abode for the tomb. But would Bramante allow it in his church? Would he be willing to share credit and attention with Michelangelo Buonarroti?

By the middle of March the sun came out. Michelangelo had the Guffatti family set three giant columns upright. Soon he would be ready to work on the Moses and the Captives.

He received a letter from the man who owned the boats in Carrara, advising him that another shipment of marbles would reach Rome early in May. Michelangelo would have to make payment before the marbles could be released. He washed, went to the Papal palace. Pope Julius, his bristling beard protruding from the high ermine collar, was in his small throne room.

Michelangelo knelt and said,

"Holy Father, the next shipment of your marbles for the tomb are on the way. The boat charges must be paid before I can have them carried home. I am without funds to meet the bill. Could you give me expense money to secure the blocks?"

"Return Monday," said the Pope curtly, and turned away.

Michelangelo took his story to Baglioni, asking if his friend knew what had caused the change in the Holy Father.

"Bramante has convinced the Pope that it is bad luck to build one's own tomb. That it could hasten the day when it has to be pressed into service."

"What shall I do?"

"Go back on Monday. As though nothing had happened."

He went back on Monday, Tuesday, Wednesday, Thursday. Each time he was received coolly, told to return. On Friday the guard at the Papal palace refused him entrance.

Michelangelo walked home, bolted the door of his house, sat down and scrawled:

> *Most Blessed Father, I have been turned out of the palace today by your orders; therefore, if you want me, you must look for me elsewhere than in Rome.*

He sent the letter to the Pope's steward, rented a horse and left for Florence.

Early the second day he dropped off his horse at an inn. He was washing in a bowl when he heard hoofs on the road and saw Baglioni at the head of a party of five couriers.

"Leo! What brings you here?"

"You! The Holy Father knew we were friends. He ordered me to head the party."

"What . . . party? I'm on my way home to Florence. . . ."

"No, you're not!" Baglioni dismounted, brushed the hair out of his eyes. He took a parchment from his saddlebag. "This is a letter from Pope Julius. He commands you to return forthwith to Rome under penalty of disgrace. . . ."

"I did not deserve to be driven from his presence."

"All will be set to rights."

"Permit me to doubt."

"I have the Holy Father's word for it."

"The Holy Father has lapses of memory."

A burly horseman asked, "Shall we truss him up, Messer Baglioni? We could sling him over his own saddle."

"I was not instructed to use force. Michelangelo, you're not the first to be kept waiting by a Pope. If Julius says, 'Wait!' you wait, if it takes a week, a month or a year."

"I'm going back to Florence for good."

"Bravo! You sound like the Florentine Lion. But now that you have asserted your independence, come back. Do not put me in a difficult position."

Michelangelo was silent; Baglioni had always been a good friend. But no one should ask another man to surrender his pride. He told Leo so. Baglioni's face became stern.

"It is not possible to defy the pontiff. You will see. Now or later. And later could be worse. I urge you not to match your will against his. How could you win?"

"If I return now I lose everything. I'm going on to Florence to get my house and my contract back. If he wishes it, I'll sculpture the Pope's tomb . . . under the shadow of the Signoria tower."

He took over his room in his father's house, checked his

marble for the Apostle Matthew where it was stored in a Duomo workshed, carried home from the foundry a still unfinished bronze David he had begun. His cartoon for the Battle of Cascina, which had come to be known as the Bathers, had been moved to the Palazzo della Signoria.

The news of the exchange in the yard of the Poggibonsi inn took only a few hours to make its way over the mountain. Gonfaloniere Soderini's face was grave when he received Michelangelo in his office.

"You're the first Florentine to defy a Pope since Savonarola. I'm afraid your fate will be about the same."

"You mean I'll be hanged from a gibbet in the piazza, and then burned?" He shivered involuntarily.

Soderini smiled for the first time.

"You are not guilty of heresy, only of disobedience. But in the end the Pope will have his way."

"Gonfaloniere, all I want to do is settle down in Florence. I'll start carving the St. Matthew tomorrow so that I can have my house back."

"Florence cannot renew your sculpture contract now. His Holiness would consider it a personal affront. No one can employ you."

"And the Bathers; can I do the fresco?"

Soderini looked up at him. "You have not been in the Great Hall?"

"The groom brought me through your apartment."

"I suggest you go out that way."

He went directly to the east side of the Council platform where Leonardo da Vinci had painted the Battle of Anghiari. The back of his hand swung up to his mouth.

"*Dio mio,* no!"

The entire lower half of Leonardo's fresco was in ruin, the colors having run sharply downward: horses, men, spears, trees, rocks, having flowed into each other in an indistinguishable chaos of color.

All Michelangelo's antagonism washed away. He felt only the deepest regret for a fellow artist who had created mightily for a whole year of his life, only to have the results wiped out.

"Gonfaloniere, how did it happen?"

"Leonardo was determined to revive ancient encaustic painting. He used wax with a solvent, and then gum to harden the mixture. When he finished, he applied heat by lighting fires on the floor. But this mural is twenty-two feet high. The intense heat on the lower half caused the wax to run . . ."

Michelangelo went to see Leonardo, who met him limping from a fall he had taken in his flying machine.

"Leonardo, I want you to know how sorry I am about your fresco. And I want to apologize for my curtness, for the wretched things I have said about you."

"You were provoked. I said slighting things about your marbles. I saw your cartoon of the Bathers. It will become the glory of Florence."

"I don't know. I've lost my appetite now that your Battle of Anghiari will not be fought beside mine."

Michelangelo had straightened out an enmity. But early in July, Gonfaloniere Soderini sent for him to read him a message from the Pope demanding that the Signoria return Michelangelo Buonarroti to Rome at once, under pain of pontifical displeasure.

Soderini put the letter down. "I'm going to have the Cardinal of Pavia write a letter by his own hand, in which he will promise you safety. Will that satisfy you?"

"No. Last night at the Salviati I met a Florentine merchant who lives in Turkey. There is a chance for me to go there and work for the Sultan."

In late August Julius left Rome with an army of five hundred knights and nobles. He made a bloodless conquest of Perugia and continued his victorious march across the Apennines.

Yet nothing happened to Pope Julius II to make him forget his errant sculptor. At the Palazzo della Signoria, Soderini shouted at Michelangelo as he entered:

"We do not wish to go to war with the pontiff on your account! The Holy Father wants you to do some works in Bologna. Make up your mind to go!"

Michelangelo knew he was beaten. Florence, which had no defense, desperately needed the Pope's friendship. No one wanted the Pope's now swollen and confident army crossing the Apennines to attack. The Signoria, the townspeople, all were determined that he be sent back to the Pope, regardless of the consequences to him.

They were right. Florence came first. He would go to Bologna, make his peace with the Holy Father as best he could.

It was November. The streets of Bologna were crowded with people who had thronged to the court of the Pope.

Michelangelo went to the church of San Petronio where mass was being said, and was recognized by one of the Pope's body servants from Rome.

"Messer Buonarroti, His Holiness has been waiting impatiently."

The Pope was at dinner in a palace. He looked up, saw Michelangelo, fell silent. So did the rest of the hall. The two men glared at each other, their eyes flashing fire. Michelangelo threw his shoulders back, refusing to kneel. The Pope was the first to speak.

"You have delayed long! We have been obliged to come to meet you!"

Michelangelo thought grimly that this was true: the

Pope had traveled a good many more miles than he had. He said stubbornly, "Holy Father, I did not deserve the treatment I received in Rome in Easter week."

A bishop, attempting to intervene in Michelangelo's behalf, stepped forward.

"Holiness, one must be indulgent toward artists. They understand nothing, outside of their trade, and often lack good manners."

Julius rose from his chair, thundered:

"How dare you say before this man things that I myself would not say? It is you who lack manners!"

Having received as close to a public apology as a Pope could proffer, Michelangelo knelt, kissed the Pope's ring. The Pope bestowed his benediction, said, "Come to my camp tomorrow. We will arrange our affairs."

He reached Julius's military encampment through heavy snows. Julius was reviewing his troops, wrapped in an enormous furred and wadded overcoat, on his head a gray woolen hood.

Julius led the way to his tent, hung with warm furs. "Buonarroti, I have been thinking I would like you to sculpture a bronze statue, a portrait in my ceremonial robes and triple crown . . ."

"Bronze!" It was an agonized cry. "It is not my trade!"

"You will do this statue as a service to your Pope."

"Holy Father, I know nothing of casting, finishing . . ."

The Pope's face was livid as he roared into a violent temper. "I command you, Buonarroti, to stop issuing ultimatums. You will create a bronze statue for me for San Petronio. Go now, and study the space above the main portal. You will create as stupendous a bronze as the niche will hold."

"Holy Father, if my bronze statue pleases you, will you permit me to resume carving the marble columns?"

"The pontiff does not make bargains!" cried Julius. "Bring me your drawings in one week from this hour. Dismissed!"

At the appointed hour he appeared before Julius, sketches in hand. The Pope was delighted.

"You see, Buonarroti, I was right: you can make bronze statues."

"Begging your pardon, Holy Father, this is not bronze, it is charcoal. But I will do my best so that I may return to the marbles in Rome. And now, if you will direct your treasurer to pay out some money to me, I shall buy supplies and begin work."

Julius turned to Messer Carlino, his papal treasurer, and said, "You are to give Buonarroti whatever he needs."

The treasurer, a sallow, thin-lipped man, gave him a hundred ducats. Michelangelo sent a messenger for Argiento, and wrote to the Signoria, asking if the two bronze casters Lapo and Lotti could be sent to him to help cast the Pope's statue.

He rented a former carriage house with a high ceiling, stone walls and an uneven orange-colored brick floor. There was a garden with a door at the back, and a walk-in fireplace for cooking.

Argiento arrived and set up his kitchen in the fireplace. Lapo and Lotti came two days later. Michelangelo put small, honest-faced Lapo in charge of buying supplies: wax, clay, cloth, brick for the casting ovens.

The hundred ducats were exhausted. Michelangelo went to the Pope's treasurer for more money.

Messer Carlino listened to Michelangelo's request and asked, "What did you do with the first hundred ducats?"

"None of your business. The Pope said he would give me enough money."

"Bring me receipted bills for the first hundred, and written estimates of what you want to spend the second hundred for. I must keep the Pope's books accurately."

"You're like the gardener's dog, that neither eats cabbage himself nor lets anyone else."

A little smile touched Carlino's lips. "It is my job to make people hate me. Then they return as seldom as possible."

"I'll be back."

Lapo quieted him. "I remember what I spent. I'll write up the bills."

He started work at white heat, driven by a fury to get finished almost before he began. There was nothing in his nature which would permit him to do a sleazy job. Much as he detested bronze, he was going to have to make the best bronze statue of the Pope that he could conceivably dig out of himself, even if it took twice as long. He would finish this giant bronze so that it brought honor on himself and the Buonarroti name!

Mail from home came irregularly. Michelangelo looked forward to news of the family, but mostly he received requests for money. His father had found a farm; it was good income property, but a deposit had to be paid right away. If Michelangelo could send five hundred florins, or even three hundred . . . From Buonarroto and Giovansimone, there was rarely a letter without the lines, "You promised us a shop. We are tired of working for someone else. We want to make lots of money. . . ."

Muttering to himself, "Me too," Michelangelo wrapped himself in a blanket in the freezing carriage house while his three assistants slept, and answered the family:

"As soon as I come to Florence, I will set you up in business by yourselves, or with a company, as you wish. I shall try to get money for your deposit on the farm."

He spent hours following Julius about, sketching him in

a variety of poses: saying mass, walking in procession, holding court, shouting in anger, laughing uproariously at a courtier's joke; until he knew every muscle, bone and sinew of the Pope's body beneath his robes. Then he returned to the carriage house and, with Lapo, Lotti and Argiento worked day and night, building the thirteen-foot-high armature of wood, then slowly adding on the clay, touch by touch, spatula by spatula, to create the model from which the bronze would be cast.

Julius arrived at midafternoon, accompanied by Messer Carlino. Michelangelo had draped a quilt over his one comfortable chair. Here the Pope sat in silence, studying his portrait.

Julius was pleased. He rose, walked around the model several times, stopped in front of the statue, looking perplexedly at his right hand, which was raised in a haughty, almost violent gesture.

"Buonarroti, does this hand intend to bless or curse?"

"The right hand lifted, Holy Father, bids the Bolognese be obedient even though you are in Rome."

"And the left hand. What shall it hold?"

"Perhaps the keys to the new St. Peter's?"

"Excellent!"

Glancing at Carlino, Michelangelo added, "I must buy seven to eight hundred pounds of wax to create the model for the oven. . . ."

The Pope authorized the expenditure and swept out to join his train waiting in the street. Michelangelo sent Lapo to shop for the wax. Lapo returned shortly.

"I cannot get it for less than nine florins and forty soldi a hundred. Better buy it at once, it is a good bargain."

Michelangelo was disturbed by a strange note in Lapo's voice. He said quietly to Argiento, "Go to the same shop and ask the price."

Argiento returned, whispered, "They are asking only eight and a half florins, and I can get off the brokerage charge."

"That's what I thought. Lapo's honest face has made a fool of me! Carlino was right. Here, take the money, get a receipt, and wait for their wagon to deliver."

It was dark by the time the donkey pulled up in front of the carriage house and the men brought in the wrapped bales of wax. When they had gone Michelangelo showed Lapo the bill.

"Lapo, you've been taking a profit from me. On everything you bought."

"Why shouldn't I?" the man demanded without change in expression. "When you pay so little."

"Little? I've given you far more than you earn at the Duomo."

"But we live so miserably! There isn't enough to eat!"

"You eat what we eat," growled Argiento, his heavy-knuckled fists clenched. "Food's expensive. If you had stolen less there would have been more for all of us."

"There's food in the restaurants. And wine in the wine-shops. I would not live the way you live."

"Then return to Florence," said Michelangelo bitterly, "where you live better."

Lapo began packing his possessions. Lotti came to Michelangelo, said apologetically, "I'm afraid I must go with him."

"But why, Lotti? You have done nothing wrong. We have been friends."

"I admire you, Messer Buonarroti, and I hope I can work for you again sometime. But I came with Lapo, and I must go with him."

The Pope announced that he would return to Rome for Lent. This gave Michelangelo only a few weeks in which to perfect the wax model and get the Pope's approval. Without experienced helpers, he had to work with no thought of food, sleep, relaxation. The Pope visited the workyard for the last time, approved the model, gave Michelangelo his benediction, and an order on a Bolognese banker to continue paying his costs.

Desperately needing a bronze caster, he wrote to the Herald in Florence, asking him to send Master Bernardino, the best in Tuscany. He arrived in a blaze of May heat, built a tremendous brick oven in the courtyard. There followed weeks of experimenting with the fires, testing the way the metals fused. Michelangelo was filled with impatience to cast, and go home.

"We must not hurry," Bernardino warned him. "One untested step, and all our work will be for nothing."

But when they finally poured in June, something went wrong. The statue came out well as far as the waist; the rest of the material did not fuse. In order to take it out it was necessary to dismantle the furnace. Aghast, Michelangelo cried:

"What could have gone wrong?"

"I don't know. This has never happened to me before."

Bernardino was as wretched as Michelangelo. "I'll start again tomorrow."

He worked heroically, night and day, rebuilt the furnace, experimented with the metals that had not fused. Finally, under the blinding heat of the mid-July sun, he poured again. Slowly, the heated metal began to run from the furnace to the mold. Bernardino said:

"There's nothing more you need me for. I leave for Florence at dawn."

Michelangelo was left to discover the results himself. He had to sit on his hands for three weeks, until the mold cooled sufficiently for him to tear it down.

Bernardino had done his job. The two halves of the statue were joined without a serious mark. The bronze was red and rough, but there were no imperfections. "A few weeks of filing and polishing," Michelangelo thought, "and I, too, will be on my way."

But there was still more delay, for the ledge on which the statue was to stand had not been completed.

At last a crew came to move the statue to the front of San Petronio. Bells rang all over the city. The whole city assembled in the square, listening to the fifes, trumpets and drums. At the hour which the astrologers had told Julius was propitious, the covering was removed from the statue. The crowd cheered, then fell to its knees and crossed itself.

Michelangelo, standing in his worn workman's shirt at the far end of the square, went unnoticed. Looking up at Julius in his niche, he felt nothing. Not even relief. He walked the streets of Bologna all night. There was a cold drizzle. He had exactly four and a half florins left. At dawn he borrowed a horse and left for Florence.

One of his first acts upon his return was to write Sangallo in Rome, asking him to have the marbles for the Pope's tomb sent to Florence where they could be worked along with the Apostles ordered so long ago. But in April he received through Gonfaloniere Soderini a direct message from Julius sealed with the Fisherman's ring, asking him to come to Rome.

"Julius has good news for you," Soderini said.

"That can only mean he is going to let me carve again."

"You will go?"

"Tomorrow. Sangallo wrote that my second shipload of marbles has been lying exposed in front of St. Peter's. I want to rescue them."

In Rome, Sangallo took him at once to the Papal throne room. The Pope beckoned him forward.

He cried, "You had no confidence in yourself. When I asked you to work in bronze you cried out, 'It is not my trade!' "

"You are generous, Holy Father," murmured Michelangelo.

"I intend to continue being generous," cried the Pope heartily. "I am commissioning you to paint the twelve apostles on the ceiling of the Sistine Chapel, and decorate the vault with customary designs."

Michelangelo was stunned. Nausea gripped him. He cried passionately:

"I am a sculptor, not a painter!"

The Pope glowered at Michelangelo, who stood before him defiant but speechless. Their eyes met and held. Then a wisp of a smile drifted across the pontiff's face, was reflected in the tiny amber sparkle of Michelangelo's eyes, the barest twitching of his lips.

"Buonarroti, you will paint the ceiling and decorate the vault. For this we will pay you three thousand large gold ducats. We shall also be pleased to pay the expenses and wages of five assistants. When the Sistine vault is completed, you have your pontiff's promise that you shall return to the carving of the marbles. My son, you are dismissed."

What further could he say? Where could he flee? There was nothing to do but submit.

Strong sunlight was streaming in from three tall windows in the Sistine Chapel, lighting the glorious frescoes of Botticelli and Rosselli opposite, shooting strong beams of light across the variegated marble floor, the side walls, one hundred and thirty-three feet long, and barrel vault, sixty-eight feet above. Taking a deep breath, Michelangelo craned his neck and looked up the more than sixty feet into the air at the enormous ceiling he was to fill with decorations.

The motive for the commission became crushingly clear to him. It was not to put magnificent paintings on the ceiling, but rather to mask the structural supports from the top third of wall into the barrel vault so that the gaze of people on the floor would be diverted from the ungainly architectural divisions. As an artist he had become not merely a decorator but an obliterator of other men's clumsiness.

But he could not fight the Pope. If he were ever to be allowed to go back to his beloved marble he would first have to paint that ceiling. He signed the contract, paid his debts, wrote to Argiento and Granacci asking them to come to Rome. Granacci agreed to help find him five assistants, but it would take time.

In the meantime Michelangelo would have to design a new kind of scaffolding that would enable him to paint a surface sixty feet above the floor and yet would never touch the ceiling or damage the paintings. He could cut no niches to anchor the ends of his planks. He solved the problem, at last, bolting the scaffolding to a cornice that ran around the chapel. Put in place and tested, the trestle proved to become stronger as more weight was added. He was jubilant. It was a tiny victory; yet it provided him with the impetus to begin the detested chore.

The group of assistants Granacci found worked well with one another. By the middle of December a seventh of the vault was completed and Michelangelo could see what the ceiling would be like when it was done. The Pope's objective would be accomplished. The brightly colored designs of the Apostles on their thrones would conceal the structural ugliness.

He and his group could apply the remaining paint without much trouble. But he could not deny that the quality was mediocre. He told Giuliano da Sangallo so.

"You have done your best under the circumstances," replied his friend.

"I'm a long way from convinced of that."

"No one will blame you. The Pope gave you a job, and you did as you were told. Who could do otherwise?"

"Me. If I walk away from this ceiling as it is, I'll despise myself."

The country around Rome was not Tuscany. But it had power, and history; the flat, fertile plains, the remains of Roman aqueducts, the villa built by the Emperor Hadrian, the towns on the slopes of volcanic hills, the ruins of Cicero's house, the forum and buried temples. He walked deeper and deeper into the past and thought of the vast ceiling of the chapel. Gradually he came to know that he would have to work alone if he were to accomplish the design being created in his mind. For he knew now that nothing would suffice for his vault but Genesis itself.

Shortly after the first day of the year of our Lord 1509, he asked Chamberlain Accursio if he might see the Pope alone for a few moments. The chamberlain arranged the meeting for late in the afternoon.

Michelangelo explained his new plan to Julius.

The Pope stirred on his throne, rose, paced up and down the room, then came to a halt before Michelangelo.

"You are a strange one, Buonarroti. You screamed that fresco was not your profession. Yet now, eight months later, you come back with a plan that will entail infinitely more time and labor."

Julius shook his head in amused puzzlement. Then he put his hand on Michelangelo's head, blessed him.

"Paint your ceiling as you will. We cannot pay you five or six times the original three thousand ducats, but we will double it to six thousand."

He told Granacci that, except for one assistant to grind

10. God Separating the Waters from the Earth,

the colors and another to lay the plaster, he would work alone.

"Working alone on top of that scaffolding to re-create the story of Genesis will take you forty years!"

"No, closer to four."

Granacci put his arms about his friend's shoulders. "You have David's courage."

detail of the Sistine ceiling, 1511.

Michelangelo went again to the Sistine Chapel to re-study the vault. He was determined to get a teeming humanity up on that ceiling, as well as God Almighty who created it. In the center space he would show the major legends of the creation story: Dividing the Waters from the Earth; God Creating the Sun, the Moon; God Creating Adam and Eve; Expelling Them from the Garden; the

11. The Creation of the Sun and Moon,

legend of Noah and the Deluge. On the ends and sides he would paint Prophets and Sibyls.

He was ready now to tear out the plaster already frescoed and start afresh, when Argiento came to him with tears in his eyes.

"Argiento, what's wrong?"

"My brother is dead."

Michelangelo put a hand on the young man's shoulder.

detail of the Sistine ceiling, 1511.

"I'm so sorry."

"I have to go home. The family farm is mine now. I must work it. My brother left little children. I'll raise them."

He paid Argiento's back wages, thirty-seven gold ducats. This was almost the last of his funds. He could not even consider asking the Pope for more funds until he had an important section of the ceiling finished. There would be

12. The Deluge, detail of the Sistine ceiling, 1508–9.

months of drawing before he could start his first fresco. And now there would be no one to cook a meal, sweep a floor or wash a shirt.

He ate his soup-of-the-country in the silent house. It would be lonelier still, all alone on the scaffolding in the barren chapel.

He began with the Deluge. By March he had the cartoon ready to be transferred to the ceiling.

Michelangelo helped his assistant Michi carry the sacks of lime, sand, and volcanic dust up the steep wall ladders to the top of the scaffolding. Here Michi made his mix. They climbed the three receding platforms, Michi laid an

13. The Creation of Man, 1511, detail of the Sistine ceiling.

area of intonaco, then fixed the cartoon. Michelangelo drew in the figures.

Michi descended, set to work grinding colors below. Michelangelo was now on his top platform, sixty feet above the floor, suffering from vertigo. He painted with his head and shoulders pulled sharply back, his eyes staring straight up. Paint dripped onto his face, the moisture of the wet

.ome, Vatican, Sistine Chapel.

plaster oozed out and dripped in his eyes. His arms and back tired quickly from the strain of the unnatural position. During the first week he allowed Michi to lay only modest areas of plaster each day, proceeding cautiously, experimenting with figures and colors. He was content to feel his way slowly until he had mastered his medium.

The Deluge took him thirty-two days of consecutive

14. The Creation of Woman, detail of the Sistine ceiling, 151

painting. During the last weeks he was completely out of funds. How was it that only he did not prosper from his papal connections?

He went to his drafting table, burying his hunger and loneliness in work, sketching the next fresco, the Sacrifice of Noah. As the figures came alive his workroom filled up with energy and vividness, vitality and color. His hunger,

ome, Vatican, Sistine Chapel.

his sense of isolation receded. He felt secure among his companions in this world of his own creating. To the silent house he murmured:

"I'm never less alone than when alone."

And he sighed, for he knew himself to be a victim of his own character.

Pope Julius came to the chapel when the first fresco was

15. The Fall of Man and Expulsion from Ede

done. He climbed the ladder, joined Michelangelo on the scaffolding, studied the fifty-five men, women and children.

"The rest of the ceiling will be as good?"

"It should be better, Holy Father, for I am still learning about proper perspective at this height."

"I am pleased with you, my son. I shall order the treasurer to pay you another five hundred ducats."

tail of the Sistine ceiling, 1509–10.

Now he was able to send money home, to buy food for the house, needed supplies for the job.

He painted furiously every day while the light held, returning home each night to work on the cartoons for other sections of the ceiling. He slept in his clothes without even taking off his boots.

When he grew dizzy from standing and painting with

his head and shoulders thrown back, his neck arched so that he could peer straight upward, his arms aching in every joint, he had a still higher platform made. He painted sitting down, his thighs drawn up tight against his belly for balance, his eyes a few inches from the ceiling, until his bones became so bruised and sore he could no longer endure the agony. Then he lay flat on his back, his knees in the air, doubled over as tightly as possible against his chest to steady his painting arm.

He thought he was going blind. A letter arrived from Buonarroto, and when he tried to read it he could see nothing but a blur.

In June 1510, a year and a few weeks after he had shown Julius the Deluge, the first half of the vault was completed. In a small central panel God in His rose-colored robe had just raised Eve from the rib of the sleeping Adam. Half of the vault was now a flood of glorious color: mustard yellows, pale sea greens, dust rose and azure blues against the mighty parade of sun-flooded flesh tones.

He had not told anyone the vault was half completed, but the Pope knew at once. He sent word to Michelangelo that he would be in the Sistine at midafternoon. Michelangelo helped Julius up the last rungs of the ladder, pointed out the Old Testament scenes he had completed.

Julius demanded that the scaffold be taken down so that the world could see how great a thing was being executed.

"It is not yet time to take the scaffold down, Holy Father. There are so many things to be finished."

"When will it be ready?" insisted the Pope stubbornly.

"When it is ready!"

Julius went red in the face, raised his walking stick in a ury and brought it down across Michelangelo's shoulder.

There was a silence while the two antagonists glared at ach other. Michelangelo went cold all over. He bowed, said formally in a voice from which all emotion had been smitten:

"It shall be as Your Holiness desires. The scaffolding will be down by tomorrow, the chapel ready to be shown."

He backed away, leaving the space open for the Pope to descend the ladder.

"It is not for you, Buonarroti, to dismiss your pontiff!" cried Julius. "You are dismissed."

Michelangelo backed down the ladder, left the chapel. A bitter end, to be beaten with a stick like a peasant. He stumbled blindly along unfamiliar streets. He had re-created the world. He had tried to be God! Well, Pope Julius II had put him in his place.

He made his way home. Michi was waiting for him, silent and owl-eyed.

"Pack your things, Michi," he said. "Get a head start. If the Pope orders my arrest, I don't want them taking you too."

"He had no right to hit you."

"He can put me to death if he wants to. Only he'll have to catch me first."

He filled one canvas bag with his drawings, another with his personal things. Just as he finished there was a knock on the door.

He opened it, expecting to see soldiers. Instead there was the chamberlain, Accursio.

"Have you come to arrest me?"

"My good friend," said Accursio gently, "do you think the pontiff would bother to strike anyone he was not deeply fond of? The Pope loves you. He asked me to bring you these five hundred ducats, and to convey his apologies."

"Who knows that the Pope sent you to beg my pardon?"

"Is that important?"

"Since Rome will know the pontiff struck me, I can only go on living here if people also know that he apologized."

Accursio rolled his shoulders. "Who has ever been able to conceal anything in this city?"

Julius chose the week of the Feast of the Assumption to unveil the first half of the vault. A crew took down the scaffold and stored it. Michelangelo spent the intervening weeks at home, making the cartoons for the prophets Daniel and Jeremiah, the Libyan and Persian Sibyls. He did not go near the Sistine or the Papal palace. Julius sent no word. It was an uneasy truce.

And, suddenly, Pope Julius was deep in war.

Two days after the unveiling, Julius left Rome at the head of his army to drive the French out of northern Italy. Michelangelo watched him leave—and worried. The Pope's chamberlain had not brought him specific permission to put back the scaffolding and commence work on the altar half of the vault. The Pope could be gone for months. What did he do in the meanwhile?

It was not until after New Year's, 1511, that he was able to start painting again.

The Pope's campaign against the French had gone badly. He had been saved from a serious defeat only by the arrival of Venetian and Spanish troops. He sent Michelangelo money and permission to finish the second half of the chapel.

Throughout the winter and spring, while the Pope's army suffered defeat again and again, Michelangelo labored from first light until darkness drove him from his scaffold to finish the four panels that were the heart of the ceiling. He knew he was racing against death, for Julius had finally returned to Rome ill, the most hated man in Italy, his resources nearly exhausted.

Michelangelo worked the more desperately, hoping, praying, striving to complete his Genesis before the collapse of his protector brought in a new Pope who might want to wipe out all traces of Julius II's reign, including the ceiling he had commissioned for the Sistine Chapel.

But in spite of the fury of his painting the ceiling panels grew slowly. Another fall and winter, spring and summer passed. And during all those months the Pope kept insisting that Michelangelo complete his ceiling quickly, quickly! Then, one day in the autumn of 1512, Julius climbed the ladder unannounced.

"When will it be finished?"

"When I have satisfied myself."

"You have already taken four full years."

"It will be done, Holy Father, when it will be done."

"Do you want to be thrown down from this scaffolding?"

Michelangelo gazed at the marble floor below.

"On All Saints' Day I shall celebrate mass here," declared the Pope. "It will be two years since I blessed the first half."

Michelangelo had wanted to touch up some of the draperies and skies in gold and ultramarines. But there would be no time now. He had Michi take down the scaffold.

On All Saints' Day official Rome dressed itself in its finest robes for the Pope's dedication of the Sistine Chapel. Michelangelo rose early, went to the baths, shaved off his beard, donned his blue hose, blue wool shirt.

But he did not go to the Sistine. Instead he walked out under the portico of his house, pulled back the tarpaulin, stood ruminatively before the marble columns he had waited these seven long years to carve.

He took up his hammer and chisel. Fatigue, memory, bitterness and pain fell away. Sunlight streaming in the window caught the first shafts of marble dust that floated upward.

BOOK EIGHT

THE MEDICI

Pope Julius II survived the completion of the Sistine vault by only a few months. Giovanni de' Medici, the first Florentine to be elected to the papacy, was the new Pope.

Michelangelo stood in the Piazza San Pietro among the Florentine nobles who were determined to make this the most lavish procession ever to be seen in Rome. Ahead of him were two hundred mounted spearmen, the captains of the thirteen regions of Rome with their banners flying, the five standard-bearers of the Church carrying flags with the papal arms. Twelve milk-white horses from the papal stables were flanked by a hundred young nobles in fringed red silk and ermine. Behind him were a hundred Roman barons accompanied by their armed escorts, the Swiss guards in uniforms of white, yellow and green. The new Pope, Leo X, mounted on a white Arabian stallion, was shaded from the warm April sun by a canopy of embroidered silk but was perspiring from the weight of the triple tiara and heavily jeweled cope.

The trumpeters sounded for the beginning of the march across the city. Riding next to his cousin, Paolo Rucellai, Michelangelo watched Leo raising his pearl-encrusted gloved hands in benediction, his chamberlains beside him throwing handfuls of gold coins to the crowds. Marbles of Rome lined the Via Papale: busts of the emperors, statues of the apostles, saints, the Virgin, placed side by side with pagan Greek sculptures.

At midafternoon Pope Leo descended from his horse by means of a ladder, stood for a moment by the ancient bronze equestrian statue of Marcus Aurelius in front of the Lateran. Then, surrounded by his College of Cardinals, flanked by Cousin Giulio and the Florentine and Roman nobles, he entered the Lateran and seated himself on the Sella Stercoraria, ancient seat of power occupied by the first Popes.

Michelangelo ate little of the elaborate banquet served in the hall of the palace of Constantine, restored for the feast. At sunset he remounted his horse to follow in Pope Leo's train back to the Vatican. By the time they reached the Campo dei Fiori night had fallen. Torches and tapers lighted the streets. Michelangelo dropped off his horse at Leo Baglioni's house, handed the reins to a groom. Baglioni had not been invited to ride in the procession; he was alone in the house, unshaven, gloomy. This time he had been certain Cardinal Riario would be elected to the papacy.

"So you made it to the Vatican ahead of me!" he grumbled to Michelangelo.

"I'd be happy never to see the inside of the Papal palace again. I cede my place to you."

"This is one game in which the winner can't cede. I'm out; you're in. There'll be glorious commissions."

It was late when he returned to his new home near the foot of Trajan's column. Just before his death Pope Julius had paid him two thousand ducats to settle the Sistine account. When this property, consisting of a main building, a cluster of wooden sheds in the rear, a stable, tower and overgrown garden with shady laurel trees, had come on the market at a reasonable price, he had bought it.

He felt easy about his future. Had not Pope Leo X announced to the courtiers about him: "Buonarroti and I were educated together under my father's roof"?

For the first time since April 1505, eight years before, he was carving. Three heroic figures for the tomb of the late Pope Julius. He carved for fourteen hours a day in his workshop, moving smoothly from the eight-foot, seated figure of Moses holding the stone tablets under one arm to the two Captives, one dying, the other heroic, rebellious. Mounds of white dust caked in his nostrils.

Balducci was advising him on the revision of the tomb contract. Pope Leo was using his good offices to persuade the Duke of Urbino and the other Rovere heirs to make the agreement more equitable for Michelangelo, to allow him more time and more money.

He had his own studio now, with six young assistants and a good apprentice-servant. He had acquired a sorrel horse for traveling the cobbled streets of Rome, ate his meals at a well-set table, went abroad in warm weather in a black cape lined with satin.

The Sistine ceiling had produced an effect equal to the unveiling of the David in Florence. From artists of every medium who had flocked to Rome from all over Europe to help Leo celebrate his elevation to the papacy, Michelangelo had rewon the painting title first earned by the Bathers: "Master of the World." The Architect Bramante was no longer art emperor of Rome. Cracks of such serious dimension had shown in his piers of St. Peter's that all work had been stopped and extensive studies undertaken to see if the foundations could be saved.

Giuliano, the only one of *Il Magnifico's* sons Michelan-

16. Moses, 1513–16. Tomb of Julius II, Rome, San Pietro in Vincoli.

gelo loved, was recalled from Florence by his brother, the Pope. At a great ceremony on the Capitoline Hill just above Michelangelo's house, Giuliano was made a Baron of Rome. Reluctantly Michelangelo left his carving, dressed in his best clothes, attended the ceremony, sitting with the Medici family. But during the winter he managed by a series of excuses which amused Leo to absent himself from the frequent, long and elaborate papal entertainments.

Only once did he break his fast: when Giuliano came to the studio to urge him to attend a reception for Leonardo da Vinci, whom Giuliano had invited to Rome and installed in the Belvedere, one of the Vatican palaces.

Entering the Belvedere, Giuliano took him through a series of workrooms extensively renovated for Leonardo's purposes.

"Look at these concave mirrors," exclaimed Giuliano, "this metal screw-cutting machine, all new. When I took him out on the Pontine marshes he located several extinct volcanoes, and sketched plans for draining the fever-laden area. He won't let anyone see his notebooks, but I suspect he's completing his mathematical studies for the squaring of curved surfaces. His work on optics, his formulations of the laws of botany—amazing! Leonardo feels he will be able to tell the age of trees by counting the rings on the trunk. Imagine!"

"I would rather imagine him painting beautiful frescoes."

Giuliano led him back toward the drawing room.

"Leonardo is a universal man. Has there been such a scientific mind since Aristotle? Art he conceives as only one aspect of human creativity."

"It is beyond my comprehension," growled Michelangelo

stubbornly. "When a man has such a rare gift he should not spend his days counting the rings on trees."

Leonardo joined them, dressed in an elaborate red blouse and lacy sleeves. Michelangelo thought he looked tired and old, his magnificent flowing beard and shoulder-length hair now white. The two men, who understood each other not at all, exchanged expressions of pleasure at the reunion.

Other guests began to arrive. Soon there was a hubbub in the room. Michelangelo stood alone at a side window overlooking the Sistine. Leonardo was astonishing the guests with new contrivances: animals filled with air which sailed over everyone's head; a live lizard to which he had attached wings filled with quicksilver, and whose head he had decorated with artificial eyes, horns and a beard.

"The mechanical lion I made in Milan could walk several steps," he announced to the guests who were congratulating him on his inventiveness. "And when you pressed a button his breast fell open, exposing a bunch of lilies."

To himself Michelangelo muttered, "This is the limit!" and rushed home, trembling to get the feel of marble between his hands.

The carving went well that winter and spring. In another year he would complete the front wall of the tomb, the Moses and the two Captives. He would have to work like a man possessed, but since he was to be possessed by marble, it seemed good and right.

Then Pope Leo summoned him to the Vatican. Leo had been kind to the Buonarroti family, naming them counts palatine, and granting them the right to display the Medici crest of six balls.

Leo, sitting at a table in his library, was examining through his spyglass a number of gems and carved cameos.

"Holy Father, you were most generous to my family," Michelangelo said.

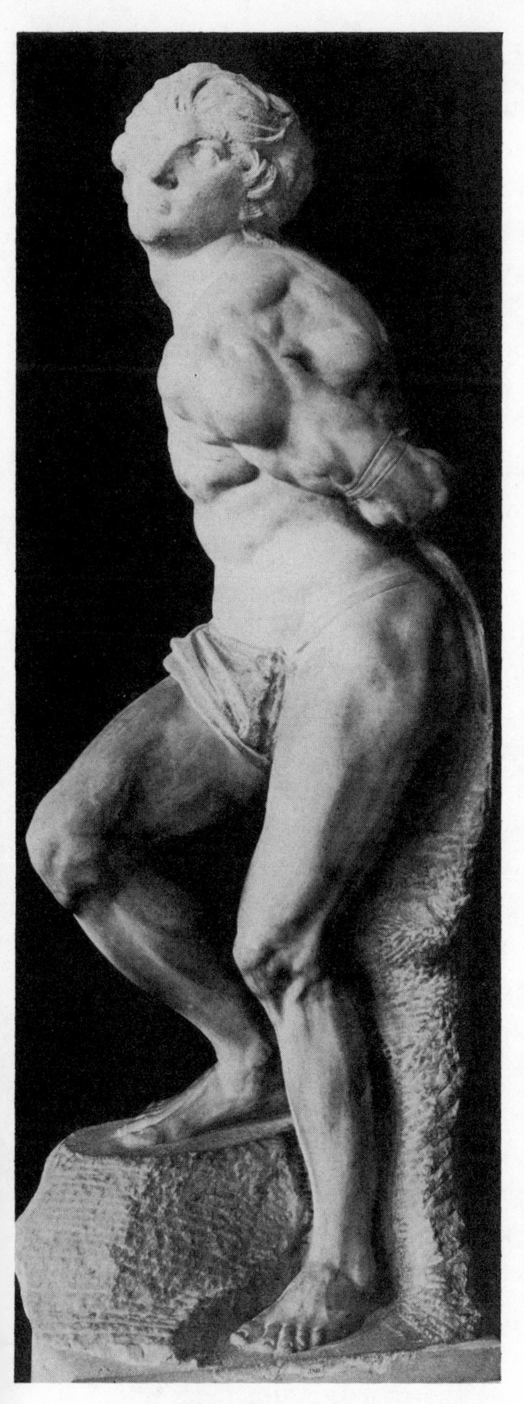

17. The Heroic Captive, 1513–16. Paris, Louvre.

18. The Dying Captive, 1513–16. Paris, Louvre.

"Good," said Leo. "Because we do not want you, a Medici sculptor, spending your time creating statues for a Rovere. We have decided to present you with the greatest art commission of our age. We wish you to undertake a façade for our family church, San Lorenzo . . . as my father thought of it . . . a glorious façade."

"But, Holy Father, the tomb for Pope Julius! I must finish it or the Roveres will prosecute me."

"A Medici artist should serve the Medici."

"And so it shall be," replied Michelangelo. "Within two years the tomb will be complete. I have everything organized . . ."

"No!" Leo's round face was flushed with anger. "There will be no two years for the Roveres. You will enter our service at once. We will protect you against the Roveres, secure a new contract which will give you more time and money. When you have completed the façade for San Lorenzo you can return to Julius's mausoleum."

"Holy Father, I have lived with this tomb for ten years. We are ready to construct the front wall, cast the bronzes, mount my three big statues. You must not stop me. It is a crucial moment for me. I have trained workmen. If I have to dismiss the men, leave the marbles lying about . . . Holiness, on the love I bore your noble father, I implore you not to do this terrible thing to me. . . ."

He dropped on one knee, bowed his head.

"Give me time to finish the work that is planned. Then I can move to Florence and to the façade in peace and happiness. I will create a great façade for San Lorenzo, but I must not be tormented in mind and spirit. . . ."

"Michelangelo," said Pope Leo, shaking his head, "you still take everything so . . . so . . . desperately. Or is it that you do not wish to create the San Lorenzo façade for the Medici?"

"I do, Your Grace. But it is a huge undertaking . . ."

"You are right!" cried Leo. "You must leave for Carrara at once, choose the blocks yourself, supervise the cutting. I will send you a thousand florins to pay for them."

Michelangelo kissed the Pope's ring, left Leo's presence, descended the steps of the Vatican palace with the tears streaming down his face.

Carrara was a one-crop town: marble. Each day the Carrarino lifted his eyes to the reassuring white slashes in the hills, and thanked God. Their life was communal: when one prospered, all prospered; when one starved, all starved. Their life in the quarries was so dangerous that when they parted from each other they did not say "Good-by," but "Go carefully."

Michelangelo liked these people. They were more like him than his own brothers: small, wiry, tireless, taciturn, with the power of men who work stubborn stone. They spoke in clipped, monosyllabic hammer strokes, a language Michelangelo had had to learn.

Michelangelo joined a stream of quarriers bound for the Polvaccio quarry, where he had found his best marble for Julius's tomb eleven years before.

As the sun edged over the mountains they reached the nearly mile-high quarry where the crew were at work as swiftly as they could raise a hammer. The steeplejacks of the quarries descended their ropes from the precipices above, cleaning the ledges of loose stone as they dangled several hundred feet in the air.

The owner of the quarry, called The Barrel from his enormous round torso, greeted Michelangelo heartily.

"Ah, Buonarroti, today we have your great block."

"Permit me to hope."

The Barrel grasped him by the arm, led him to the area where water-soaked wooden pegs had been driven into a

V-shaped incision and, in the natural course of swelling, had forced an opening in the solid marble cliff which the quarriers were now attacking with levers and sledge hammers, driving the pegs deeper to dislodge the marble from its bed. The foreman cried, "Fall below!" Workmen sawing blocks fled to the edge of the quarry. The topmost block ripped from its hold with the sound of a falling tree, landed with tremendous impact in the level work space below, splitting according to its cracks.

When Michelangelo came forward and studied the huge jagged block he was disappointed.

"A beautiful piece of meat, no?"

"It is good."

"You accept?"

"It is veined."

"The cut is near perfect."

"I must have perfect."

The Barrel lost his temper.

"You cost us cash. A month we quarry for you, and not one ducat we see."

"I will pay you much money . . . for statuary marbles."

"God makes marble. Complain to Him."

"Not until I am convinced there are not whiter blocks behind these."

"You want me to cut down my whole peak?"

"I will have thousands of ducats to spend for the façade of San Lorenzo. You will have your share."

The Barrel turned away, a scowl on his face, grumbling something which Michelangelo could not catch, but which sounded as though the owner were calling him, "The Big Noise."

Michelangelo picked up his jacket and dinner, struck out for another quarry, using an old goat trail that gave him but a few inches of security as he moved down the cliff. He reached the quarry at ten o'clock.

He was disappointed again.

"A beautiful block," said the owner, hovering near. "You buy?"

"Perhaps. I will try."

Though he had replied courteously, the owner's face set in a grim expression. Michelangelo was about to move on to the next quarry when he heard the sound of the horn, echoing up and down the valleys. The quarriers froze in their positions.

One of their members had been hurt, perhaps killed. No further work would be done until the following morning, and none then, if there should be a funeral to attend.

Michelangelo circled to the bottom of the town, and admitted himself to his two-room apartment at the rear of the apothecary's house. Apothecary Francesco di Pelliccia was the second best-educated man in town, having been trained at the neighboring University of Pisa.

He had gone to attend the injured man. There was a doctor in Carrara but few of the quarriers used him, saying, "Nature cures and the doctors collect."

Signora Pelliccia had saved Michelangelo some of their midday dinner. He was finishing the soup when a groom arrived with a note from the Marquis Antonio Alberico II of Carrara, requesting that Michelangelo come at once to the castle.

It was a fortress bastion built in the twelfth century with crenelated defense towers, a moat and thick stone walls to withstand siege. Lately it had been converted to an elegant marble palace, with frescoes and furnishings from all over Europe.

The marquis was waiting at the head of a majestic

flight of stairs. He was tall, courtly, commanding, with a long thin face and a luxuriant beard.

"It was kind of you to come, Maestro Buonarroti," the marquis said, leading Michelangelo to his paneled library. "Do you remember a name that the owner of the quarry called you?"

"I thought I heard him call me 'The Big Noise.' What can it mean?"

"In Carrarino it means to be a complainer, not to accept what is handed to you. The owners say that you don't seem to know your own mind."

"They're partly right," Michelangelo admitted ruefully. "Pope Leo promised me a thousand ducats to buy marbles, but nothing has arrived."

"May I make a suggestion? Sign two or three modest contracts for marbles to be delivered in the future. The owners will be reassured. A number of them who have quarried blocks just for you fear they have cut too much and may have to idle the men. These people have little reserve. A few weeks' beans and flour separate them from hunger. Threaten this thin margin and you become their enemy."

"It is a narrow precipice. I will do as you suggest."

Within the next weeks he signed two contracts. Tension vanished as he promised The Barrel and Pelliccia to buy heavily as soon as money arrived from the Pope. But he could not get rid of his own tensions. Although the Rovere heirs had buckled under to the Pope's demands, writing a third contract which further cut down the size of the tomb and extended the time limit from seven to nine years, Michelangelo knew they were outraged. Pope Leo had blandly assured the Roveres that he could continue to carve the tomb marbles while he did those for the façade; but no one, least of all Michelangelo, was fooled by this promise.

Winter rains turned the mountain trails into flooding river beds. Then the snows fell. All work stopped in the mountains. Letters from friends implored Michelangelo to come to Rome where the Pope was clamoring to see the designs for San Lorenzo.

He reached Rome as the city was preparing for Christmas. He went first to his house and was relieved to find everything as he had left it. His Moses seemed nearer to completion than he had remembered. If only he could steal off a month . . .

He received a hearty reception at the Vatican. He spread his sheets of paper on a desk.

"But one thing must be changed," the Pope said.

"What is that, Your Grace?"

"The marbles must come from Pietrasanta. They have the finest statuary marble in the world."

"Yes, I have heard. But there is no road. The Roman engineers tried to open one and failed."

"They did not try hard enough."

Michelangelo surmised that something more than marble was involved.

"The Carraresi are a rebellious lot," the Pope explained. "They have not co-operated with the Vatican. The people of Pietrasanta and Seravezza consider themselves loyal Tuscans. They have signed over their quarries to Florence. Thus we shall secure the purest statuary marble for only the cost of labor."

"I don't believe it is humanly possible to quarry in Pietrasanta, Holiness," protested Michelangelo. "The blocks would have to come out of stone precipices a mile high."

"You will make the trip to the top of Monte Altissimo and report on what you find."

He returned to Carrara, to his rooms behind Pelliccia's apothecary shop. When the Pope's thousand ducats were at last sent to him, he put out of his mind any worry about the Pietrasanta quarry and began buying marble almost in a fever.

Then came a stinging letter. The Pope wanted Pietrasanta marbles.

He told no one of his destination, arranging to have a horse ready at dawn to take him to Pietrasanta. He tarried for a moment at the morning market to buy an orange. Above him towered Monte Altissimo, Highest Mountain.

There was a narrow wagon road between Pietrasanta and the hill town of Seravezza. Here he found a room for the night, and a guide, called Antò.

They left Seravezza in the pitch-dark. Where the trail ended they had to cut through thickets of underbrush. They climbed straight up dark stone ranges, rock formations that looked as though they had been made as steps for the gods. They descended deep into gorges, clammy cold from centuries without sun, then climbed on hands and knees up the next range.

By midmorning they emerged at the top of a shrub-covered promontory. Between Michelangelo and Monte Altissimo was only a sharp hogback, and beyond this a canyon at the foot of the mountain where they would have to cross a river.

Michelangelo sat on a boulder looking upward at the fearsome Alps.

"With the help of God, and the whole French army, one might get a road built to this point. But how could anyone build a road up that perpendicular wall? Let's start climbing, Antò. I want to see how good the marbles are that we can't bring down."

The marbles were perfect: outcroppings of purest white statuary. He found a quarry where the Romans had dug, fragments of a marble block they had excavated. After the battle to keep their footing up the rocky ravines and gorges until they had passed the snow line, it was clear to Michelangelo why the emperors had used Carrara marble to build Rome. Yet he ached to set hammer and chisel to this shining stone, the purest he had ever seen.

It was dusk by the time he reached Carrara. When he entered the Porta Ghibellina the townspeople in front of their shops suddenly became busy. In the Piazza del Duomo a group of men talking in a tight circle hunched their shoulders toward each other as he passed. He walked into the apothecary's shop where Pelliccia and his son were grinding medications on a slab of marble.

"What has happened? I left yesterday morning a Carrarino. I return tonight a Tuscan."

"It's your trip up Monte Altissimo."

"I shall report to His Holiness that no marbles can be brought down from Monte Altissimo."

He was more amused than concerned when he learned that Baccio d'Agnolo and Bigio had been granted five hundred ducats to go into the Seravezza mountains and lay out a road. He knew them both; they could not lay out a corpse.

He sent his report to Rome. The answer came back.

"His Holiness wills that all work to be done on the façade of San Lorenzo shall be carried out with marble from Pietrasanta, and no other."

Within an hour a crowd began to gather. The apothecary's dining-room windows were of floor-to-ceiling height, the center pair being glass doors. Michelangelo stood behind the curtained doors listening to the murmur grow in intensity as the quarriers continued to jam into the square. Then someone spied him behind the curtains. A movement went through the crowd. They began shouting.

"Big Noise! Big Noise!"

Michelangelo threw open the glass doors and shouted, "This is not my doing. You must believe me."

"Liar! You have sold us."

"Have I not bought marble from you? I will suffer more than you."

"You will not suffer in the belly!"

The cry acted like a signal. A hundred arms were raised. Stones filled the air like hail. Fragments of white marble broke one glass door, then the other.

A large stone struck him on the forehead. Blood began to trickle down his face. He made no move to stanch the flow. The crowd saw what had happened, and within minutes the piazza was deserted, with only the white stones and broken glass to tell what had happened.

He rented a house in Pietrasanta. He was told that the Wool Guild was sending an expert to build his road.

It was March, he had about six months of good weather before snow and ice closed down the mountains. If he could start the marble he had bought in Carrara toward Florence he could spend the winter carving them.

But the Carrarini balked him at every turn. They would not ship his marble, although he had paid for it. Even the Pope was powerless to help. He could not force the men to load the barges. How, Michelangelo wondered, was he going to get his costly marbles off the Carrara beach? However, now he had the quarry at Pietrasanta to open. He would have to leave the columns where they were. Later he could try again.

First he must assemble a crew of stonecutters. He set out for Settignano to the Topolinos. If his Topolino family would not help him, no one would. He laid out his situation fully, omitting none of the hardships or dangers.

"Could one of you come along? I must have someone I can trust."

"We can't let you go alone," said Bruno slowly. "One must come."

Gilberto, the youngest of the brothers, scratched the bushy hair on his chest. "I have the least skill but most strength. I will do?"

"You will do. I am grateful."

Over the next days Michelangelo assembled a crew but his heart sank when he gave instructions for leaving the following morning. Of the twelve stonecutters there was not one quarrier in the lot! How could he tackle a savage mountain with this inexperienced crew?

The first weeks of quarrying were a total waste. His stonecutters knew nothing about the ways of marble. Even Gilberto knew only how to fashion building blocks from the serene stone of Settignano. It was infinitely more durable, not so easily shattered as marble. His stonemasons did their best, but they made mistakes. Michelangelo learned by trial and error, leaning heavily on his years of watching the men of Carrara, trying to absorb generations of skill in a few months.

By now it was close to June. The Wool Guild had not yet sent a superintendent to build the road. Unless it was started immediately it could not be completed before winter storms shut them down. At last the builder arrived.

The Guild had chosen Bocca, a brute of a man, hairy from his skull to his toes, because of his reputation for pushing through contracts in record time.

Within ten days he had mapped the simplest possible route to the base of Monte Altissimo. The only trouble was that the road was not directed toward those places where the marble was to be found. After Michelangelo had lowered his twenty-ton blocks down the ravines of Monte Altissimo by hand, he would still be a considerable distance from Bocca's road!

"You see, Bocca, I could never get my blocks to your road. It doesn't reach the quarries."

"I'm road. You're marble."

It was a warm night, the stars hanging low over the sea in brilliant clusters. Michelangelo walked for miles while he wrestled with his problem.

He could complain to Pope Leo, have another road builder sent in. But what assurance would he have that the second contractor would be any better?

He must build the road himself!

He mapped the road, laid out stakes, dug the footings. At two points he chose to tunnel through solid rock rather than to try to push the road up a hogback and down into the valley again. For a terminus he chose a spot at the base of two ravines down which he planned to lower the blocks.

At the end of June his accountant said:

"You have to stop building your road."

"Stop . . . but why?"

"There's no more money."

"I can't stop now. Use my other money."

"But you may never get it back."

"Until I get the marbles out, the Holy Father won't let me be a sculptor. Spend my money for the road. When the Wool Guild sends in cash, pay me back."

By mid-September the road could be used. He had at last managed to bring out a magnificent block and a column. He started to move it down the ravine, well filled over the months with marble chips to provide a smooth sliding base. The column was roped half a dozen times around its width and length, crowbarred onto wooden rollers. Down the length of the draw, on either side, nests of stakes had been driven into the ground. The ropes from the column, tied around these stakes, were the only hold the crews would have on the block.

Down it went, held by some thirty men. Michelangelo, imitating the calls of the Carrara crews, a series of sung and shouted notes, directed the men handling the rollers to run with the one at the rear, when the end of the marble had passed, and put it under the front; and the men at the stake nests, holding the ropes with all their might until the column had slid past them, to run down the trail to the next stakes to tie up their ropes and apply the brake. Hours passed, the sun rose high in the heavens, the men sweated, swore, strained.

Down the long steep ravine the column slid, the crew exerting all its strength to hold it back, to slow its movement. By late afternoon they were only thirty-five yards from the road. Michelangelo was jubilant; very soon now they would slide the column onto the loading platform, from which it would be moved onto the special wagon drawn by the team of thirty-two bulls.

He never quite knew how the accident happened. An agile young Pisan named Gino had just kneeled to put another roller under the front of the column when suddenly something snapped, and the column started to move on its own.

There were shouts: "Gino! Get out! Quick!"

But it was too late. The column rolled over Gino, swerved toward Michelangelo. He threw himself over the side of the ledge, rolling a number of feet before he could break his fall.

The men stood paralyzed as the flawless column picked up speed, smashed its way downward, hit the loading platform and broke into a hundred pieces on the road.

Gilberto was leaning over Gino. Blood stained the mar-

ble-choked draw. Michelangelo went on his knees before the boy.

"His neck is broken," said Gilberto.

"He is still alive?"

"No. Killed instantly."

In his mind Michelangelo heard the mournful sound of a horn echoing from peak to peak. He picked up Gino's dead body, stumbled blindly the rest of the descent down the white passage. Someone brought his mule to the loading station. Michelangelo mounted, still holding Gino, while the others led the funeral procession into Seravezza.

Torrential rains inundated the piazza. All work was shut down. The crews returned home. Michelangelo's accounting showed that he had spent thirty ducats beyond the eight hundred advanced to him at the beginning of the year for marble. He had loaded not a single block. The lone consolation was the attendance of a group of Carrarini quarriers and owners at Gino's burial. Apothecary Pelliccia linked his arm through Michelangelo's as they left the cemetery.

"We're deeply sorry, Michelangelo. The death of the boy brought us to our senses. We treated you badly. But we too have suffered from the loss of contracts from agents and sculptors waiting to buy from the Pope's quarries."

Now the Carrarini would transport the blocks, still sitting on the beach at Carrara, to the docks of Florence. He packed his few personal belongings and returned to Florence. He was still too shaken to attempt even the simplest carving, so he began to build a new studio on land he had bought.

The winter was mild. By February his studio was ready. He brought half a dozen of his nine-foot Carrara blocks for Julius's tomb from the Arno storehouse, set them upright so that he could study them. He had only to return to Pietrasanta, excavate the columns he needed for San Lorenzo; then he could settle down on the Via Mozza for years of concentrated work for the Medici and Roveres.

He did not ask Gilberto Topolino to go back to the quarries, that would have been unfair; but most of the others agreed to join him. Rather than being frightened by Pietrasanta, the masons felt that with the road completed and the quarries opened the hardest work was already done. Still disturbed by the unexplained accident that had killed Gino, he evolved a system of iron rings which could be driven into the surface of the block, giving the crews a surer grip on the marble as it was brought down the ravine.

In good time they detached the marble from the mountain. The Pope had been rightly informed, there was enough magnificent marble here to supply the world for a thousand years.

There were no more accidents. In the ensuing weeks he directed five superb blocks to the beach.

Then suddenly he was recalled to Florence. He rode his horse into Florence late the following afternoon. He was to report at once to the Pope's cousin, Cardinal Giulio, in the Medici palace.

"Your Grace, why have you recalled me? In a matter of months I would have had all nine of my giant columns on the beach of Pietrasanta."

"There is enough marble now."

Michelangelo was unnerved by an undertone of hostility in the cardinal's voice.

"Enough . . . ? I don't understand."

"We are abandoning the façade for San Lorenzo."

Michelangelo turned white, speechless.

Giulio continued: "The floor of the Duomo needs repaving. Since the Duomo and Wool Guild Boards paid the cost of the road, they are entitled to the marbles you have excavated."

"To pave the Duomo floor? With my marbles? With the finest statuary marbles ever quarried! Why do you humiliate me in this way?"

Cardinal Giulio answered icily, "Marble is marble. It should be used for what is needed next. Right now the cathedral needs paving blocks."

Michelangelo clenched his fists to stop his trembling. "It is nearly three years now since His Holiness took me off the Rovere tomb. In all that time I have not been able to carve one inch of marble. Of the twenty-three hundred ducats you have sent me, I have spent eighteen hundred on the marbles, quarries and roads. I do not reckon the costs, the three years I have wasted in this work, the great insult put upon me, my house in Rome, which I left, and where marbles, furniture and blocked-out statues have suffered upwards of another five hundred ducats. I will not reckon all these things, regardless of the terrible loss to me. I only want one thing now: to be free!"

Cardinal Giulio had listened carefully to Michelangelo's catalogue of complaints. His thin, smooth face grew dark.

"The Holy Father will review these doings at the proper time. You are dismissed."

Michelangelo stumbled down the long hallway, his feet carrying him to what had been *Il Magnifico's* studio. He thrust open the door, entered, stared at the room. He cried aloud to the long-departed spirit of Lorenzo:

"I am ruined!"

BOOK NINE

THE WAR

Where did a man go when he had been destroyed? Where else but to work, bolting the door of his studio, standing the dozen blocks around the walls as though they were armed soldiers guarding his privacy.

The new studio had ceilings thirty-five feet high, tall windows to the north, spacious enough to allow him to carve several of the tomb figures at the same time. This was where a sculptor belonged, in his workshop.

The tighter he bolted his studio door against the intrusion of the outside world, the more evident it became that trouble was man's natural state. News reached him that Leonardo da Vinci had died in France, unwanted and unhonored by his countrymen. A letter from Rome told him that Raphael Sanzio was ill, obliged to turn more and more of his work over to apprentices. Pope Leo's political judgment had proved unsound in the backing of Francis I of France against Charles V, the newly elected Roman Emperor. In Germany, Martin Luther was challenging papal supremacy by crying:

"I don't know if the Christian faith can endure any

other head of the Universal Church on earth . . . save Christ."

As the months passed he broke into four nine-foot blocks simultaneously. These were to be part of his Captive theme for Julius's tomb: the somnolent Young Giant, the Awakening Giant, the Atlas holding God's earth on his shoulders, and the Bearded Giant, old and tired.

By spring the four Captive-Giants had come alive in the marble. Then Pope Leo and Cardinal Giulio decided to build a sacristy onto the church of San Lorenzo in which to bury *Il Magnifico* and his brother Giuliano. Unembarrassed by the fact that they had canceled his contract for the façade, Pope Leo and Cardinal Giulio sent Michelangelo an offer to make sculptures for the new chapel.

"I am no longer their sculptor," cried Michelangelo. "In another two years I can complete Julius's tomb. The Rovere family will owe me some eighty-five hundred ducats."

"You need the good will of the Medici," the Pope's messenger said.

"I also need money . . . which I don't get from the Medici."

He went on carving his Giants while the Medici increased their pressure on him to do the tomb. In the end they had their way. He could not afford the disfavor of the Vatican. Either he worked for the Medici, or he might not work at all.

He drew a new concept: one austere sarcophagus on either side of the chapel, each holding two reclining allegorical figures: Day and Night on one, Dawn and Dusk on the other; two male, two female; great brooding figures which would represent man's cycle within the days of his life.

This plan was accepted.

In late November Pope Leo caught a chill. By December 1, 1521, the first Medici Pope was dead in the Vatican. Michelangelo attended the requiem mass. He joined in the prayer for Leo's soul. Later, he whispered to Granacci:

"Do you suppose that heaven can offer any part of the entertainment Leo provided himself at the Vatican?"

"I doubt it. God would not spend that much money."

With Leo dead, the project of the Medici chapel became cold and wind-swept as the streets of Florence. The College of Cardinals elected Adrian of Utrecht as Pope.

Cardinal Giulio had fled to Florence, for Pope Adrian was a highly moral churchman who had disapproved of the Medici pontificate. He listened sympathetically to the complaints of the Rovere family, agreeing that they should file suit against Michelangelo Buonarroti for failure to fulfill his contract with Pope Julius's heirs.

Michelangelo was trapped. The Roveres did not care about the money, they were out to punish him for abandoning the Rovere tomb in favor of a Medici façade and chapel.

He sought out Granacci, demanding:

"What is it that I lack? I have talent, energy, enthusiasm, self-discipline, singleness of purpose. What am I missing? Luck? Where does one search for the leaven of luck?"

"Last out the bad times, my friend, then you will be alive to enjoy the good."

God alone rescued him. He gathered Pope Adrian to his everlasting reward. Cardinal Giulio de' Medici garnered enough votes to get himself elected. He called himself Pope Clement VII and sent word immediately after his coronation: Michelangelo must resume work on the chapel.

He was like a man who had been through a dangerous illness.

Pope Clement put him on a lifetime pension of fifty ducats a month, assigned him a house across the piazza from

19. The Young Giant, about 1519. Florence, Academy.

20. The Awakening Giant, about 1519. Florence, Academy.

21. Atlas, about 1519. Florence, Academy.

22. The Bearded Giant about 1519. Florence, Academy.

the church of San Lorenzo as a workshop. The Rovere heirs were persuaded to drop their lawsuit. Orders and commissions began pouring in.

Michelangelo heard stories of how Clement was strengthening the cause of the anti-Medici party by making fatal errors of judgment, even as Leo had. In the incessant wars among the surrounding nations he consistently backed the wrong side . . . though, truth to tell, Clement changed sides so often that neither Michelangelo nor Europe could keep up with his intrigues.

Michelangelo locked himself inside the sacristy, thinking of nothing but the marble.

But Cardinal Passerini of Cortona, appointed by the Pope, ruled Florence autocratically. Clement rejected all appeals from the Signoria and the old families to replace him. The Florentines were waiting only for an advantageous moment to rise, seize the necessary arms and drive the Medici out of the city. When the army of the Holy Roman Empire, sweeping southward to invade Rome and punish Pope Clement, marched thirty thousand strong on Bologna, after which it planned to conquer Florence, the city rose in a mass, stormed the Medici palace and demanded arms to defend itself against the coming invasion, shouting:

"Guns! Guns to the people!"

The Cardinal of Cortona appeared in an upper window and promised arms. But when he learned that the Pope's army was approaching Florence, he ignored his promise and rushed out to meet it. Now Michelangelo joined Granacci in the piazza where crowds were calling:

"The people, liberty!"

Florentine soldiers guarding the Signoria made no attempt to prevent a committee of citizens from entering the government palace. Then Niccolò Capponi, whose father

had led the earlier movement to drive out Piero de' Medici, stepped onto a balcony and announced:

"The Florentine Republic is re-established! The Medici are banished! All citizens are to be armed and summoned to the Square of the Signoria!"

Cardinal Passerini arrived with a thousand of the Duke of Urbino's cavalry. The Medici party opened a gate for them. The committee inside the palace bolted the doors. Urbino's cavalry attacked the doors with long pikes.

A heavy wooden bench came hurtling down from the parapet. Michelangelo saw that it was headed straight for the David.

"Look out!" he screamed, as though the statue might dodge.

He was too late. The wooden bench struck. The left arm holding the slingshot snapped off below the elbow. The arm fell to the stone of the piazza, broke.

The crowd drew back. A hush fell over the throng. He felt himself moving toward the sculpture. The crowd opened, murmuring:

"It is Michelangelo. Let him pass."

He stood below the David, gazing up into the pensive, resolute yet beautiful face. Goliath had not scratched him; but the civil war inside Florence had come within inches of destroying him completely. Michelangelo's arm ached as though it too had been amputated.

Out of the crowd Giorgio Vasari, one of Michelangelo's young apprentices, and Cecchino Rossi sped toward the David, picked up the three marble fragments of the arm and hand and disappeared down the narrow side street.

In the stillness of the night there was a knocking on Michelangelo's door. He opened it to admit Vasari and Cecchino. They began talking at once.

"Signor Buonarroti . . ."

"... we have the three pieces hidden ..."

"... in a chest in Rossi's father's house."

"They are safe."

Michelangelo gazed at the two shining young faces before him, thinking:

"Safe?" What was safe in a world of war and chaos?

The Holy Roman Emperor's army reached Rome, breached the walls and forced Pope Clement to flee to the fortress of Sant'Angelo where he remained a prisoner while the German, Spanish and Italian troops looted, ravaged and burned Rome, destroying sacred works of art, smashing altars, melting bronze figures for cannon, stained-glass windows for lead, lighting fires on the inlaid marble floors of the Vatican, dragging a statue of Pope Clement into the street and hacking it to pieces.

"What of my Pietà? My Sistine ceiling?" groaned Michelangelo. "What of my studio? The Moses and the two Slaves? They can be lying in a thousand pieces."

The Florentines agreed that the Medici must be deprived of their power. With Pope Clement a prisoner, the Republic could once again be proclaimed.

The Republic of Florence was triumphant. Trade was active, the city prosperous, the people happy in their regained freedom. Few cared what happened to Pope Clement, still a prisoner at Sant'Angelo. But Michelangelo was vitally interested in Pope Clement. He had put four years of loving work into the sacristy.

At the end of 1527 the tide turned again. A virulent plague decimated the Holy Roman Emperor's armies. A French army invaded Italy to fight the Holy Roman Empire.

With warm weather, the plague struck Florence. People came down with crushing headaches, pain in the back and limbs, fever, vomiting, and in three days were dead. If they dropped in the streets they were left there; if they died in their houses their families fled. Thousands of Florentines perished. The city became a morgue.

Though he had nursed his brother, Buonarroto, who died of the sickness, Michelangelo himself escaped and the plague abated.

People filtered down from the hills. Shops reopened. The Signoria returned to the city.

Once again Pope Clement interfered. Having returned to the Vatican by making an alliance with the Holy Roman Emperor, he resumed power and sent an army against independent Florence to wipe out the Republic. Michelangelo was summoned before the Gonfaloniere.

"Since you are a sculptor, Buonarroti," he said in a rushing voice, "we assume you can also be a defense engineer. We need walls that cannot be breached. Since they are of stone, and you are a man of stone . . . I appoint you an officer of the Militia. Confine yourself to the south of the city. We are impregnable from the north. Report at the quickest possible moment."

He explored along the several miles of wall. Neither the walls nor defense towers were in good repair, nor were there ditches on the outside to make the enemy approach more hazardous. More towers for cannon were needed, additional height to make scaling a longer task. The anchor of the defense line would have to be the campanile of San Miniato, from whose height the defenders could command most of the ground over which the enemy troops have to charge.

He returned with his report and was given permission to begin work. It went ahead at full speed, for the Pope's army was reported moving on Florence from several directions. A hundred farmers, working in teams, threw up the walls as fast as they could get the bricks squared. The stonemasons cut, chipped, shaped, shoring up weak

stretches, adding height to the walls and towers, erecting new areas at the more vulnerable spots.

His work was inspected and he was elected to the Militia Nine, as Governor General of the Fortifications.

There was no further thought of sculpture. Nor could he cry, "War is not my trade." Florence had called on him in its time of crisis. He began a series of ditches as deep as moats and secured permission to level all buildings between the defense walls and base of the encircling foothills a mile to the south.

General Malatesta of Perugia had been brought to Florence to serve as one of the commanding generals. He quarreled immediately with Michelangelo.

"You have already burdened us with too many walls. Take your peasants away, and let my soldiers defend Florence."

Malatesta seemed cold, devious. That night Michelangelo roamed the base of his ramparts. He came upon the eight pieces of artillery that had been given to Malatesta to defend the San Miniato wall. Instead of being placed inside the fortifications, or on the parapets, they lay outside the walls, unguarded. Michelangelo awoke the sleeping general.

"What do you mean by exposing your artillery pieces that way? We guarded them with our lives until you arrived. They could be stolen or destroyed by anyone who stumbled upon them."

"Are you the commander of the Florentine army?" demanded Malatesta.

"Just of the defense walls."

"Then go make your brick, and don't tell a soldier how to fight."

He returned to the walls but he could not put Malatesta out of his mind. Everywhere he went he heard stories against the general: he had yielded Perugia without a battle; his men would not fight the Pope's troops at Arezzo; when the armies reached Florence, Malatesta would surrender the city. . . .

He settled his effects in the tower of San Miniato, gazed through the powdery light of a full moon at the hundreds of enemy tents marking the encampment of 30,000 men a mile away. He was awakened at dawn by artillery fire. As he had expected, the attack was concentrated against the tower of San Miniato. If it could be knocked down, the Pope's forces would pour into the city. One hundred and fifty pieces of artillery fired steadily. Whole sections of brick and stone were blasted out by the exploding cannon balls. The attack lasted for two hours. When it was finished Michelangelo let himself out by a tunnel and stood at the base of the bell tower, surveying the damage.

He asked for volunteers and in full view of the papal troops refitted the fallen, shattered stone into the walls. For some reason, perhaps because they did not know how much damage they had inflicted, the enemy troops remained in camp. He sent out runners to collect crews of masons and quarriers, at dusk set them to rebuilding the tower. They worked all night; but it took time for cement to harden. If the enemy artillery opened fire too soon, his defense would be leveled. He gazed up at the campanile, its crenelated cornice wider by four feet all around than the shaft of the tower. If there were a way to hang something from those parapets, something that could absorb the impact of the iron and stone cannon balls before they could strike the tower itself . . .

By first light a company of militia was beating on the doors of the wool shops and the warehouses. Next they hunted the city for mattress covers. He worked fast. By the time the sun was up he had dozens of stout covers stuffed with wool and suspended by ropes across the face of the tower.

When the Pope's officers turned their artillery on the campanile, it was too late. Their cannon balls struck the heavy paddings which, although they gave with the impact, hung four feet beyond the wet stone walls and served as a shield for Michelangelo's newly cemented blocks. The cannon balls fell harmlessly into the ditch below. After firing until noon, the enemy abandoned the attack.

Heavy rains began to fall. The open mile of cleared fields between his walls and the enemy became a bog. There could be no attack now.

Michelangelo spent the days on the parapets; at night he slipped into the sacristy and carved by candlelight. The chapel was cold, full of shadows; but he was not alone. His figures were familiar friends: the Dawn, the Dusk; telling him that as long as art lives, man does not perish.

In the spring the war was resumed, but none of the battles except the one against starvation took place in Florence. The papal army had cut off supplies from the sea.

Meat vanished first, then oil, greens, flour, wine. People began eating asses, dogs, cats. Summer heat baked the stones, the water supply failed, the Arno dried up, the plague struck again. By mid-July five thousand were dead within the city.

Florence had only one chance to survive, through its heroic general Francesco Ferrucci. Plans were laid for him to attack and lift the siege. The last sixteen thousand men within the walls who were able to fight took the sacrament, vowing to storm the enemy camps on both sides of the city, while General Ferrucci struck from the west.

General Malatesta betrayed the Republic to the Pope's generals. Ferrucci was defeated and killed.

Florence capitulated. Malatesta's troops opened the

gates. Pope Clement's representatives entered the city to take control in the name of the Medici. Those members of the government who could, fled; others were hanged. All members of the Militia Nine were condemned.

"You'd better get out of the city this very night," a friend urged Michelangelo. "The Pope will show no mercy."

Michelangelo was thoughtful. "I know a tower on the other side of the Arno. No one will suspect it. I'll take refuge there until Malatesta clears out with his troops."

He made his way by back passages to the Arno, crossed the river to the bell tower of San Niccolò, knocking at the house next door, which belonged to the sons of old Beppe of the Duomo workyard, to let them know he was taking refuge. Then he locked the door of the tower behind him, climbed its circular wooden staircase and spent the rest of the night staring over the hills at the deserted enemy camp. At sunrise he was still leaning against the stone walls gazing sightlessly at the terrain he had leveled to protect the city-state.

Lorenzo had said that the forces of destruction were everywhere. That was all Michelangelo had known since the days of Savonarola: conflict. And here he was, cowering in an ancient bell tower, afraid to come down for fear he would be hanged. What an inglorious end for the pure bright fire that had burned in him.

Between midnight chimes and cockcrow he walked along the upper marshes of the Arno, returning to find that food and water had been left for him. Florence knew where he was hiding, but hatred for Pope Clement was so intense that he was not only safe but had become a hero.

On a mid-November day he learned that the Pope had pardoned him. His pension was restored. He was to return to work on the Medici tomb.

His studio in the Via Mozza had been thoroughly ransacked by papal troops, but nothing had been stolen. In

23. The Tomb of Lorenzo de' Medici, about 1524–31. Florence, San Lorenzo, Medici Chapel. (Dawn and Dusk)

24. The Tomb of Giuliano de' Medici, about 1526–34. Florence, San Lorenzo, Medici Chapel. (Day and Night)

the chapel he found the scaffolding removed, probably to keep the clergy of San Lorenzo warm; but none of his marbles had been disturbed. After three years of war he could resume work.

By September, nine months after he had come down from his tower, he had finished the figures of Day and Night, Dawn and Dusk.

The rains started, the chapel became cold and raw. Again his flesh vanished, he was down to bone and gristle, under a hundred pounds as he picked up hammer and chisel to attack the remaining figures.

"It won't do, you know." Granacci reproved him, a Granacci who himself had grown lean over the misfortunes of his city. "Death from overindulgence is a form of suicide, whether it's from work or wine."

"If I don't work twenty hours a day I'll never finish."

He developed a high fever. When it passed he was so weak his legs could barely hold him.

The Pope sent a carriage and driver to Florence, ordering Michelangelo to come to Rome to recuperate in the warmth of the more southerly sun, and to hear about an exciting new project he had envisaged. Clement invited Michelangelo's friends in the Florentine colony for dinner at the Vatican, had several comedies played to amuse them. Clement's solicitude for his health was genuine, almost like that of a beloved brother. Then the Pope revealed his desire: would Michelangelo like to paint a Last Judgment on the vast altar wall of the Sistine Chapel?

Michelangelo would need time to decide.

In the meantime he must return to Florence and complete the statuary for the Medici Chapel.

In June 1534, on his ninetieth birthday, Lodovico died, surrounded by his three sons. Michelangelo felt strangely alone. He had loved his father; the world would seem

25. The Medici Madonna, 1524–34. Florence, San Lorenzo, Medici Chapel.

empty without him. Lodovico had caused him endless anguish, but he was proud he had been able to fulfill his father's ambition.

That night he stood alone in the Medici Chapel, the two tombs ready to be set in place, the Madonna and Child already on the side wall.

Was the chapel finished? After fourteen years?

Standing amidst his exquisitely carved sarcophagi, he felt he had carved everything he had wanted to carve, and said everything he had wanted to say. The Medici Chapel was complete. He believed that *Il Magnifico* would be gratified.

He picked up a piece of drawing paper, wrote instructions for his three helpers to mount Day and Night on their sarcophagus, Dawn and Dusk opposite. He left the note on the plank table under a piece of scrap marble, turned and went out the door without looking back, and packed his saddlebags.

He mounted his horse, crossed the city and left Florence. At the top of the rise he stopped, turned to look back at the exquisite city of stone nestled under its red tile roof. It was hard to take leave of one's city; hard to feel that, close to sixty, he could not count on returning.

Resolutely he turned the horse south toward Rome.

BOOK TEN

THE LAST JUDGMENT

Two days after Michelangelo reached Rome, Pope Clement VII died in the Vatican. The city poured into the streets in a paroxysm of joy. The hatred of Clement, which continued to manifest itself during the elaborate funeral ceremonies, was based on his responsibility for the sack of Rome. Only the day before, Michelangelo and Benvenuto Cellini had visited with Clement. He had been in good spirits, discussing with Cellini a new medal he was to strike, and with Michelangelo the design for the Last Judgment. Michelangelo felt a sense of loss for this last of his childhood friends from the Medici palace.

With his new apprentice-steward, a quiet young man named Urbino, he went to his house. Most of the furniture and some of the marble blocks for Julius's tomb had been stolen. But the Moses and the two Captives had not been injured. The house itself was dilapidated but it could be repaired.

He asked himself over and over again whether he was relieved to have the crushing burden of the Last Judgment off his shoulders. The altar wall of the Sistine would have required a minimum of five years to paint, for it would be the largest wall in Italy ever painted in a single fresco. Yet as his ducats poured out for the repairs and refurbishing of his house he saw that he would soon be in need of money.

His old friend Balducci, as wide as he was tall, but of hard flesh and red cheeks, exploded:

"Of course you're in trouble! Spending all those years in Florence without my financial wizardry. But you're in safe hands now. Turn over to me the money you earn, and I'll invest it so that you'll be independently wealthy."

"Balducci, there is something about me that seems to alienate money. Ducats say to themselves, 'This man will not give us a secure home in which we can multiply. Let us go elsewhere.'"

Early the next morning the head of the Rovere family came to call, followed by a servant with a box containing the four contracts for Julius's tomb. He was a ferocious-looking man. He informed Michelangelo that the wall had been prepared for Julius's tomb, then took from the top of the leather box the latest agreement and flung it at Michelangelo's feet.

"There will be no more Medici to protect you. If you do not complete this last contract by May of next year, as specified in the agreement, I shall force you to fulfill the earlier contract: twenty-five statues, larger than life."

He stormed out, but in the matter of completing the Rovere tomb the fates were as much against the Roveres as against Michelangelo. On October 11, 1534, the College of Cardinals elected Alessandro Farnese to the papacy.

As Pope Paul III he sent a courier to ask Michelangelo Buonarroti to come to the Vatican palace that afternoon.

Michelangelo entered the small throne room, knelt, kissed the Pope's ring.

"I wish you to enter our service," the Pope said.

Michelangelo paused for the stonemason's rest count of one two three four.

"How can I serve Your Holiness?"

"By continuing your work on the Last Judgment."

"Holy Father, I cannot take so large a commission."

"Why not?"

"I am bound by contract to the Rovere family to complete Pope Julius's tomb."

"Put the tomb out of your mind. I wish you to complete the Sistine Chapel for the glory of our pontificate."

Michelangelo backed out of the small throne room. Returning to his house, he sank into an old leather chair. Urbino, answering a knock at the door, admitted two Swiss guards, tall blond giants in identical yellow-and-green costumes, who announced that Michelangelo Buonarroti would receive, the following midmorning, a visit from His Holiness Paul III.

"I will find charwomen, master," announced the imperturbable Urbino. "What refreshment does one serve the Holy Father and his train? I have never seen a Pope before, except in procession."

"I wish that that was the only place I had ever seen one," grumbled Michelangelo. "Buy raisin wine and cookies. Use our best Florentine tablecloth."

The Pope arrived with his cardinals and attendants. Paul smiled at Michelangelo, went quickly to the Moses. The cardinals surrounded the figure in a field of red cassocks. The Cardinal of Mantua, the acknowledged art authority of the Vatican, declared in a voice compounded of awe, pride and gratification:

"This Moses alone is sufficient to do honor to Pope Julius. No man could want a more glorious monument."

Pope Paul turned to Michelangelo, "You see, my son, I was not being unreasonable. Paint the Last Judgment for me. I will arrange for the Rovere family to accept the Moses and these two Captives from your hand."

Michelangelo had not lived through four pontificates without learning when he was outmaneuvered.

The next morning he walked slowly to St. Peter's. As far as he could tell, little had been accomplished in the eighteen years since he had left Rome except the repair of the giant piers and the building of the lowest foundation walls. Two hundred thousand ducats from all over Christendom had been poured into the concrete; but mostly, Michelangelo had learned, into the pockets of contractors who were erecting St. Peter's as slowly as was humanly possible.

The tiny chapel of Mary of the Fever had not yet been removed to make way for the transept. He entered, stood before his own Pietà. How beautiful Mary was. How exquisite and tender. And the son on the mother's lap, how sensitive the face.

He fell to his knees. For a moment he wondered if it was wrong to pray before his own creation; but he had carved these figures so long ago, when he was only twenty-four. He could not remember any of the actual detail of carving the block. It was as though someone he had known ages ago had done the work.

In the Sistine Chapel he stood alone beneath the tumultuous array from Genesis, making a detailed survey of the altar wall. It was a fifty-five-foot-high wall, forty feet wide, with painted tapestries in the bottom zone, above the table-altar two frescoes; in the next area two tall windows corresponding to those on the side walls, with portraits of the first two Popes; then, in the topmost or fourth compartment, his own two lunettes in which he had painted the early ancestors of Christ.

The wall was fire-blackened at the bottom, pitted and broken at the second height; above, there was spoilage from damp, and an over-all soiling of dust, grime and smoke from the candles burned on the altar. He disliked destroying the Perugino frescoes, but since he was also obliterating two of his own paintings no one could think him vengeful. He would seal up the two diverting windows, build a new brick wall which he would engineer to slant outward a foot from ceiling to floor so that dust, dirt and smoke would no longer adhere.

Pope Paul gave his consent to Michelangelo's building plans. Michelangelo found himself liking the Farnese Pope more and more, developing a feeling of friendship for him. Paul was a Latin and Greek scholar. He intended to avoid the wars of Julius, the international blunders and intrigues of Clement. He also was blessed with an astute sense of humor. Pope Paul, wishing to give him security, issued an order which declared Michelangelo Buonarroti to be the *Sculptor, Painter and Architect of All the Vatican,* with a lifetime pension of a hundred ducats a month.

Michelangelo was happy during these months of steady drawing in the studio that Urbino had redone with a touch of color in the walls. Through the medium of his drawing hand he was beginning to glimpse the finished fresco.

Every man, woman and child was to stand out in stark clarity, to achieve his full human dignity; for each was an individual and had worth. This was the key to the rebirth of human learning and freedom that had been sired in Florence, after the darkness of a thousand years. Never would he, Michelangelo Buonarroti, a Tuscan, be responsible for reducing man to an indistinguishable part of a mass, not even en route to heaven or hell!

Though he would not have admitted it, his arms were weary after the ten years of continuous carving on the Medici Chapel. The more he studied his vault in the Sistine, the

26. The ceiling of the Sistine Chapel, 1508–12. Rome, Vatican, Sistine Chapel.

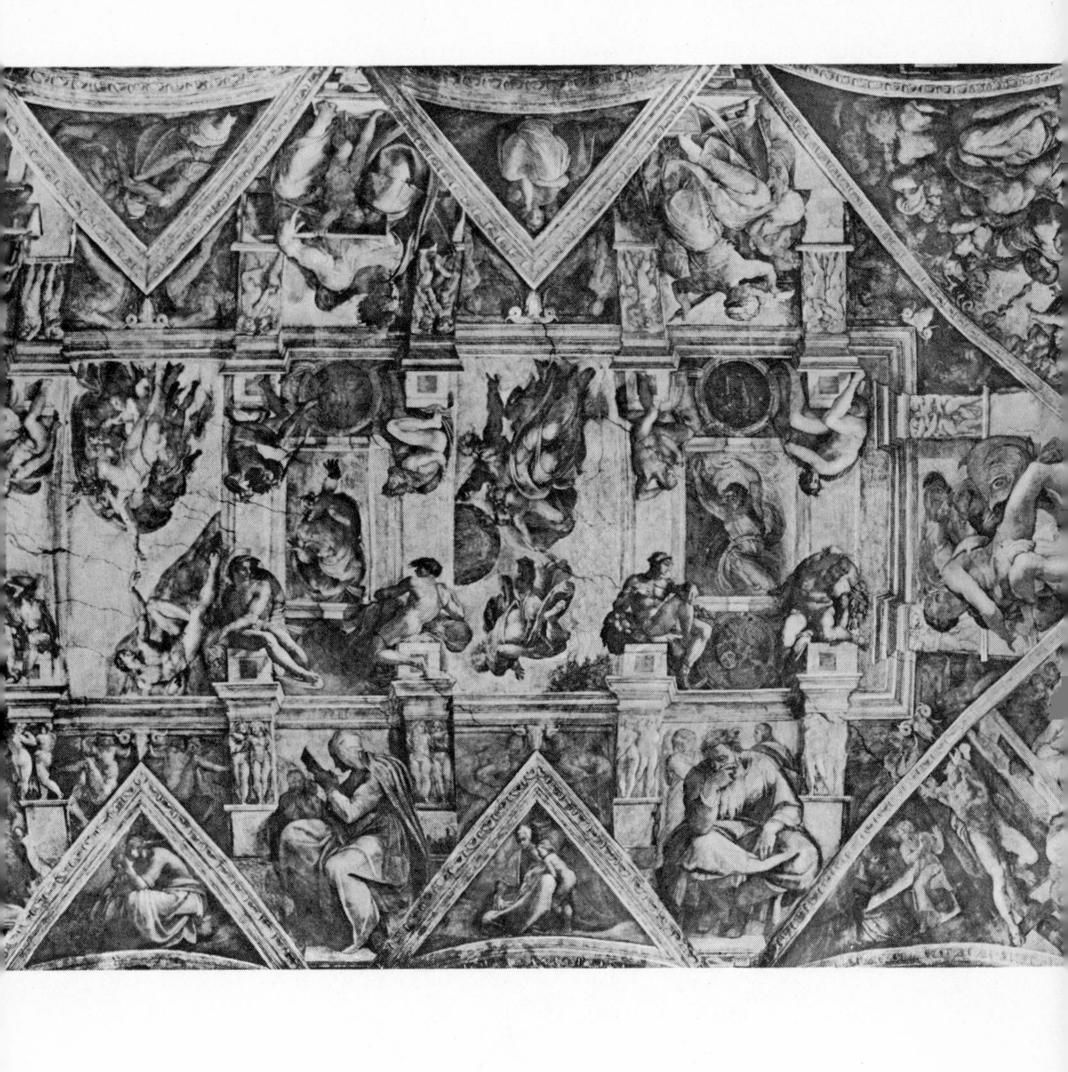

more he came to think that painting might become a noble and permanent art, after all.

By fall, one year after he had reached Rome, his Sistine wall was rebricked and dried, the over-all design for it completed and enlarged to wall size. It showed more than three hundred "men of all races," as the Gospel According to Matthew put it; a tumultuous horde of humans surrounding Christ in inner intimate circles and outer remote ones; vertical shafts of bodies rising upward on one side, descending on the other. On the bottom at the left was the yawning cave of hell.

On the vault he had painted his Genesis in bright, dramatic colors; the Last Judgment would be confined to quieter monotones, flesh tones and brown.

Now, ready to begin the fresco itself, all feeling of spent years, of fatigue and uncertainty about the future vanished. He tackled the wall with vigor. All his figures except those of Christ and the Virgin were nude. He was painting them as God made them. By day he locked himself into the Sistine, with only Urbino by his side on the high scaffold. At night he read the Bible, Dante and Savonarola's sermons. His days and his nights fitted together as parts of a whole.

On the outside, it looked as though Judgment Day had arrived for Pope Paul. Cardinal Niccolò, now one of the most influential cardinals at court, brought the news to Michelangelo: Charles V of Spain and Francis I of France had once again declared war on each other. Charles was traveling north from Naples with his army, the one that had sacked Rome and crushed Florence. Pope Paul had no army or means of resistance; he was preparing to flee.

Michelangelo ignored the outside world and its politics.

He could not swear how many days, weeks, months passed as 1537 gave way to 1538. Each morning Urbino laid the needed field of intonaco; by nightfall Michelangelo

27. Christ and the Virgin, detail of The Last Judgment, Sistine Chapel.

had filled it with a body tumbling downward toward hell. Each day at noon Urbino had the woman servant, Caterina, bring hot food which he reheated on a brazier on the scaffold before serving Michelangelo.

"Eat well. You need your strength."

"Urbino, you know I'm too wrought up to eat in the middle of a day's work."

". . . and too tired to eat at the end of one. Look what I have here, a salad that sings in the mouth."

Michelangelo chuckled. To indulge Urbino, he ate, and was surprised at how good it was.

When Michelangelo began to falter, after months of intensive work, it was Urbino who made him stay at home and rest. When the head of the Rovere family died, Michelangelo was immensely relieved even though he knew he would have to confess the sin of rejoicing over another man's death. But before long his son arrived at the studio. Michelangelo watched him standing in the doorway, looking exactly like his father.

"*Dio mio,*" he thought, "I inherit the sons of my enemies."

But he was wrong about the young duke.

"I have come to put an end to the strife," he said quietly. "I have never agreed with my father that your failure to complete my granduncle's tomb was totally your fault."

"You mean that I can call you my friend?"

"And admirer. I often told my father if you had been allowed to continue your work you would have completed that tomb even as you did the Sistine Chapel and the Medici Chapel. You shall be harassed no more."

Michelangelo sank into a chair. "My son, do you know from what you have just delivered me . . . ?"

"But by the same token," continued the young man, "you

will readily understand our earnest wish to see you finish the holy monument to my uncle, Pope Julius. Because of the reverence we bear Pope Paul, we shall not interrupt you while you are completing your fresco; but, being finished, we ask that you give yourself to the monument, doubling your diligence to remedy the loss of time."

"With all my heart! You shall have your tomb."

By the end of 1540, when Michelangelo had completed the upper two thirds of the fresco, he hired a carpenter to lower the scaffolding. Pope Paul heard the news, arrived at the locked Sistine door unannounced. Urbino, who answered the banging on the door, could not refuse to admit the pontiff.

Michelangelo came down from the new, low scaffold, greeted Pope Paul and his Master of Ceremonies, Biagio da Cesena, with cordial words. The Pope stood facing the Last Judgment, walked stiffly toward the wall without removing his eyes. When he reached the altar he sank to his knees and prayed. He rose to his feet, made the sign of the cross over Michelangelo and then the Last Judgment. There were tears of pride and humility on his cheeks.

"My son, you have created a glory for my reign."

"It is disgraceful . . . !" spat out Biagio da Cesena.

Pope Paul was astounded.

"And totally immoral! I cannot tell the saints from the sinners. There are only hundreds of nudes. It is shameful."

"You think the human body shameful?" asked Michelangelo.

"In a bath, no. But in the Pope's chapel! Scandalous!"

"Only if you wish to create a scandal, Biagio," replied Paul firmly. "On Judgment Day we shall all stand naked before the Lord. My son, how do I express my overwhelming gratitude?"

Michelangelo turned to the Master of Ceremonies with a conciliatory gesture, for he wanted to make no enemies for his fresco. Biagio da Cesena broke in roughly.

"One day this sacrilegious wall will be annihilated."

"Not while I live," cried Pope Paul, furious. "I will excommunicate anyone who dares touch this masterpiece!"

They left the chapel. Michelangelo asked Urbino to mix some intonaco and lay it on the blank spot on the extreme lower right-hand corner of the wall. There he painted a caricature of Biagio da Cesena, representing him as the judge of the shades of Hades, with the ears of an ass, and a monstrous snake coiled around the lower part of the torso. It was a lethal likeness.

Word leaked out somehow. Biagio da Cesena demanded a second meeting before the fresco.

"You see, Holy Father," cried the Master of Ceremonies, "the report was true. Buonarroti has painted me into the fresco with a repulsive serpent."

"It's a covering," replied Michelangelo. "I knew you would not want to be portrayed wholly naked."

"A remarkable likeness," observed the Pope, his eyes twinkling. "Michelangelo, I thought you said you could not do portraiture?"

"I was inspired, Holiness."

Biagio hopped up and down on either foot as though it were he instead of his picture standing over the fires of hell.

"Holiness, make him take me out of there!"

"Out of hell?" the Pope turned surprised eyes on the man. "Had he placed you in purgatory, I should have done everything in my power to release you. But you know that from hell there is no redemption."

The following day Michelangelo learned that no one ever

28. Minos the Judge in Hell, detail of The Last Judgment, Sistine Chapel.

got the last laugh. He was on the lowered scaffolding painting Charon with the protruding eyes and horns for ears, whipping the damned out of his boat and into the fiery depths, when he felt dizzy, tried to grasp a support rail, fell to the marble floor. There was a moment of excruciating pain. He revived to find Urbino splashing cold, sandy water from the bucket onto his face.

"Thanks to God, you're conscious. How badly are you hurt? Is anything broken?"

"How would I know? If I'm so stupid, I should have broken every bone in my body. For five years I work on this scaffold, and at the very end I fall off."

"Your leg is bleeding where it struck this piece of lumber. I will find a carriage."

"You'll find nothing of the sort. Nobody is going to know what an idiot I am. Help me up. Now put an arm under my shoulder. I can ride the horse home."

Urbino put him to bed, pressed a glass of wine to his lips, then washed out the wound. When he wanted to go for a doctor Michelangelo stopped him.

"No doctor. I'd be the laughingstock of Rome. Bolt that front door."

Despite all that Urbino could do by way of hot towels and bandaging, the wound began to fester. Michelangelo developed a fever. Urbino was frightened.

"If I let you die . . ."

"The thought has its compensations, Urbino. I wouldn't have to go climbing scaffolds any more."

"How can you tell? Perhaps in hell a man has to do forever the thing he most hated to do in life?"

Urbino went for Dr. Baccio Rontini. When Michelangelo refused to allow them to enter the front door they forced a back door of the house. Dr. Rontini was irate.

"For sheer perverse idiocy, no one can rival a Florentine." He probed the infected wound. "Another day or two . . ."

It took a week to get him back on his feet; he felt like a bag of meal. Urbino helped him up the scaffolding, laid a patch of intonaco in the sky just below St. Bartholomew. Michelangelo painted a caricature of his own drained, woebegone face and head, suspended in the middle of an empty skin, and held aloft by the hand of the saint.

"Now Biagio doesn't have to feel too badly," he observed to Urbino as he gazed at his empty, hanging carcass. "We've both been judged, and recorded."

He painted the bottom third of the wall, the simplest part since there were fewer figures: the symbolic graveyards and hell, with the long dead rising from their tombs, one of them a skeleton trying to join those in the sky; and the too long alive, being driven into the fires.

Several months later, on an intoxicating April evening when the wild scents of spring filled the air of Rome, Michelangelo asked Urbino to light his way to the Sistine, for he had a sudden wish to see the Last Judgment by

29. An Upward-Floating Soul, detail of The Last Judgment, Sistine Chapel.

30. A Damned Soul, detail of The Last Judgment, Sistine Chapel.

night. Urbino went ahead with a taper to let warm wax drip onto the scaffolding and make a base for the two candles he was carrying.

The Last Judgment sprang cyclonically to life in the flickering half-world of the chapel. Judgment Day became Judgment Night. The three hundred men, women and children, saints, angels and demons, many of whom had been submerged in the full light of day, pressed forward to be recognized.

Michelangelo remembered the lines from Genesis that concluded the description of God's creation of the earth, *And God saw all that He had made, and found it very good.*

He looked steadily at his painting on the altar wall. He saw all that he had made and he found it very good.

31. Ecclesia Receiving One of the Elect, detail of The Last Judgment, Sistine Chapel.

BOOK ELEVEN

THE DOME

On All Saints' Eve, exactly twenty-nine years after Pope Julius had consecrated the Sistine ceiling, Pope Paul said high mass to celebrate the completion of the Last Judgment.

On Christmas Day, 1541, the chapel was thrown open to the public. Rome streamed through the Sistine, terrified, shocked, awe-stricken. Michelangelo's studio was thronged with Florentines, cardinals, courtiers, artists and apprentices. When the last of the guests had disappeared Michelangelo realized that two groups had not been represented: Antonio da Sangallo and the artists and architects who centered around him, and Cardinal Caraffa and his followers, who hated Paul.

Very soon war was declared. An unfrocked monk, Bernardino Ochino, censured Pope Paul by demanding:

"How can Your Holiness allow such an obscene painting as that of Michelangelo's to remain in a chapel where the divine office is sung?"

But the Pope rallied to his support by asking him to fresco two walls of the chapel named after him, the Pauline.

He wanted a Conversion of Paul on one wall, a Crucifixion of Peter on the opposite.

Antonio da Sangallo, nephew of Michelangelo's old friend, Giuliano da Sangallo, had inherited the title of Architect of St. Peter's. He was not a good architect and was jealous of Michelangelo. When he began pouring foundations for a ring of chapels on the south side of St. Peter's, the long-smoldering feud between them burst into flame.

According to Michelangelo's measurements, the corresponding wing to the north, toward the Papal palace, would of necessity replace the Pauline chapel and part of the Sistine.

"I simply cannot believe my eyes," cried Pope Paul when Michelangelo drew him a plan of what was going on. "Why would Sangallo want to tear down a chapel he designed and built himself?"

"His plans for St. Peter's keep expanding."

"How much of the Sistine would his chapels replace?"

"Approximately the area covered by the Deluge, the drunkenness of Noah, the Delphic Sibyl and Zacharias. God would survive."

"How fortunate for Him," murmured Paul.

The Pope suspended work on St. Peter's on the grounds that there was insufficient money to continue. But Sangallo knew that Michelangelo was the cause. Sangallo entrusted to his assistant an attack on the Last Judgment as giving comfort to the enemies of the Church and causing converts to Luther. Yet travelers coming into the Sistine fell on their knees before the fresco.

The next foray came when Sangallo submitted his design for the third-floor windows and cornice of the Farnese palace which he had been building in sections over a long period of years for Cardinal Farnese before he became Pope Paul. Michelangelo had frequently seen the palace under construction. He had thought the design ponderous, belonging to the fortresslike bastions of another age. Now Pope Paul asked Michelangelo to write him a candid criticism of the palace.

As a result of his letter the Pope threw open to competition the design of the top floor. Michelangelo entered the competition.

His cornice was sculpture, carved and brilliantly decorated. The arches and slender columns of the windows gave the palace the elegance it needed to carry its ponderous body of stone.

Pope Paul studied all the designs in the presence of Sangallo and other competitors. He looked up and announced:

"I wish to praise all of these drawings as ingenious and very beautiful. But surely you would agree that it is most true of the divine Michelangelo?"

Michelangelo had saved the Farnese palace from mediocrity and dullness, but gossip had it that he had done it to replace Sangallo as architect of St. Peter's; that now all he had to do was walk into Pope Paul's throne room and announce that he wanted to take over the building.

"I shall do nothing of the sort," Michelangelo declared.

Urbino finally assembled the single-wall tomb of Pope Julius in San Pietro in Vincoli. Michelangelo considered the monument a failure; but the Moses sitting in the central bay of the marble wall dominated the church with a power equaled only by that of God in the Genesis and Christ in the Last Judgment.

He set up an architectural office in a spare room of the house, then completed the Conversion of St. Paul for the Pauline chapel.

He had Urbino lay a fresh coat of intonaco for the Crucifixion of Peter. While it was drying he closed out the world, selected a marble column and with hammer and

chisel blocked out a descent from the Cross; a Christ supported on one side by the Virgin, on the other by Mary Magdalene and behind a portrait of himself as Nicodemus, who had helped take Christ down from the cross.

Reputations in Rome were made and broken in the time it took a man to crack a walnut. When Michelangelo refused to take advantage of his victory to force Sangallo out of St. Peter's, the city forgave him for criticizing the Farnese palace.

As he was completing the sketch of the Crucifixion of St. Peter, church bells started tolling mournfully over the city. His servant woman burst into the studio, crying:

"Master, Sangallo is dead!"

". . . dead? He has been building in Terni . . ."

"He caught the malaria. They just brought his body back."

Pope Paul gave Antonio da Sangallo a spectacular funeral. His coffin was carried through the streets with great pomp, followed by the artists and craftsmen who had worked with him over the years. In church, Michelangelo

stood with Urbino listening to the eulogizing of Sangallo as one of the greatest architects since the ancients who had built Rome.

The superintendent of St. Peter's suggested that Giulio Romano, sculptor and architect, disciple of Raphael, be called from Mantua and appointed architect of St. Peter's. Pope Paul cried:

"It shall be Michelangelo Buonarroti. None else!"

Michelangelo was summoned by a groom, rode his stallion to the Vatican.

"My son, I am appointing you architect of St. Peter's."

"Holiness, I cannot assume the post. I might have to tear down everything Sangallo has built, dismiss Sangallo's contractors. Rome would be solidly against me. I have the Crucifixion of St. Peter to complete. I am over seventy years old. Where will I find the vital force to build from the ground up the mightiest church in Christendom?"

Pope Paul was unaffected by Michelangelo's tale of woe. His eyes gleamed.

"My son, you are but a youth. When you reach my august

32. Head of Pietà. Rome, St. Peter's.

age of seventy-eight you will be allowed to speak of your years. Not before! By that time you will have St. Peter's well on its way."

Michelangelo's smile was on the wan side.

He left the Vatican and, after watching the sunset, went to St. Peter's. The workmen had gone home. He went over Sangallo's foundations. Much of what his predecessor had built was unsafe and would have to go.

His tour of inspection ended just as night closed down. He stood in the dark before his Pietà. He truly wanted to rescue St. Peter's, make it a glorious monument to Christianity. It was his church; if not for him, it might never have been conceived. Then was he not responsible for it?

An old woman came into the chapel, placed a lighted taper before the Madonna. Michelangelo reached into the long basket of candles, selected one, lighted it, placed it beside the other.

Of course he must build St. Peter's! Was not life to be worked, and suffered, right to the end?

He refused to accept any pay for his services as architect. He painted from first light until dinnertime in the Pauline chapel, then walked to St. Peter's to watch the leveling. The workmen were sullen and ill disposed toward him . . . but they followed the schedule he set. The superintendent and contractors who had worked under Sangallo put so many obstacles in his path that Pope Paul had to issue a decree declaring Michelangelo superintendent as well as architect. From that moment the fabric began to grow with a momentum that amazed Rome.

He did not lack for projects. In the eyes of the world he was truly the "Master." Duke Cosimo urged him to return to Florence to create sculptures for the city. The King of France deposited money in a Roman bank in his name against the day when he would carve or paint for him. The Sultan of Turkey offered to send an escort party to bring him to Constantinople to work there.

He spent the better part of the daily hours in the Pauline, painting. Tiring of paintbrushes, he returned home to pick up hammer and chisel, glorying in the sheer freedom of being able to carve, creating the collapsed Christ and behind him Nicodemus with his own white beard, deep-sunk eyes, flattened nose, a cowl over his head, the mouth sensitive, poetic: the new Descent from the Cross he hoped would be placed on his own tomb.

Then, after weeks and months of lavishly outpoured energy, he would suddenly fall ill, with what he could not tell. At such times he would grow cranky with his closest friends and relatives. Then he would recover and say to Urbino:

"Why do I behave so cantankerously? Because my seventies are fleeing so fast?"

Granacci, his oldest friend, had died; so had Balducci, Leo Baglioni and his brother Giovansimone.

Then Pope Paul, too, died. The new Pope, who took the name Julius III, poured such a vast fortune into his own pleasure and entertaining that he used up the income set aside for St. Peter's. All work ceased.

Michelangelo was livid, but there was nothing he could do. He went for a walk about the city. When he returned, relaxed and refreshed, Urbino was waiting for him with a worried expression.

"Master, I do not like to bring you further problems, but I must now leave you."

Michelangelo was too astonished to answer.

"Leave me?"

"You remember the girl I chose, in Urbino, ten years ago?"

Michelangelo shook his head in disbelief. Was it already ten years?

33. Pietà, about 1548–55. Florence, Cathedral.

"She is eighteen today. It is time for us to marry."

"But why go? Bring your wife here, Urbino, we'll fix up an apartment for you, buy furniture."

Urbino's eyes were round.

"Are you sure, master? For I am forty now, and I should have children as quickly as possible."

"This is your home. I am your family. Your sons will be my grandchildren."

He gave Urbino two thousand ducats in cash so that he could be independent, then an additional sum to fix up a room for his bride and to buy a new bed. In a few days Urbino returned with his wife, Cornelia Colonelli, a sympathetic girl who took over the management of the household and ran it well. She gave Michelangelo the affection she would have brought to her husband's father. They named their first son Michelangelo.

In March 1555 his friends gave him a party for his eightieth birthday. The walls of the studio were lined with drawings and projects for another eighty years ahead. . . .

Two weeks later Pope Julius III died, and was succeeded by Pope Marcellus II, who lived only three weeks to enjoy his pontificate. His successor was Cardinal Caraffa, an old and bitter enemy of Michelangelo's. He called himself Paul IV.

No one knew quite how he had been elected. He was a thoroughly disagreeable man, violent of nature, intolerant of all about him. Pope Paul IV, knowing how completely he was hated, said:

"I do not know why they elected me Pope, so I am bound to conclude that it is not the cardinals but God who makes the Popes."

It was his ambition to wipe out all heresy in Italy. His Board of Inquisition tortured and condemned accused people without trial, locked them in dungeons in the cellars, burned others in the Campo dei Fiori. Michelangelo considered he would be fit fuel for the fires, but he made no attempt to flee. The Pope did not molest him . . . until the day of reckoning.

Pope Paul IV received him in a small, monastic room with whitewashed walls. His expression was as severe as his robe.

"Buonarroti, I respect your work. But heretical frescoes like your altar wall must be destroyed."

". . . the Last Judgment?"

He half slid to the corner of a bench, sat staring blindly at the whitewashed wall before him.

"Decent people are shocked by the nakedness of saints and martyrs, of hundreds of men and women fully exposed. . . ."

"They are the narrow-minded, Holy Father, ignorant of the true nature of art. The fresco is not evil. Never has there been a wall more permeated with a love of God."

"Very well, I will not demand that the wall be torn down. We will simply give it a coat of whitewash. Then you can paint something over it, something simple and devout, that you can do quickly."

He was too crushed to fight back. Not so, Rome. His friends, including a number of cardinals, began a campaign to save the wall. Then Daniele da Volterra, one of Michelangelo's most enthusiastic followers, came to the studio with high color in his cheeks.

"Master, the Last Judgment is saved. There will be no coat of whitewash."

Michelangelo collapsed onto his leather chair, breathing hard.

"I must go out and thank personally every last person who helped me. . . ."

"Master," interrupted Daniele, with eyes averted, "we

have had to pay a price. The Pope agreed not to destroy the wall . . . providing breeches were put on everybody's nakedness."

"Breeches?"

"And petticoats on the females. All must be clothed from the hips to the knees."

"If in my earlier years I had given myself to make sulphur matches," swore Michelangelo, "I should now suffer less."

"Master, let us try to be sensible about this. The Pope was going to call in a court painter . . . but I persuaded him to let me do the job. I will injure the wall as little as possible. Don't be angry with me."

"You are right, Daniele. I have spent a lifetime portraying the beauty of man. Now he has become shameful again, to be burned in a new bonfire of vanities. Do you know what that means, Daniele? We are returning to the darkest, most ignorant centuries of the past."

"Look here, Michelangelo," said Daniele placatingly, "I will use so thin a paint that the next Pope can have all the breeches and robes removed without harming anything beneath . . ."

"Go then, and wrap their winding sheets about them."

Sigismondo died in Settignano, the last of his brothers. He had outlived his generation. Urbino was taken ill and died and his wife, Cornelia, took her children to her parents' home. The house seemed desolate.

The eighties, he decided, were not the most pleasant decade in the span of man. When he left Florence at sixty he had feared that his life might be over; but the sixties had flown by. During his seventies he had been so deeply immersed in the Pauline chapel frescoes, the carving of the Descent, his new architectural career, and St. Peter's, that no day had been long enough to accomplish his tasks.

But now, as he became eighty-one, and moved toward eighty-two, he could no longer see as well as he used to; his step was not as firm; stamina was giving way to a series of minor disturbances, sapping his strength, interfering with his drive to finish St. Peter's, to create a glorious dome for it.

Then he went down with a severe attack of kidney stones. Dr. Colombo pulled him through, but he was confined to his bed for several months and was obliged to turn over the designs for one of the chapels to a new superintendent. When he recovered, he found that the new superintendent had misread his plans, making serious errors in construction. He was overcome with shame and remorse; this was his first failure in the ten years of building.

He called on the Pope at once; but quick as he was, his enemies had been there before him.

"It is true?" Pope Paul asked as he saw Michelangelo's face. "The chapel will have to be pulled down?"

"Most of it, Holiness."

"I am saddened. How could such a thing happen?"

"I have been ill, Holy Father."

"I see. Perhaps you are too old to carry such a heavy responsibility. For your own sake you should be relieved of the crushing burden."

Michelangelo was silent for a moment, thinking backward.

"Holiness, for thirty years I watched good architects pour foundations. They never got St. Peter's off the ground. In the ten years I have been the architect, the church has risen upward like an eagle. If you dismiss me now, it will be the ruin of the edifice."

The Pope's lips twitched.

"Michelangelo, as long as you have the strength to fight back, you shall remain the architect of St. Peter's."

That night there was a meeting at Michelangelo's house.

Because he had nearly died, a group of his oldest friends insisted that he build a complete model of the dome. Up to now he had made only fragmentary sketches.

"I have heard you say," one of his friends said, "that you wanted to progress St. Peter's so far that no one could change its design after your death."

"That is my hope. But I have not yet conceived the final dome. I shall have to find it. Then we shall build a wooden model."

Everyone left. Michelangelo walked to his drawing table, pulled up a wooden chair. A dome, he thought, was not a mere covering; any roof would serve that utilitarian purpose. A dome was a major work of art. It was a vault of man, created in the image of the vault of heaven. The perfect dome went from horizon to horizon in man's mind, covering it with grace. It was the most natural of all architectural forms, and the most celestial.

Some people said the earth was round; for a man like himself whose travels had been confined between Venice and Rome, that was hard to prove. He had been taught that the earth was flat, ending where the dome of heaven came down to its circular boundaries. Yet he had always observed a peculiar facet of that supposedly anchored-down horizon: as he walked or rode to reach it, it receded at an equal pace. . . .

Just so, his dome. It could not be finite. No man standing beneath it must ever feel that he could reach its boundaries. He wanted his dome too to be mystical, so beautiful it would reassure man of God's presence . . . a sentient form which man could not only see and feel but enter. Under his dome a man's soul must soar upward to God even as it would in the moment of its final release from his body.

His mind and fingers were moving with force and clarity.

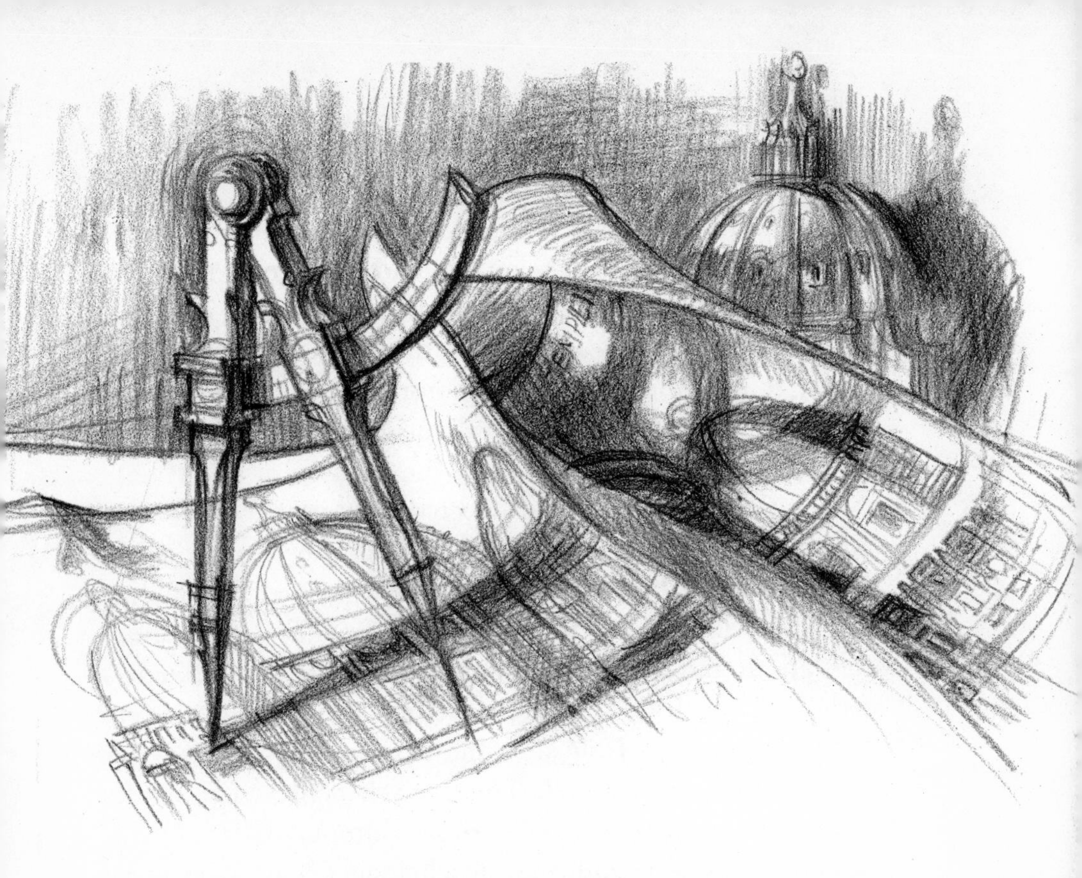

He laid aside his charcoal and drawing pens, started modeling. Over the weeks and months he made a dozen models, destroying them, moving on to new designs. None of the results satisfied him.

At last it came, after eleven years of thinking, drawing, praying, hoping and despairing, experimenting and rejecting: a structure soaring, lilting heavenward, three hundred and thirty-five feet. . . . It was a dome unlike any other.

He hired a carpenter to build the model, of linden wood, one fifteen-thousandth of the projected size. The giant dome would rest on the piers and on the arches that the piers supported, and on a circular cement base. The buttresses would be held by a framework of wrought iron. Eight ramps along the lower drum would afford a means of carrying materials on the backs of donkeys up to the dome walls. The engineering plans took months to draw, but Michelangelo had the skill.

Pope Paul IV died suddenly. Rome burst into the most violent insurrection Michelangelo had yet seen at the death of any pontiff. The crowd knocked down the ex-Pope's statue, dragged its head through the streets for hours, then threw it into the Tiber before storming the headquarters of the Inquisition to release all prisoners and destroy the documents assembled to convict the accused of heresy.

The College of Cardinals elected sixty-year-old Giovanni Angelo Medici, from an obscure Lombardy branch of the Medici family. Pope Pius IV had been trained as a lawyer. He was brilliant and a man of integrity. The Inquisition, foreign to the Italian character, was ended. Through a series of legalistic conferences and contracts the Pope brought peace to Italy and the surrounding nations, and to the Lutherans as well. The Church achieved peace for itself and reunited Catholicism in Europe.

Pope Pius IV reconfirmed Michelangelo's position as architect of St. Peter's, providing him with funds with which to push the arches upward.

It was clearly a race against time. He thought he could finish the dome in ten to twelve years. That would bring him to a round century mark. Nobody lived that long; but despite his attacks of kidney stones, pains in the head, disorders of the stomach, aches in the back, bouts of dizziness, he did not feel any true diminishing of his power. He still took walks in the country. His eyes were clear and penetrating. He would get that dome built.

While the cathedral structure rose through its giant columns, arches and façades, Michelangelo went back to carving the Descent from the Cross. One day as he stood before it, darkness flooded over him. After a lapse of time he regained consciousness; but he was confused. He knew that something had happened, but he could not collect his thoughts. Had he dropped off to sleep? Was he not quite

34. Detail of the Pietà, about 1548–55. Michelangelo's Self-Portrait at the Age of About Eighty.

awake? Then why did he feel a numbness and weakness in the left arm and leg? Why did the muscles on one side of his face feel as though they were sagging?

He called his servant. When he spoke to her, he noticed that his speech was slurred. The elderly woman gazed at him, wide-eyed.

"Master, are you all right?"

She helped him into bed, then put on a shawl to go for the doctor. Michelangelo could see by their expressions that something serious had occurred though they pretended that he had just overtired himself. Dr. Donati gave him a warm drink, stirring in a foul-tasting medicine.

"Rest cures everything," said the doctor.

"Except old age."

He awakened to find deep night outside his window. He lifted himself gingerly. The headache was gone and he could see clearly the work that was still required on the Descent. He rose, put a goat candle in his cap, returned to his carving. The confusion was gone from his mind. It was good to have the feel of marble at his fingertips.

He worked all day, had supper, then threw himself on the bed for a few hours of sleep before rising to begin polishing.

He forgot all about the attack.

Two days later, as he stood before his marble he was struck again. He dropped his hammer and chisel, stumbled to the bed, fell on his knees, with his face sideways on the blanket.

When he awakened the room was full of people. Facing him was the statue which throbbed with a life all its own. He thought:

"Man passes. Only works of art are immortal."

He insisted on sitting in a chair before the fire. Once when he was left alone he slipped a robe over his shoulders and started walking in the rain in the direction of St. Peter's. One of his newer apprentices met him in the street, asked:

"Master, do you think it right to be about in such weather?"

He allowed himself to be taken home, but at four the next afternoon he dressed and tried to mount his horse for a ride. His legs were too weak.

Rome knew he was dying and came to bid him farewell. Those who could not be admitted left flowers and gifts on the doorstep. Dr. Donati tried to keep him in bed.

"Don't hurry me," he said to the doctor. "My father lived to his ninetieth birthday, so I still have two weeks to enjoy."

"As long as you're feeling so intrepid, what about a carriage ride in the morning? The last work on the drum is complete. To celebrate your ninetieth birthday, they're going to start the first ring of the dome."

"Thank God. No one will ever be able to change it now. But all the same, it's sad to have to die. I would like to start all over again, to create forms and figures I have never dreamed of."

As he lay sleepless in bed, he thought, "Life has been good. God did not create me to abandon me. I have loved marble, yes, and paint too. I have loved architecture, and poetry too. I have loved my family and my friends. I have loved God, the forms of the earth and the heavens, and people too. I have loved life to the full, and now I love death as its natural termination."

Dusk was falling. Alone in the room, Michelangelo began to review the images of all the beautiful works he had created. He saw them, one by one, as clearly as the day he had made them, the sculptures, paintings and architecture succeeding each other as swiftly as had the years of his life:

The Madonna of the Stairs and the Battle of the Centaurs, Sts. Proculus and Petronius; the wooden Crucifix for Prior Bichiellini; the Sleeping Cupid with which he had tried to fool the dealer in Rome; the Bacchus he had carved in Jacopo Galli's orchard; the Pietà for St. Peter's; the Giant David for Florence; the Holy Family teased out of him by Agnolo Doni; the cartoon for the Battle of Cascina, called the Bathers, to compete with Leonardo da Vinci's; the Madonna and Child for the merchants of Bruges, carved in his own first studio; the ill-fated bronze portrait of Pope Julius II; Genesis, painted for Julius II on the vault of the Sistine; the Last Judgment for Pope Paul III to complete the chapel; the Moses for Julius's tomb; his four unfinished Giants in Florence; the Dawn and Dusk, Day and Night for the Medici Chapel; the Conversion of Paul and the Crucifixion of Peter for the Pauline chapel; the Pietàs sculptured for his own pleasure . . . and as the pictures came to a stop and stood still in his mind's eye, St. Peter's.

St. Peter's. . . . He entered the church through its front portal, walked in the strong Roman sunshine down the wide nave, stood below the center of the dome, just over the tomb of St. Peter. He felt his soul leave his body, rise upward into the dome, becoming part of it: part of space, of time, of heaven, and of God.

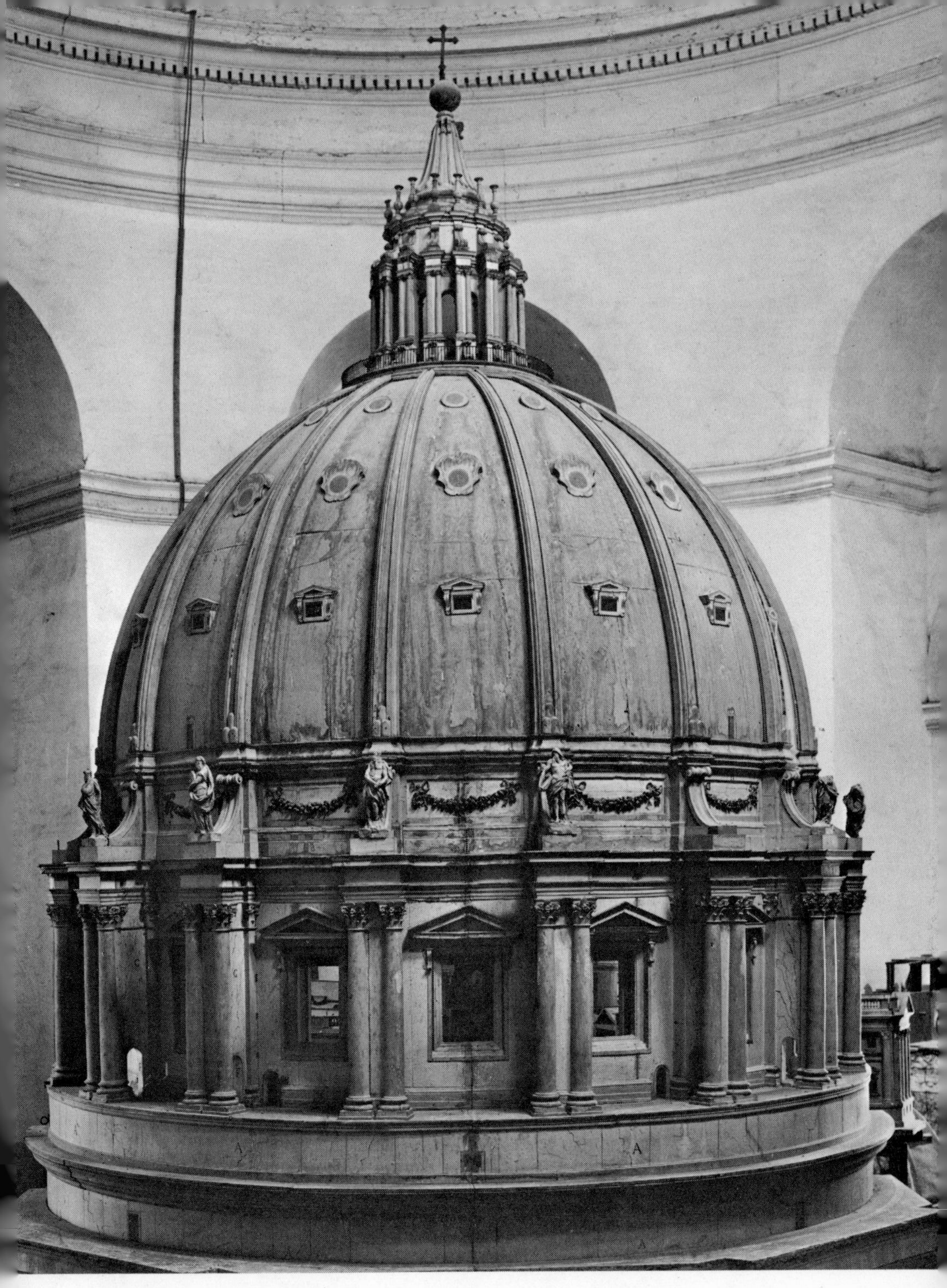

35. Michelangelo's model for St. Peter's Dome, 1558–61. Rome, Vatican, Museo Petriano.

NOTE

This biographical novel is documented by several years of living and researching in the source materials of Florence, Rome, Carrara and Bologna. The work actually began eight years ago when I had the entire body of Michelangelo's four hundred and ninety-five letters, as well as his records and art contracts (Milanesi edition, Florence, 1875), translated into English, a task not before attempted, to create a solid base for the novel. A considerable amount of material is here published for the first time. The sources are now on record at the library of the University of California at Los Angeles.

I am deeply indebted to the scholars in the Renaissance field. The late Bernard Berenson afforded me expert counseling on the Michelangelo bibliography, and opened his magnificent library at I Tatti, in his own words, "night or day." Ludwig Goldscheider, the British authority, gave warmheartedly of his precious time and materials. Aldo Fortuna, the Florentine archivist, shared his lifetime of Renaissance documentation. Cardinal Tisserant made available the superb Michelangelo collection in the Vatican Library. Professor Giovanni Poggi unlocked the Buonarroti family record books, which go back many years before Michelangelo's birth. Dr. Ulrich Middledorf, director of Der Kunsthistorisches Institut in Florence, facilitated our work in his library, as did the directors of the Bibliotheca Hertziana in Rome.

In Carrara, I am grateful to Bruno and Mario Taverelli for the opportunity to study the quarries at close range, and for their indefatigable efforts to document the Carrarino dialect and mores. In Bologna, I am indebted to Professor Umberto Beseghi for leading me to the best of the Bolognese source materials. Stanley Lewis, the Canadian sculptor, was my guide in Florence to Michelangelo's techniques; there he also taught me to carve marble. He has answered an unending stream of questions about the thinking and feeling of the sculptor at work. Charles and Carmela Speroni corrected manuscript and galleys, as a labor of love.

Lastly, I want to acknowledge my considerable indebtedness to Charles de Tolnay, whose monumental five volumes constitute the definitive art history on Michelangelo's work. Michelangelo's sonnets are quoted from the J. A. Symonds translation.

PRESENT LOCATION OF MICHELANGELO'S WORKS

TITLE	YEAR	LOCATION
Madonna of the Stairs	1491	Casa Buonarroti, Florence
Battle of Centaurs	1492	Casa Buonarroti, Florence
Sts. Petronius and Proculus, and the Angel	1495	San Domenico, Bologna
Bacchus	1497	Bargello, Florence
Pietà	1498–1500	St. Peter's, Vatican City
Bruges Madonna	1501–4	Church of Notre Dame, Bruges, Belgium
Statues for Piccolomini Altar	1501	Cathedral, Siena
David	1501–4	Accademia, Florence
Doni Holy Family	1503	Uffizi, Florence
Pitti Madonna	1504	Bargello, Florence
Taddei Madonna	1504–5	Royal Academy, London
St. Matthew	1505–6	Accademia, Florence
Tomb of Pope Julius II	1505–45	San Pietro in Vincoli, Rome
Sistine Ceiling	1508–12	Vatican Palace, Vatican City
Heroic and Dying Captives	1513–16	Louvre, Paris
Moses	1513–42	San Pietro in Vincoli, Rome
The Risen Christ	1518–21	Santa Maria sopra Minerva, Rome
The Four Unfinished Captives (Giants)	c. 1519	Accademia, Florence
The Medici Chapel	1520–34	Florence
The Laurentian Library	1524–34	Florence
Dawn	1524–31	Medici Chapel, Florence
Dusk	1524–31	Medici Chapel, Florence
Madonna and Child	1524–34	Medici Chapel, Florence

TITLE	YEAR	LOCATION
Duke Lorenzo	1524–34	Medici Chapel, Florence
Night	1526–31	Medici Chapel, Florence
Duke Giuliano	1526–34	Medici Chapel, Florence
Day	1526–34	Medici Chapel, Florence
Victory	c. 1526–30	Palazzo Vecchio, Florence
David-Apollo	1502, 1531	Bargello, Florence
The Last Judgment	1536–41	Sistine Chapel, Vatican City
Brutus	c. 1539	Bargello, Florence
Rachel	1542	San Pietro in Vincoli, Rome
Leah	1542	San Pietro in Vincoli, Rome
Conversion of Paul	1542–45	Pauline Chapel, Vatican City
Crucifixion of Peter	1546–50	Pauline Chapel, Vatican City
St. Peter's	1547–64	Vatican City
Farnese Palace: third story, cornice and courtyard	1547–50	Rome
The Capitol	1547–64	Rome
Pietà (Deposition from the Cross)	1548–55	Duomo, Florence
Palestrina Pietà (Entombment)	c. 1550–56	Accademia, Florence
Rondanini Pietà	1555–64	Castello Sforzesco, Milan
Porta Pia	1561–64	Rome
Santa Maria degli Angeli	1563–64	Rome

The following works by Michelangelo have been lost: Mask of a Faun, 1490; Santo Spirito Crucifix, 1494; Hercules, 1494; Little St. John, 1496; The Sleeping Cupid, 1496; Cupid for Jacopo Galli, 1497; Bronze David, 1502–8; Battle of Cascina cartoon, 1504–5; Bronze Statue of Julius II, 1506–8; Leda and the Swan, tempera panel, 1529–30.

Of Michelangelo's many wax and clay models, only a few have survived, and there is disagreement about the authenticity of some of these. Five models are generally accepted: the clay River God in the Accademia in Florence; the clay Victory group or Hercules and Cacus, a clay male nude, and a clay of the Awakening Giant in the Casa Buonarroti in Florence; the clay Giant, repaired with red wax, in the British Museum, London.

The following are disputed and doubtful, although several critics accept them as Michelangelo's work: a clay allegorical female figure, and a clay Giant in the Casa Buonarroti; a red wax Young Giant at the British Museum, London; a clay Night and Dawn in the collection of Dr. Alejandro Pietri in Caracas, Venezuela. Less authenticated are two wax Captives at the Casa Buonarroti.

The major collections of Michelangelo's drawings are to be found in the Casa Buonarroti and Uffizi in Florence; the British Museum in London; the Louvre in Paris; the University Galleries in Oxford, England, and the Royal Library at Windsor Castle, in England.